Apache Blue Eyes

A Novel by
Denis J. LaComb

Apache Blue Eyes

Published by BAMs2 Publishing
A division of Sharden LLC

Credits:
Editing and cover design
by Vida Raine

ISBN: 1494809060
ISBN-13: 978-1494809065

DEDICATION

This novel is dedicated to Sharon; my wife, best friend, and lifelong partner.

To my children, Brian and Melanie, who continue to inspire me as parents and 'just good people.'

Also to Vida, for taking this raw material written so many years ago and through her deft editing helping to craft a story that I hope my readers will enjoy as much as I loved creating.

TABLE OF CONTENTS

Chapter One

He was alone under a blazing noonday sun. There was little water left, few loads, and all the while he was being watched by two Navajo warriors. They lay motionless in a grove of cottonwoods nestled near the base of a feeder canyon. Their black eyes watched the white enemy coming closer. The rider had entered their break from the main canyon a half mile back. He rode easily in the saddle as if he were familiar with the land. There was no urgency to his canter. If he was aware of the danger, it did not show.

The man was dressed in badly worn chinos the color of sunblasted sand, a patched calico shirt and dirty leather boots. A layer of alkali dust said four or five days in the saddle, perhaps more. He was neither a drifter nor a tenderfoot. Beneath each leg was a rifle scabbard; one held a Sharps buffalo gun, the other a new 16-shot Winchester.

It was the man's face that was different. It was shaped like that of an Indian; bony and high cheekboned, sun-blackened carmine - but the eyes beneath his black shaggy hair identified him as white. They were startlingly blue, like the rare pure-blue turquoise stone. The eyes missed nothing as they darted back and forth across rock and brush, crack and crevice surrounding him.

The rider drew rein long enough to dig a long brown cigarrito out of his shirt pocket, light it, and nudge his desert bred mustang into movement again. During that brief interval, the two Navajo guards moved up to the end of the tree line, drawing arrows to their bowstrings. Though the sounds of their movement had been lost to the wind, the rider noticed it.

As the rider drew nearer to the tree line, he drew rein and whipped out the Winchester, levered it and laid the piece across his saddle. He called out in a loud, clear voice.

"Chee Bear, you can show yourself, I come in peace to see my father."

The two Navajos broke cover, their horn bows drawn at the ready. They edged out of the tree line.

The man did not move. His hand lay cradled across the rifle. The Navajo approached cautiously, angling out until they were well over ten feet apart when they came abreast of the man. The older of the two warriors spoke. "So, Belinka, you return. I did not recognize you at first. It has been many seasons since you left our people. Why are you back? This is Navajo land. You are a white man now…you are no longer Diné."

"I have come to see my father. I will not stay."

"Are you alone?"

"You know that I am."

The braves released their taut bowstrings, slipping the arrows back in their buckskin quivers. Chee Bear motioned toward the end of the canyon behind him. "Your father is with the old men and women. Do not stay long. I do not want you here when the sun falls. You must be far away or I cannot assure your safety."

"And if my father wishes me to stay?"

Chee Bear stiffened his back, cutting a knife stare at the old friend he had long since disowned for siding with the whites. "I have spoken. Your father is no longer an important man among our people; but he is still a Navajo, even if you are not. Go before I change my mind"

Ree Bannon; no longer Navajo, but never a white man, met the glare of the young chieftain head-on. He held it firm for a moment then kicked his horse into a canter and rode past. Ever the hunter, his precautionary once-over revealed he was not alone. A dozen or more warriors had quietly begun their decent from the rim above. If there was to be trouble, he would be hopelessly trapped and outnumbered.

Bannon rode deeper into the canyon. The hooves of his pony clicked on the shale and loose rocks, echoing tiny pings that bounced off the stone walls. He passed through a narrow opening in the canyon and emerged into a hidden valley.

It was a half mile long and barely a quarter mile wide at its broadest point. The canyon walls slanted sharply toward an upland desert. At the far end the wall rose sheer for several hundred feet. At its base, a tiny spring ebbed forth life-giving water which ran down a narrow creek bed the length of the valley between two rows of willows and reeds. A few scattered cottonwoods laced the foliage. Several hogans crouched on the banks of the stream, lining the gravel banks like upturned pods.

Ree saw several old men and women, drawn by curiosity, gathering outside their hogans. Dogs, mangy curs all of them, barked and snarled. The mustang ignored them as did its rider. The Navajo were whispering amongst themselves about the stranger in their presence. There were a few old men with ancient muzzleloaders and hunting bows. Ree did not turn around. He knew by now the warriors on his tail had melted into the background and were watching his every movement.

Bannon recognized the withered old mule outside his father's hogan. He rode up to it and dismounted, keeping the horse between himself and the Navajo. It didn't go unnoticed. The people gathered in a loose circle around the structure of adobe covered logs. Ree ignored them.

Stooping down low, the half-breed entered the gloom of the hogan. There was a pungent odor of a pinion log smoldering. It was dark inside and at first Bannon could not make out the shadowy figure sitting back in one corner.

"You have come, my son. My heart is glad."

Ree approached the figure and seated himself respectfully in front. He touched fingertips to his brow, a sign of Indian respect for an elder. There was no sound in the dark room, save that of the flies buzzing and the low murmur of the old ones outside. Ree's adjusted eyes saw the sand painting in front of his father. When death seemed close, the medicine man performs a curing ritual centered on the sand painting. They had done it for his father.

Ree studied the man in front of him. A red bandana was wrapped around the old man's wrinkled forehead. He wore a faded, ragged calico shirt and matching trousers. He was bent with age and sickness. His cheeks were like parchment and his eyes sad with age. Still, he managed a weak smile as he watched his son.

Bannon's mother had been the only survivor of an Apache raiding party on her family's remote cabin. After she was violated by the Apache, she was left for dead. Anza, a Navajo hunter, found her wandering in the desert and took her home. Nine months later, she gave birth to Ree. Although Ree carried Apache raider blood, Anza welcomed Ree as his son. Anza was an honorable man whose love for Ree's mother surmounted all obstacles.

The rigors of Navajo life were too much for her and she died when Ree was still a young boy. Anza raised Ree alone as Navajo, but Ree was never accepted by the tribe. Anza taught Ree to hunt and trap and live off the land. In his teen years, Ree and his father engaged in brutal skirmishes against neighboring Apaches and the Mexican Rurales.

While Ree was neither white man nor Indian; he was a skilled warrior, born and bred in the Indian ways. However, Ree wanted no part of the battles and dying, so he left the tribe and spent the next ten years trying to eke out a living hunting and trapping in the white man's world, with only half the blood required to be successful.

Here he sat before Anza, his father, for what he knew would be the last time. The old man was crippled with arthritis and a festering bullet wound that had never healed properly. He had little time left to live.

With his only son before him, Anza was growing more alert. It was plainly written in his rheumatic eyes and gnarled fingers that shook as he tried to light a cigarrito. Ree leaned forward and steadied his father's shaking hands.

Anza spoke then. The words disjointed and with strained effort. "I would offer you tiswin or meat but there is none. I have not been on the hunt for a long time. The others take care of me now." He paused, his watery eyes seeking those of his son. "It is not the way for a Navajo warrior to live. Sometimes I wish for death to find me so that I may journey to Dinétah, old Navajo land."

Ree spoke softly and slowly. "It troubles me to see my own father suffering as you must be. I offer you all that I have, though it is not much. Come with me to the mountains. It will be like the old days when we hunted and trapped there, just you and me. Our mother and father, the earth and the sky, are all the companions we need. Will you come with me?"

"Is it the white man's way to run away from death?" Anza said sharply.

"I have learned many things since I left, but disrespect is not one of them. If I have offended you, I am sorry."

Anza's shoulders sagged. "It is nothing," he said with a bowed head. "My tongue still rattles away before my brain commands it to speak. I did not call you here to see me like this or to hear of my troubles." He paused long enough to gaze with now steady eyes upon his only son. "You are no longer of the Diné. You know this as well as I. You are a man of two tribes and neither one will accept this. You are living as a white man but your blood is native. Because of that, I called for you. You are still my son - my own. I want you to go on a mission for me; for our people. Before I die, I must know that my brother's wish is satisfied."

"My uncle? I thought him long since dead."

"So had all of us, but he was alive a month ago. He returned to our village with a strange tale that he only shared with me. It was about a cave in the mountains. The chain is called Sangre de Cristo by the whites and lies somewhere between the villages of Santa Fe and Taos Pueblo. It is a wondrous cave filled with the treasures from the black invaders of years ago."

"You mean the Spanish. The ones they called the conquistadors?"

"Yes, the same. You must find that cave and close it so that the whites do not find those treasures and use them against our people."

Bannon had traveled the mountains and plateaus between Santa Fe and Taos Pueblo many times. He knew of its many hidden canyons and lost valleys. There were too many places to count where a treasure might be hidden. "How will I find this cave?"

Anza bent closer to his intent son. "Your uncle found this cave by accident several months ago when he was hunting. It was filled with ancient weapons and gold and silver. The Spanish must have hidden it there when the Apaches chased them from this part of the country. Their intent was clearly to return and use those weapons against our people and the gold and silver to finance their domination over us. Yet they never returned. My brother was the first to lay eyes on that treasure since the Spanish left it many years ago. He is dead now and I am too old to find that cave. You must do this for us ... both of us."

"What happened to my uncle?"

"He was on his way back here to enlist help to close the cave when he was ambushed by a group of miners. He escaped into the rocks but was badly hurt. He killed one of the miners, so the others just left him to die. He crawled away and it was several days before he gained enough strength to move again. For four days, he walked and crawled and rested. His mind began to leave him so he made a map of the cave's location. He used Navajo symbols to identify the mountain and the cave's location. He did not want to forget what he had found."

"Do you have the map?" Ree asked anxiously.

Anza shook his head disappointedly. "No, my son. My brother did not have the map when our warriors found him in the hills. Before he died, he said a miner had come across him hiding in a cave. The miner searched my brother and found the map. Although it was marked in Navajo, he still took it and then left my brother to die. Your uncle remembered that very clearly. He did not live long after he was brought back to camp, but he remembered that miner and where it happened."

"And where was that?"

"The Salt Mountains," Anza said with firmness to his voice. "That miner must still have the map though it does him little good. My brother is gone now but you are still alive to carry out his wish. That is what I ask of you."

Bannon sat in silence for a long time. He pictured his uncle struggling through the high country, pushing himself to make it back to the village and help. He also thought of his own father, old and gnarled, sure to die soon, wanting desperately to see that the wish of his brother was carried out. Ree looked up with strength and determination. "I will do as you wish."

"It shall be the last thing I ask of you. We are both changed persons. You with the white man's ways and myself with age and the shadow of death over me. I think we shall not see one another again."

Ree arose, bent under the low ceiling. His fingers were clenched on the felt hat in his hand. "I do this because I am still Navajo ... and proud of it. I will do this for our people."

Anza bowed silently.

Ree touched fingertip to brow and left. He squinted cat's eyes as he reentered the harsh brightness of the day. A crowd was still gathered there. He swung to saddle, looking straight ahead, never once making contact with the black eyes peering up at him.

He rode out of the canyon village at a canter, past the warriors at its entrance and out of the mountains. He rode at a steady pace, letting the mustang find its own gait. He was heading for Apacheria but it didn't worry him. He'd already hunted and traveled through the Mules, the Whetstones and the Dragoons right under the noses of the wary Apache. This would be no different. He would ride toward the little mining town of San Lacita and then swing west northwest toward the Salt Mountains and the miner who had his uncle's map.

Chapter Two

Eli Dunn didn't like running his stage to San Lacita at night. Not when the darkness could be crawling with hostiles. Many times he'd heard the claims that Apaches didn't attack at night. He knew that if the odds were on their side, they'd attack any time of day or night.

Nestled on the creaking Concord seat box, next to the slouch-hatted driver, was another frontier veteran. He was whiskered like Eli and cradled a ten gauge L.C. Smith shotgun firmly in his huge paws. John Montgomery, like his partner Eli, wore the tattered buckskin uniform of a frontiersman. His boots were Apache design with pointed toes and laced with fringe. He carried a large Sheffield knife in his wide belt. It was eight inches of cold steel etched with "Death to Abolition" and grips of checkered ebony and mounts of German silver.

In the darkness of the New Mexico night, the tension lines drawn on both their faces were hidden; but the worry was there - and with it a caution that ran with their darting eyes crossing and crisscrossing the blanket of black before them.

Eli Dunn had come out of the gumbo mud of Deadwood when his family died of the smallpox plague of '68. He served his time on a slew of Diamond R bull trains before he decided to chuck long hauls for a steady job running a stage. And steady work it was; except when the Cherry Cows and Mescaleros were on the warpath again … like now.

"You think we'll make San Lacita before dawn," John Montgomery asked Dunn. It was asked halfheartedly, with little hint of concern in his voice.

The old gaffer puckered his lips and sent a stream of tobacco juice flying into the night. Slowly, choosing each word, he answered. "Before we lost that hitch, I'd have expected to. Now I don't know. It don't seem too likely. We probably won't be through Jeopardy Pass until just about sunup."

The journey from Black Horse Springs to San Lacita should have been a seventeen hour extended run. The horses would have been worn but not hocked out. If it hadn't been for the whippletree cracking, Eli would have made it easily before dawn. Safe inside the town at daybreak and a bellyful of breakfast to boot. As it stood now, he would still be far out in the desert by dawn. That was not a good sign with rumors of raiding Apaches flying thicker than a swarm of flies on fresh cut buffalo meat. Both men knew the consequences of that broken hitch. Neither had to voice it to the other.

Dunn slowed the teams to a walk trot. He glided them into a wash, followed its dry, gritty course for a while then swung them up and out of the depression toward a series of mounds; blurred and formless in the starlight. The horses were held to a walk. No sense in pushing them any harder than had to be on that stretch of the run. There was plenty of flat, even land up ahead. The night air was cool and still. A Southerly breeze blew lightly. Only the crunch of pebbles and scraping of larger stones against the iron wheel rims broke the silence.

Inside the heavy mail coach, five passengers attempted to sleep with little success. They were silent but alert. The window passengers kept peering out into the starlit darkness even as their heads bobbed back and forth against the horsehair headboards. Four of the passengers were rugged men of the land, three miners and a cowboy on the drift. They wore the scruffy clothes of their profession; canvas trousers, woolen longsleeved underwear and coarse shirts. They smelled of the land and hard work and hard times. A bottle moved between the three miners and when it was empty another took its place.

They occasionally gave silent head bows to the fifth passenger, and were repeatedly ignored.

She was of Spanish blood and very beautiful. It showed in her high cheek bones, perfect nose and full robust figure. It was a shape not at all concealed by the expensive riding breeches she wore or the blouse of fine fabric. She ignored the miners' leering stares and their mutterings with an air of confidence and self-assurance uncommon for a woman alone in the wilderness. She was dark skinned but unlike most Spanish, her hair was lighter brown. A closer examination of her face revealed a smaller mouth and nose than most latins. Over the delicate blouse, the girl wore a vest of lightly tanned calf skin and in one pocket a bulge stood out. None of the trio had missed that when she boarded the stage back in Black Horse. It was probably a knuckleduster, a small caliber derringer. It was not a dangerous weapon at a distance but a killer close up.

At the girl's feet sat a canvas bag. It had been placed on board by a large vaquero who had escorted the girl over from a Don's rig. That was the girl's sole possession. She gazed out her window, not bothering to recognize her fellow passengers. The others could sense a haughtiness about her. Highbred, they thought, and a father with a lot of land and cattle. Yet alone as she was, the girl displayed no signs of nervousness. If she did have a little derringer in her vest pocket, odds favored her being a crack shot with it. Not a man onboard was of a mind to try to find out. They drank and fantasized and that was about all.

Atop the Concord, driver and guard were engaged in a muffled conversation, their voices unusually low. Each cut sharpened eyes into the darkness for any signs of trouble. Overhead a half moon sailed along with the constant sway of the coach.

Eli's deft hands held the leather reins easily in between his fingers. With them, he could communicate with the leaders, the wheelers and the swing team in between. Except for the clip-clop of shod hoofs scraping against rock, the rhythmic motion was hypnotic; the cadence, swinging back and forth could set the most alert skinner into a dangerous state of drowsiness.

"Another three hours and it'll be sunup," Montgomery stated. Eli acknowledged, snapped the reins, and moved the teams into a faster trot. The guard reached over and removed a wad of tobacco out of the driver's vest pocket. "I owe you," he said, gnawing off a piece.

Eli slowed the teams over a potholed stretch of ground, feeling out where each dip and rut was. He guided the horses around each obstacle. The thought of breaking a wheel spoke or spring axle weighed heavily on him.

The coach creaked and groaned as the driver missed his mark and slammed down into a deep rut. Inside, the passengers held onto the hanging straps and stiffened their legs against the pitch and roll of the stage. The girl held her own, snuggled tightly against one side of the bench seat. She left a space between herself and the middle aged cowboy who smelled badly of whiskey and many days without a bath.

Once past the broken stretch, Dunn pushed the teams into a canter and moved them up a long pull to the top of a ridge far in the distance. On topping the ridgeline, he reined back and leaned down toward the cab.

"Ten minute rest stop, folks." he announced with a wiry grin, "Don't stray."

All John Montgomery could say for Dunn's humor was "shit."

As the passengers began to stumble out of the stage, Eli swung down from the leather thorobraces to check harnesses and straps. He put feed bags on the leaders and water bags for the rest. The leaders were only a little lathered and strong enough for the rest of the journey. This blowing out halt was necessary if the horses were to make it all the way to San Lacita without another stop. Once out of the close, confining walls of the stage compartment, the three miners lit cigarettes and stood in a group talking. The cowboy ambled away into the brush.

Claire moved up to the teams, casually running her fingers over a big chestnut. His flanks and shoulders were dry but for a few patches of sweat. He turned his muzzle to the girl. Claire rubbed his neck and he nickered in reply. She turned and gazed out across the vast desert. The night air was strong with the perfume of pinion nut, mesquite and bear grass. With that sweet smell came the hard, rank odor of sun burnt rock and sand. There was scrub brush scattered everywhere. The low wail of a distant coyote made the girl feel cold and alone.

"No need to worry, Ma'am, he's just lonesome."

The girl spun around, her hand instinctively flew up to her vest pocket. It was Eli, grinning through tobacco stained teeth. He stood a few feet away, checking the leader's cinches.

"You scared me."

"Sorry, Ma'am, didn't mean to. I just noticed you like horses. Come from a ranch, do you?"

Claire's shoulders softened a bit. She released a faint smile. "Yes, I do," she answered. "My father has a rather large spread near Santa Fe. That's where I'm going now."

Eli scratched his whiskers. "None of my business, Ma'am, I'm just a driver; but don't you think it's mighty dangerous for you…I mean a woman traveling by herself? Rumors say 'paches are making big trouble again."

Claire's eyes sparkled with youthful confidence and composure. "I've been with my uncle for several months," she said, "but I had enough of that polite hospitality. I'm anxious to get home..." adding under her breath, "to see my father again."

Eli wasn't sure what to say in response. He pursed his lips and set his eyes off in the same direction as the girls.

"Have you been on this route for a long time?" the girl asked.

"Yes, Ma'am, long enough … and before that a jerk line twelve for a while. I guess I've been skinning mules most of my born days."

"How long will it take us to get to San Lacita?"

"Well, I figure we got twenty miles of salt flats with good running, then some rough country again. We should be in San Lacita just after dawn. Your father and I can rest a little easier, I expect." He gnawed off a piece of tobacco and turned back to his team.

"Have you ever been a buffalo hunter?" Claire asked.

Eli turned back, his furry eyebrows registering surprise. "Yes Ma'am; buff, hide hunting, and wolfing - done 'em all. Why do you ask?"

Claire seemed more relaxed. "Oh, just idle curiosity," she admitted. "My father often hired hunters such as you to work for him…especially those that came off the Staked Plains. He always said they were always among the best. Did you hunt there?"

"Among other places... You name it and chances are I've been there."

The girl demurely dropped her eyes for a moment, then raised them again. "My name is Claire LeFonte."

"LeFonte is French, isn't it?"

"On my mother's side. My given name is Claire LeFonte Martinez."

Eli dragged off his slouched hat. "Eli Dunn, at your service, Ma'am! You need anything, you just let me know."

Claire's face broke into a wider smile. Her teeth were shiny white in the darkness. "Thank you, it's good to see a friendly face." With an affirmative nod, she turned back toward the stage. She followed the others into the tiny cramped compartment.

"Eli, what was you and that young Miss chattering on about?" John Montgomery asked.

Dunn snapped the reins, moving the teams out. He gazed out beyond the leaders in a trancelike state. John Montgomery began again but Eli cut him off. "John, let's just say we was talking of lavender and lace and pretty memories like that."

The shotgun guard didn't understand but knew Dunn well enough not to pry. So he turned instead and checked the rigging over some heavy trunks he and the cowboy had positioned just behind the driver's seat box. They were not large but rather long and heavy. In case of trouble, the luggage would be the only protection either driver or guard might have.

The next two hours dragged by. A dusty moon still hung above the stage, illuminating some of the rough cut stage trail while concealing the rest in splashes of black and gray. Inside all five passengers had settled down to make an attempt at sleeping. The miners leaned against one another, wrestling on their butt-sore bench for a little comfort. Claire nestled into her corner, with a vapid gaze out the window. The cowboy followed suit out of his.

Eli and the guard went an hour without a word between them. Another hour passed before John Montgomery stretched a bony finger toward the low terraced foothills up ahead. "That'll be Jeopardy Pass, I reckon. If trouble's coming, it could be there." Eli spat out another long stream of spittle. "Let them know below. We'll be going through pretty fast. Be rough riding for a while."

John Montgomery leaned over his seat rail, braced against the pitch and roll, and shouted above the pounding hooves, "Bad spot up ahead, folks, gonna be rough going for a while. No need for alarm, just hold on tight."

Eli snapped his lines and the horses' cadence increased. The old Concord swayed and rolled as its wheels hit rocks and ruts, bouncing over them. They entered the first of a series of low lying hills and rolled toward a break in the ridges that formed the entrance to Jeopardy Pass.

Both driver and guard kept their eyes darting back and forth, scanning the landscape for signs of trouble. It was deathly still. Once past a jumble of boulders and siltstone, the ground smoothed out a bit and the coach evened out its sway. Eli brought the teams back to a canter and held them steady. On both sides of the faint deer trail, the ground stretched only a hundred yards or so before meeting loose piles of rocks and boulders beyond the boulders, upthrusts of basalt and rocky outcroppings grew until they towered several dozen feet above the stage route.

John Montgomery tightened grip on his piece and checked the load for a third straight time. His Sheffield was loose in its scabbard. Even self-assured, confident Eli Doreen cupped both sets of reins in one calloused palm and checked his .44 old model cap and ball Colt. If he could have gotten to the new Winchester repeater at his feet, he'd have checked that also. "Gettin' too old for this kind of life," he mumbled under his breath. "Why the hell can't I settle down? Anywhere but on this damn stage." The thought was a recurring one and he never had an answer for himself.

After ten minutes the land began to close in tighter. The narrowing desert trail was growing pockmarked with washed out ruts and stray boulders that had tumbled down from above. Eli braced his feet against the front boot footrest and snapped the teams a little harder. The old coach creaked and groaned and rolled ahead.

"What's that?" John Montgomery exclaimed. He swung his piece out, pointing up ahead - then Dunn saw it. A riderless horse sprawled alongside the roadway. There were two feathered arrows buried deep in its shoulder. A thick crust of blowflies hung over its body. The carcass was still saddled but its rifle scabbard was empty. Blanket, lariat and utensils lay scattered about the ground - but no sign of its owner. "What do you think?" John Montgomery asked.

Eli held steady. He puckered his lips and let loose with another reddish stream into the wind. The teams pounded on toward the carcass at an even cadence. They were good stock. They wouldn't spook at the smell of a dead horse. He kept them rolling.

"We don't stop," Dunn muttered as they closed in on the dead beast. Both sets of eyes followed the still form until they had passed and it was behind them. Nothing stirred on either side of the pass. Darkness hid all movement, any sign of the missing rider or lurking Apaches.

"Apaches didn't grab him back there," John Montgomery announced. "There go his tracks!"

Eli could see the faint trace of footprints heading out of Jeopardy Pass in roughly the same direction as they were traveling. The driver pulled a dirty bandana out of his shirt pocket and wiped his forehead. He let out another warp of lines. The teams slowed their pace and went at their own gait. The last of the steep sided hills moved slowly by. They were out of the pass.

"If he ain't hanging from an Apache torture pole or skinned in some gully around here, I'd say he's probably up ahead, plodding along."

Eli shot his partner a look. "Apaches don't let gringos get away like that. They got a reason for letting him get away. Just so we aren't that reason!"

Up ahead the country was crosshatched by scrub filled draws, wandering arroyos and rocky mounds thrusting up in unexpected spots. The moon moved behind gathering clouds and the darkness grew. The tracks, if there were still some, were now hidden by rough ground and heightened darkness.

The Concord rolled on for another half hour then moved into broken country. The old wild horse trail twisted its way around arroyos and gullies then snaked a path up and over a low rising stretch of ridgeline. Both driver and guard watched the rising hills up ahead, narrow eyed.

Overhead the sky was beginning to change from solid darkness to a lighter tone.

Predawn.

A line of gray outlined the horizon and grew more distinct as each minute passed. In less than an hour it would be dawn. If the Apaches were to attack, it would be soon.

Eli believed he had seen the survivor's tracks in patches of sand along the roadway but he couldn't be sure and he had no intention of stopping to see. No one could be seen up ahead. Just the outlines and ghostly forms of sagebrush and sentinel cactus.

The teams were slowing a bit. Dunn could feel it in their response to his reins. He couldn't see the dark patches of sweat on their shoulders and flanks but he knew they were there. The horses would have to make it without another rest stop. If they didn't reach San Lacita within the hour, Elise would have to chance playing them out entirely. If they went bad, his element of speed was gone. That was a risk he'd have to take. He couldn't afford another stop … not now.

A short while later, the foothills up ahead began changing colors to dove gray and lavender. Deep alkali draws, drifting sand spits and gigantic saguaro cactus were becoming more pronounced all around them. An early morning breeze was beginning to pick up. Eli slowed the teams to a cadence that wouldn't wear them out so quickly. A faint opalescent haze hung low over the surrounding hills. Scattered sage-choked gullies lay on both sides of them. Except for the pounding hooves and creaking coach, silence lay heavy over the land.

Tension was mounting as the first rays of sunlight cracked the distant horizon and sent streaks of pale yellow light across the desert.

"There he is!"

Montgomery stuck his finger into the morning wind. Two heads popped out the cab windows. A murmur arose from within.

Outlined against the saddle of a distant rise stood a tall man. He was frantically waving a rifle over his head.

"Son-of-a-bitch," Eli swore to himself, "he made it."

In the early morning light, they could see he was a young man. He was clean shaven, carrying no gear and only had his rifle. He stood alone, stark against the gray horizon. He began a dogtrot down the slope, dragging his hat off as he came. His boots made tiny puffs in the powder dry soil.

Eli reined back the teams. The stranger came alongside the leaders and slapped hat against leg.

"Damn, it's good to see you folks!" he exclaimed.

"Found your horse back in the canyon, figured you was a goner."

"Yeah, Apaches jumped me back there," the man said, swinging his Winchester over one shoulder. "Thought they had me for a while … but then they just disappeared."

Suddenly three horses flung back their heads with pricked ears.

"Ambush!" John Montgomery snarled, rising up.

"Get in!" Eli shouted at the man.

The tenderfoot froze, shaken by their sudden reaction. He realized why he'd been spared back in the canyon. He swung around, leveling his piece.

But it was too late.

An arrow struck his midriff, doubling him over. War whoops and gunfire shattered the stillness. A party of painted Apaches broke out of a shallow gulch several hundred yards away.

"There!" Montgomery shouted, aiming his scattergun at a gully close by. He fired both barrels, tearing an Apache archer in half with eighteen rounds of buckshot.

The teams made a convulsive leap forward as Montgomery leapt off his seat box and gathered the stranger in his arms. Eli yanked back the reins, restraining the excited brutes. John Montgomery swung the cowboy's slack body toward the open stage door and pushed him up into waiting arms. Above him, Eli's short barreled Winchester fired in levered cadence at the screaming body of red men whirling toward them.

"Come on," Dunn shouted but his voice was lost amid war whoops and the sharp crack of colts firing out the cab windows. John Montgomery was half way up the front boot when Dunn let the restraining reins go loose. The teams seemed to explode forward, slamming into their breastbands. The stage snapped into motion, throwing passengers into one another. On top, John Montgomery braced his legs against the floorboards and fired at the low lying riders swirling toward them. A shell whizzed past his face, burning the air. Another exploded in the front boot. Splinters flew about his body.

Inside the cab, confusion ensued. The men tried to return fire but instead were tossed one way then another as the stage lurched drunkenly, rolling in and out of wide cut chuck holes.

Claire was aware of fierce yipping outside and shells smashing through the coach frame. She was desperate to find the revolver she had neatly tucked away inside the canvas bag. Despite the bucking seat bench and slugs flying by, she managed to squeeze low into a corner and was methodically combing through her bag.

Then it happened.

A miner opposite her emptied his gun at the approaching horde then leaned back to reload. He snapped open the cylinder and reached back to his belt loops. There was a shot from outside the window. The man's face exploded into splinters of blood and bone. His mouth flew open but made no sound as he slumped forward, landing face first into Clare's lap.

Claire sat petrified, frozen in horror at the dead man's shattered face lying against her. She could feel blood running down her legs. A wave of nausea swept through her throat. She wanted to scream but could only choke and gag. No one saw her. No one noticed. The cab was thick with dust and gun smoke. Beads of perspiration formed along her forehead and lips. The miner's head rocked in unison to the pitch and roll of the ride.

Then a bullet exploded above Claire's head and sent her pitching back, slamming her face against the window frame. It seemed to knock her back to reality. She fought her churning stomach and slowly regained some composure. Gently Glare leaned the limp body back into its corner. She gripped the man's revolver, loaded it quickly and fired it at the closing riders.

The Concord careened crazily over the crest of a limestone ridgeline and nearly tipped as one set of wheels plowed into soft sand on its shoulder. Dunn swung over to one side, bracing against Montgomery who was resting his rifle along the back of his seat. The guard fired twice, trying to time his shots with the lurching of the stage. Both shots went wild. He waited patiently, trying to align his bobbing sights on the riders who were quickly closing to within a scant dozen yards behind them.

Eli drove the teams like he had never done before. The creaking Concord groaned with each rut smashed into and rocked drunkenly on its axle springs. It rolled up the sharp grade of a granite slope and nearly flew over its top. The spooked horses, restrained only by the tough, rock solid arms of Dunn, ran right at the point of panic. Bits in their teeth, bellies to the ground, they swung into a sharp turn and sent the coach rising off one side again.

Inside the bouncing cab, the three men were settled into their positions, picking their shots. Each window had its gunner, one high, one low, firing methodically back at the Apaches. Claire realized her shots were in vain. She was wasting ammunition. So she slipped down, kneeling on the blood spattered floorboards and tried to help the wounded cowboy they had picked up. She cradled his head in her blood soaked lap and tried to comfort him as best she could. His lackluster eyes rose up to hers. He tried to smile but the effort only brought up a tiny trickle of blood out the corner of his mouth.

The initial onslaught of Apache gunfire had diminished as their attackers stretched out behind the stage. Riders raced along the roadway and its shoulders, trying to close the final distance to their coup. Four braves edged up closer, flanking the stage and hanging low on their mounts. John Montgomery brought down one pony and sent its rider tumbling into the dirt, but at a price. Even with breech-loading Springfields and Maynards, the Apache fusillade was costly.

The other three warriors fired into the cab, splintering window frames and blasting huge holes in both door panels. One miner slumped over his post, arms dangling in the wind. The cowboy ducked the furious onslaught then looked up and caught a slug through his arm. He tried a border shift, flipping the revolver to his good arm. A second slug slammed into his chest knocking him back against the headboards. He began bleeding profusely. On top, the two trunks behind Dunn and Montgomery caught a dozen slugs and held firm. Wood chips flew off into the wind.

The close up attackers swung back, only to be replaced by others who wove erratically in and out, closing in to riddle the cab and then swinging away again. John Montgomery sought them out. As they swung back in, he blasted two more out of their saddles.

Suddenly, the war party swung away. It began veering off to the right and away from the stage. The warriors shouted and waved their weapons but the attack was off. The gap lengthened between stage and attackers. Driver and guard sat dumbfounded, not believing their eyes. The stage lurched over a low lying crest and rolled down a gently sloping grade. The Apaches fell farther and farther behind. Finally they were gone and the stage was alone again.

When Eli was certain it wasn't just another Apache trick, he slowed the teams to a canter. They were already stepping short, stumbling over the hock-high sage. He reined back farther, bringing them to a walk trot. After a few minutes, certain the team's breathing had settled, Dunn drew back on the reins. The horses came to a staggering halt. Flanks and shoulders glistened in the early morning sun. The brutes hung their heads and blew out, some tossing their manes. A silence swept over the stage and its passengers. It seemed to hang above them like a shroud of death.

As Dunn tended to the jaded mounts, John Montgomery, buoyed by three sure kills, swung down off the splintered seat box and went back to the cab. He yanked open the coach door. A body slumped against his face. It was the cowboy, his chest scarlet with blood. His eyes were open. The man tried to speak but no words came forth. Montgomery looked past him at the carnage and felt sick.

Claire was on the floorboards, cramped in tightly against the far door. A revolver stuck out of her shirt. She was trying to aid the stranger they had picked up. Slumped across from her, a miner was applying a rough tourniquet to his bleeding arm. On his one side, a fellow miner hung half out the shattered window frame. On the other side, the corpse was sickening. Of the six passengers jammed tightly into the cab, two were dead, two more dying and one was wounded.

Only Claire escaped without a scratch. Her face was spotted with droplets of blood and her hair hung in tangles around her cheeks. Her skirt and blouse were scarlet and sticky. Yet she uttered no complaints as she tried to listen to the tenderfoot's incoherent words.

"Christ Almighty," John Montgomery swore softly under his breath, swallowing hard. He laid the slack body back inside. His hands were wet with blood. The guard reckoned he had seen it all during his years on the trail. From Apache torture victims to violated womenfolk but never that close up...not with death's rank odor hung heavy with the acid tang of gunpowder and smoldering wood.

"Eli, come here quick," the guard shouted, climbing inside. The girl looked up, saying nothing. Montgomery lifted the miner gently back inside the cab. He too was dead. The guard helped the surviving miner out the door and onto the ground. The arm was not badly hurt. The bleeding had mostly stopped.

Driver and guard carried the slack body of the stranger out of the cab and laid him in the shade of the wagon wheel. He was breathing poorly, the feathered shaft rising and falling with each gasp. Claire took a canteen from the boot and wiped the man's forehead. He stirred a little then fell back into his surface coma.

"How much farther do we have to go?" Claire asked softly, so as not to wake the dying man.

Eli scratched his balding head and rubbed his whiskers. "Another hour maybe less but these horses can't be pushed anymore. They're about played out right now."

"Will they come back?" Claire asked then, raising her worried eyes up the driver's vest to rest on his hard face.

The same question was hammering away at the back of Dunn's mind. And he had no answer for the girl or himself. He just didn't know. "Rightly don't know, Ma'am and that's the honest truth. I never seen Apaches break off an attack just like that. It ain't their style. If they'd stuck with us, good chance we wouldn't be here right now. It's mighty peculiar, that's what it is."

John Montgomery indicated his silent agreement with a nod. There was nothing more that had to be said. It wasn't like the Apaches. It didn't make sense. And anything that didn't hang right by the driver and guard worried them more than a pack of Apache wolves baying down their rifle barrels anytime.

They knelt around the man for a few more minutes. Nothing else stirred in the early morning sunlight. The sky was green tinted and lovely. It promised to be a hot day again but still a nice one for those still alive.

Eli arose, Montgomery followed him up. Driver and guard checked their loads and cast worried eyes in the direction of the Apaches. "Let's go, Eli, the guard said, "I got me several snorts waiting for breakfast. Maybe lunch too."

Dunn turned to the girl. "You'll have to stay inside with the others, Ma'am. I expect they'll be needing you. We don't dare leave anyone behind, even those that is dead. Apaches do horrible things even to dead people."

"I understand," Claire said, "It's alright."

They gently lifted the drifter back inside and helped the miner settle in. The teams moved out, slower this time, with little pull on the harnesses. Eli let them find their own gait and settled back for the ride to San Lacita.

Chapter Three

Jud Courtough watched the three gunmen ride past the Santa Fe stage line stables and move up the long slope toward Bald Mountain Pass. As the riders grew smaller, he surveyed to make certain no one had seen him. It could cause talk if the sheriff was seen waving off three posted criminals. There was no movement among the wood and adobe back structures, but for a few mangy curs scavenging for food. Courtough was alone in the shadows of San Lacita's back street. An early morning breeze was his only companion.

The sheriff pinned a small tin star back on his vest and tilted his stained Stetson, cocked low over watchful eyes. He casually retraced his steps to the front porch of the saloon. Reclaiming a familiar chair, he tilted back against the wall and shoved a long thick cigar into the corner of his mouth. He scratched a match against his boot, drew in deeply on the cheroot and settled into his favorite posture; a drowsy slump. Although tall and big boned, Jud Courtough cut a low, harmless looking figure as he nestled in his chair and dozed. His pencil thin mustache curled with each puff sucked in and blown out. His gray eyes lay hazy and somber. In spite of all the lazy expression he might muster, the sheriff's mind was working overtime - especially since money, lots of it, was involved.

The trio he had sent off wouldn't reach the miner's cabin until late that afternoon. Even if they were quick about rifling the cabin and finding the gold, there was no guarantee they'd be back before midnight. Courtough had lots of time to kill and plenty of people to see him doing it. He didn't need any loose talk to pin him in with that robbery and probable killing. His presence in town would make short work of that gossip, and it wouldn't jeopardize his motives for tracking the men who did it.

Jud Courtough had a sweet thing going and he didn't want to ruin it. Not yet. Not until he had his share of the gold and was clear of San Lacita. After that, the town be damned. He spoke good cow pen Spanish. Mexico City could be his next home. He could drink tequila all day and watch those fine Spanish ladies dancing at the bailes all night. Jud was a sheriff and outlaw at the same time. He had made something out of the job of sheriff where only failures had existed before. Like it or not, no one could complain about the job Jud had done. They might question his methods, but never his results.

Courtough had drifted into San Lacita a short two months earlier. It was at a time when the mining settlement was on the verge of breaking wide open. San Lacita lay nestled in the valley of Rita del Conchas where it diverged out from the foothills of the Cebolleta Mountains in the West. San Lacita was a town of mud boxes and crudely constructed wooden structures. Its buildings were dingy and dilapidated. Hurriedly fashioned, they were unable to withstand the changes of seasons; the blazing summer heat and the winter winds. It was a motley town of traders, speculators, gamblers, horse thieves and itinerant miners. Mining ruled the town's very existence.

When Jud arrived, the mines were going twenty-four hours a day. A steady stream of newcomers arrived daily. Tough, rowdy crowds of nearly every nationality roamed around town at will. Gunfights and innocent killings were commonplace. None of the merchants or mill owners could control them. What the town needed was a sheriff. After three candidates were killed in less than a week, applicants quickly dried up.

Jud had been five days in the saddle when he arrived. Tired, hungry, and broke; he was mean enough to hand wrestle a puma for a quick snort. The first saloon he wandered into gave him just that opportunity. A huge, heavy set miner, having spent ten hours getting tough drunk, met Jud in the doorway. He tried to shove Courtough back outside. Jud sidestepped and knocked the high grader back. Roaring out a stream of curses, the miner whipped out a long barreled .45 but before he could clear leather, Jud shot him three times. Two of the man's companions drew against Jud. He cut them down with a single shot apiece. As they lay dying on the sawdust floor, Courtough rifled their pockets in front of everyone. 'Just claiming the spoils', he announced. Not a sound came from the crowd. As he arose, a shout of approval went up and hands came slapping against his back. Jud had unknowingly eliminated the town's number one sheriff killer. He owned the town that day; all the liquor he could down and a job as lawmaker if he wanted it. No questions would be asked. It paid twenty-five dollars a month, free lodging at the hotel and all the meals he could stomach there. Jud Courtough had found himself a home…for the time being.

Word of the gunfight spread quickly. Several drifters came to test the new sheriff's skills. He gave them no quarter and killed every one. He seemed to welcome each opportunity at proving his gun handling. When three drunken horsemen galloped through town one night, firing at anything moving, Jud was waiting for them at the end of Main Street. He picked each one off with a carbine at close range.

Rumor spread that a professional gunfighter from Montana was heading for San Lacita, hired by a dissident gang wanting to claim the town for its own. Courtough called on three old companions in crime; the Lanker brothers, Curt and Eddie and their simpleminded friend, Gus. They bushwhacked the gunfighter outside of town. When he disappeared, Jud claimed another problem eliminated and no one dared question him on it.

After the gunfighter incident, the town began to settle into its own routine. The Lanker gang proceeded robbing and horse stealing but never around San Lacita. It became their hole-in-the-wall, their ace against any posse set out against them. Jud took his cut and let them be. Gunfights ceased in town. Things became practically peaceful. Jud began getting restless, itching for a fight - then he heard about the gold.

A detailed plan to rob the stage line office was forgotten when Jud got word that a miner had struck something, probably gold, in the Salt Mountains. The mountains were not more than a day's ride outside of town. His informant, a reservation spy, had mapped out a route to the miners cabin for a jug of whiskey. That was where the trio was heading now - to find out if it was true about the gold and to get whatever they could. *It shouldn't be long,* Jud thought. Soon he'd be heading for Sonora and those fine brown-skinned ladies. Jud blew a perfect smoke ring and shelved the stub back between his teeth.

Sunlight was beginning its assault on the horizon. Bright yellow streaks broke over the sunbaked spine of Lucero Mesa in the east. Up and down the rutted street, San Lacita was gradually beginning to awaken. From his vantage point, Sheriff Courtough could see the general store owner spreading his wares out front. The hotel was disgorging a nightly fill of hungover drifters and lobby dwellers. Old Avery's Harness and Hardware Store was just drawing its blinds.

On the rolling timbered slopes, a short distance below Main Street, the ore reduction mills were just starting up their machines. Months before, the incessant racket had kept the air humming day and night. Now the mills rumbled only during daylight hours and rumor had spread that the mines were beginning to play out. Behind Main Street, skirting the west side of town, the big ore wagons were beginning to shuttle back and forth between the mills and the silver mines scattered on the mountain slopes above. Even there the traffic was lighter than when Jud had first arrived. If new veins weren't reached soon, most of the town could die overnight. The daily traffic of rigs, ore wagons, murphys and freighters were filing into their regular channeled flow through town. More townsfolk were filling the wooden sidewalks.

The proprietor opened his door behind the sheriff and said hello. Jud waved him off with a nod and went back to his vacant staring. A short while later, two men ambled by and one stopped in front of the lawman.

"Sheriff, have you heard anything about the stage from Black Horse Springs? It's overdue by a couple of hours."

Courtough didn't bother to look up. He shrugged his shoulders and muttered, "I don't run the stage, mister, that isn't my concern. Albuquerque runs the line. I keep the law!"

"Yes, but I hoped you might have heard something," the man persisted.

"Just got up myself," Jud lied. "I haven't heard a thing." He leaned back further, his hat blocking out the men entirely. They stood for a moment then turned and walked off, mumbling under their breath.

Within an hour, Jud heard several others talking about the missing stage as they walked by. He caught several hard stares but ignored them. Realizing he hadn't eaten breakfast, Courtough got up, stretched his legs and went into the cantina for his morning snort. After two shots of aguardiente and some Mexican sweet cakes, Jud settled into his corner stool and smoked another cheroot. Halfway through the cigar, he heard shouting and the stage pounding into town. The shouts persisted. Something had happened to the stage.

Even Jud Courtough; level headed, no regrets gunfighter, had to look twice at the old Concord parked across the street. The paneled coach body was peppered with bullet holes and feathered shafts. Apache arrows! The teams were played out, heads hung, withers gone limp. There was not the strength to pull a bolt of cloth left in them. Passengers were being lifted gently out of the cab. Jud didn't have to be closer to see the pall of death over there.

Eli and John Montgomery came back from unhitching the teams to be led away. A sneer curled the side of Courtough's mouth. His bad luck! The two of them had been his nemeses since their last trip to San Lacita. They knew of his reputation outside of town. They could cause trouble if they wanted to … and they knew he knew it. It was a Mexican standoff with neither side risking too much. It made the sheriff uneasy and trigger-happy. Just one incident, one opportunity to gun them down. It never came. They were too quick for that, so he tolerated them for the meantime.

Jud crossed the street and pushed through a crowd of curious onlookers. "Driver, what happened?"

Dunn looked up from his charge with a knit brow and rasped, "What's it look like, Courtough, Injuns, of course."

"I can see that, old man! Where did it happen?"

Eli faced Courtough. "They jumped us this side of Jeopardy Pass. Left the man on foot and laid up in ambush. When we stopped, they hit us. Clean as that."

"What delayed you in the first place?" Jud asked.

"You worried?" John Montgomery mused from inside the cab.

Eli spoke before the sheriff could react to the curt remark. "We broke a hitch outside of Black Horse. It didn't seem enough to turn back for so we fixed it there. It ended up delaying us a good three hours."

"Damnable luck," he muttered to no one in particular.

Courtough was through. He had done his job, asked the questions, pretended to be full of concern. Those who didn't believe him wouldn't say so in public. Those that did couldn't harm him. He felt satisfied.

Turning away from the coach, Jud caught sight of something stir inside the cab … a swirl of hair, a beautiful face. He turned and saw Claire emerge from the stage with disheveled hair and blood-spattered clothes. She stood for a moment, framed in the splintered doorway. She was helping the last man out. It was the cowboy with an arrow deep in his gut. The girl leaned against the door frame, doggedly tired.

Jud moved quickly. He reached out a strong arm, "Ma'am, let me help you," he said in his most commanding voice. The girl said nothing, her face expressionless. She accepted his hand and stepped down.

Courtough looked down on the girl, the soft dark eyes, and her robust figure. His mind whirled with the musings of this fine specimen of a woman and what she was doing in a rot-gut town like San Lacita. She was not dressed like most female passengers he had encountered. She was young, feminine and pretty. He needed no more encouragement.

"All right, show's over," Jud announced. "Break it up, folks. Doc Smithson's got to tend to these wounded." He turned to Claire again. "May I escort you over to the hotel? I expect you've had a mighty rough time of it out there. You'll want to rest up. Maybe a room, if you're staying in San Lacita." The voice was forceful but lacking sincerity. Though Jud tried his best, women weren't his expertise.

Claire smiled weakly. "You're very kind, sheriff, but I want to see what I can do to help the doctor. Thank you anyway."

Jud stood there a moment, a smile painted on his leathery face and then he turned and pushed past the crowd, and crossed back to the cantina. *She's a looker alright,* he thought, as he took two stairs at a time and snapped back the batwing doors. A fine class of woman. The kind he hadn't seen except in penny papers. That kind of breeding came from money. Lots of it.

Inside Doc Smithson's tiny office, the two wounded men were laid out, Eli and John Montgomery stood awkwardly in the doorway until motioned outside by the little man who retained Claire as emergency nurse. They left without hesitation, but not without words.

"Ma'am."

Claire looked up, her tired eyes falling on Eli. "Yes, what is it?"

The driver dragged off his slouched hat. "Beg your pardon, Ma'am, none of my business…but…well, the sheriff. He's one bad hombre. I mean it isn't wise to tell him anything. You don't know him like I do. He's bad medicine, especially around womenfolk."

"What do you mean bad? He is the law around here, isn't he?"

Eli wrinkled his lips, seeking the right words. "What I mean is, Ma'am, he's the law alright. Only because no one else wanted the job or was mean enough for it. He isn't a regular appointed marshal. He's a gunfighter, a shootist and an opportunist above anything else."

Claire's lips curled in an understanding smile. She could read the old man's honest intent. "But why tell me all this?" she inquired innocently.

"Lands sakes, Ma'am," Eli said in astonishment, "That man's got his eyes set on you like a wolf to a lamb. If he hasn't tried to get friendly with you yet, he will shortly. That's a certainty."

Claire stepped closer. "I do understand what you're saying. Thanks for your concern. I can handle myself. Really!" Her determined eyes sought out Eli's. He understood the look. "Now I must go back inside … you understand."

Claire helped Doc Smithson remove the arrow shaft and apply quinine to the wound. It was of little good. The cowboy was hemorrhaging internally, coughing up lots of blood. His eyes rolled in pain. There was little left to do for him.

They worked in silence. The doctor motioned for his instruments, Claire responded.

A fly buzzed above their heads unnoticed. It was hot and stuffy inside the tiny windowless room. Outside, the regular wheeled traffic had settled back to its noisy, dusty pattern. The arrowhead was removed after an hour of painstaking labor. There was nothing more that could be done. Doc Smithson motioned Claire away from the bed.

"You've done all you can, now why don't you try to get some rest." The oldster's kindly face, beneath a sweep of tousled white hair, smiled appreciatively. He led her toward the door. Without braving a final peek at the dying boy, Claire stepped out into the shade of the Ramada. It was cooler outside. The harsh sunlight hurt her eyes. She stood for a moment, drained by the morning's experience. Gradually, her head and stomach began to settle.

Voices drifted past from close by. It was Eli and John Montgomery talking in a heated exchange about something. Drawn by curiosity and the need to be with friends, Claire walked to the corner. As she peered around the corner of the building, Eli was running at full steam.

"One thing don't make sense. Them was Chiricahuas and Mescaleros riding side by side. Apache tribes don't mix unless it's for something big. And what are Cherry Cows doing this far East? Something strange about them warring together. I don't like it." The perplexed driver returned to whittling a stick.

John Montgomery sat on his haunches, scratching idly in the dirt with a twig. "I don't particularly care what kind of Injun I blast out of the saddle, Cherry Cow or otherwise, but I want to know why they pulled back when they did."

"Perhaps they'd had enough," a soft voice said.

Driver and guard turned quickly, half off their haunches.

"That's right dangerous. Sneaking up like that," Montgomery warned,

"Oh hell, John, We're just gettin' old and deaf. Please do sit down, Miss." He pointed to an old chair propped up against the side of the building. The girl sat down and leaned forward.

"I was also wondering about the attack. Why did they stop it when they did? It isn't Apache style."

"You know about the Apache, do you ma'am?" Eli asked.

Claire's eyes caught Eli's and held. Penetrating and direct, they would not turn away. "I told you my father has a large ranch near Santa Fe. We've had our share of trouble with the Apache; especially during those years when the soldiers were gone. If it hadn't been for father's vaqueros, it might have been a lot worse. Still, I've seen what they do to prisoners. We've lost men to ambushes and had to go out to find them." Montgomery eyed the girl, surprise and disbelief in his eyes. "You, Ma'am, you went out with them hunting Apache?"

"I did."

"Well, I'll be a..."

"So I know it isn't like the Apache to stop an attack when they obviously have the upper hand."

Eli's hand snapped. The stick plunged into the ground. All eyes turned to him. Irritation had gotten the best of him. "No, it isn't like the Apaches. For the life of me, I can't figure out why they done that. This means they could be laying for us out there again; waiting for a fresh load of scalps to line their lodges."

"If you're thinking of not leaving San Lacita tonight because of me, don't. I intend to leave as soon as possible. It might just as well be on your stage as not."

Eli's furry eyebrows rose a bit, a smile creased his lips. "I do believe you mean that, Miss. Tonight it is then. We'll leave as soon as it gets dark. At least that'll give us some chance of reaching the relay station before dawn. Still, I wish we had the Army here for escort."

"If the U.S. Army were here, they might make us stay put," Claire volunteered.

"She knows her stuff," Montgomery laughed out loud, "She sure do."

Chapter Four

The sun was beginning its descent. Streaks of light split through the heavy cloud cover. Just above the mountain's timberline; Curt, Eddie and Gus found the miner's place. They reined in below the saddle of a ridge bordering his cabin. Gus bellied up the slope and eased into some brush to avoid being skylined.

There was no one in sight. A stream gurgled noisily down the mountainside. Tall aspens rustled and waved their branches, but nothing more. No smoke out of the chimney. No stock animals around. Nothing.

The tiny log cabin was nestled in the folds of an alluvial fan swept off the mountain's peak centuries before. Where a powerful stream once ran; a shallow, rock-filled creek now churned past the hut and disappeared into pine draws below. Behind the one room affair, the land buckled and seemed to thrust itself several hundred feet straight up. The cliff face was clear of cuts and crevasses, sliced neat and clean a century ago.

Except for a wheelbarrow and pick axe laid up against the cabin wall and a shifting trough in the creek, there were no signs to identify it as a miner's cabin. No corral for pack animals, no picket lines, no hung meat, no chiseled scars against the smooth cliff face. Nothing to indicate the area was rich in gold.

"Well?" Curt prodded Gus.

Gus shrugged his shoulders. "See for yourself, boss, no one is around. He must have the mine someplace else." The Lankers moved up to the saddle to have a look for themselves. A dozen plots ran helter-skelter through Curt's mind but he remained calm and placid on the outside.

This had to be it, the outlaw reasoned. The directions had led him straight to the spot where the Apache spy had said the cabin would be. The informant hadn't been wrong before. He most likely wasn't wrong this time either. Gus wiggled back down the slope.

"Come on, let's go in," Eddie said, moving behind Gus.

The brother mumbled something down to Gus and together they turned to the horses.

"Wait!" commanded Curt.

"Well, are we going in or not?" Eddie snapped back at his brother.

"Damn it, don't go off half-cocked like you usually do. If he's seen us, likely as not we'll get a load of buckshot riding straight in there."

"So what do you want us to do?"

Curt slid down the slope. "We split up and come in from three different directions. If he's there we can plug him from one side or the other. Courtough doesn't want any witnesses to this job and neither do I. If the miner isn't around, then we'll wait for him inside."

Gus signaled his understanding. With his child's mind, there was little logic that he'd argue with. Killing was one impression that made a difference. Gus understood that. He liked it - particularly when Curt let him tease the victim first. He really liked it then.

Eddie wasn't buying his brother's argument. "Whatta we gotta kill him for?" he groused. "Let's grab the gold if there is any and get the hell outta here. That miner isn't gonna go to town and shout he was robbed. Why these hills would be crawling with hill nuttys in a matter of days. Hell, if the old goat gets robbed, he'll just mine some other vein someplace else. We can come back and hit him again. Why ruin our opportunity to get a lot of gold?"

"Because that's what the boss wants, that's why." Curt answered evenly.

"Well the sheriff can shove it," Eddie snarled.

Curt watched him go and cursed under breath. His younger brother was impulsive. He'd be trouble someday. Either his big mouth or too-quick-to-reason mind would land him in jail or worse.

Shrugging his shoulders, Curt sent Gus off in the opposite direction.

Eddie topped the ridgeline behind a cover of fir and aspen. He moved slowly down into a grove of pine opposite the cabin. The gurgling creek seemed the loudest at that point. Eddie waited an impatient ten minutes and then spotted Curt approaching from along the mountain's alluvial fan and Gus coming through some trees in the opposite direction.

An eerie sensation chilled Eddie's body for a moment, then vanished. It seemed a pair of eyes were creeping down his neck. When he spun around with his gun at the ready, there was nothing.

Eddie nudged his mount into the cold creek and crossed toward the cabin. His rifle was still in its scabbard but his hand was loose and ready. No sound came from within the cabin. A breeze was blowing the sack curtain out through the only window. The oak door swung easily in the wind. It creaked back and forth on its leather hinges.

The trio walk trotted their mounts to within ten yards of the cabin and stopped. Eddie dismounted slowly, facing the door and slapped his hat against dirty Levis. "Hello in there," he called. The air was still. Only an ever present mountain breeze and the babbling creek broke the high mountain solitude.

"Curtis."

Lanker looked over at his brother. Eddie was nervously looking around, fingering his shotgun. He spoke as he twisted in the saddle. "You get the feeling that someone is watching us? Like maybe that miner heard us coming and lit outta here. Maybe he's in those trees, watching us."

"Oh hell, you think too much. Don't strain yourself." He swung off his horse and followed Gus to the cabin. As he approached the creaking door, he had to admit that Eddie was right. There was something strange up there on the mountainside. Call it intuition. Call it a gunfighter's gut reaction. Something didn't hang right. The uneasy feeling followed Lanker into the cabin.

It was dark and dank inside. A musty odor hung thick and heavy in the close quarters. The only light penetrating its somberness came through the door and one tiny window. Gradually Curt began to recognize the smell of burnt coals, grease and freshly out wood. It all mingled with the chilling dampness of the high country. Furniture was scarce and homemade; one wobbly chair, a corner bunk, a small table and an unfinished grading box for the creek. The only tools around were several hand drills, all old and worn - nothing fancy, and nothing extra. Not one thing that didn't have its place and function.

But there were no weapons. Day old coals in the fireplace said the owner hadn't been around since morning if then.

Curt and Eddie combed the messed up bunk and cluttered table while Gus went to look 'round the perimeter. Not even a knife could be found.

"No sign of trouble," Eddie remarked, "You think he's just gone for the day, making his way back now?"

"Oh hell, I don't know," The elder brother growled, irritated at the questioning. "One thing's certain, this place hasn't been open overnight which means he left this morning and didn't expect to be gone long. He would have closed up if he was going to a mine for the day. Otherwise varmints would most likely get in here and scavenge around for food. I got me a feeling he's either watching us close by or someone else got to him before us. Either way he isn't coming back."

Eddie looked up from by the fireplace. His brother was framed in the doorway, staring out at the dying vestiges of sunlight slipping over the distant mountains. Eddie felt a chill don his spine. And it wasn't from the dampness. He followed Curt outside only too glad to be out of the spooky cabin.

Gus was coming out of a pine grove several hundred yards away. His shotgun was shouldered. He came back, panting from the slope's steep grade. Worry ruled his face. "Hey, boss, I got me the same feeling as Eddie did...like I was being watched."

"What did you find down there?" Eddie asked.

"Horses caught the scent of something. I speculated it might be a puma or bear, but I couldn't find any tracks or signs." He paused to look around again. "They smelled something. I know that for certain."

Eddie squinted at the surrounding hills, taking in the hundreds of dark patches and extending shadows slashed in the landscape. There were hundreds of places where someone could be watching them. "I don't like it, Curt. Let's find what he's got around here and get the hell back to town."

Gus piped up. "Yeah, I think we…"

"Gus," Curt snapped, placing a firm hand down hard on the man's shoulder. "You aren't supposed to think. Just do what I tell you to do."

Gus arched his back; his face was flushed with anger, but his simple mind couldn't hold on to the sting of Curt's statement and he slumped back to his normal slouching stance. Gus was confused momentarily, and then he acquiesced. He'd do whatever the boss told him to do.

"Now go scout out back of the cabin. Look for tracks leading away from here," Curt ordered.

The feeble-minded outlaw obediently shuffled off.

The Lankers moved down to the creek but found nothing. The grading box was wearing badly but they saw no sign of gold. Even the pan was still sitting on the corner of the box, filled with gravel and small pebbles.

"Hey, boss, I found him."

Curt and Eddie sprinted back toward Gus. He was straddling the edge of a depression. The draw was on a slope above the cabin, well hidden from the lower level. At the bottom of the draw, they found the miner sprawled on his back. His woolen shirt was soaked with blood. His legs were twisted in odd shapes, indicating he had probably broken his back. One glimpse up the slope and Curt saw a goat's trail and the miner's hat still resting on its edge.

They leaned over the pale figure. He was still alive, breathing unevenly in long laboring gasps.

"What happened, Mister?" Curt asked, leaning closer.

There was no sound above the feather light breathing.

Even in the early evening chill, sweat beads formed on the miner's forehead and upper lips. He knew he was dying…and taking a long time to do it. The outlaws gave him water but it ran off his lips. His cheeks were like parchment. He had been shot in the chest but it was the broken back that would kill him. They could only assume he was bleeding internally. There wasn't much the trio could do even if they were of a mind to.

"Who did this to you?" Curt questioned, feeling panic creep in. "We know you got gold. We came to warn you about this. We're your friends. Do you

36

understand we're your friends?" Lanker was banking on the man being delirious. If he could be tricked into believing they were his friends, perhaps they could still find out where his gold was hid, if he had any at all."

"Map!" the harsh, crooked voice gasped.

Curt and Eddie leaned over closer to the dying lips.

"Whatta he say, boss?" Gus called from the edge.

"Damn it, Gus, shut up!" Lanker growled.

"What map, Mister?" Eddie asked, trying again to ply water down the man's gullet. "He took it…the map."

"Who took it? We'll get it back for you. We're your friends."

The miner's eyes widened, glassy and unfocused. They were open but unseeing. The lips trembled as blood bubbled up over them. Death was close. The man was growing more delirious. "…took my map," he uttered.

Curt could feel anxiety creeping up his throat. He wanted to grab the man and shake some sense out of his words. He wanted to slap him across the face, but reason held. He calmed his voice. "What about your gold? Where did you hide it? We'll help you protect it!"

The voice cracked, coughing blood, and then steadied again. "No gold…map is gold. He took map. Di…"

Gus shouted from the rim. "Hey, boss, I found footprints. It must be the guy that shot him. Should I follow them?"

"Yes!" The brothers snapped in unison.

The miner lapsed into unconsciousness. They laid him back down and walked to the top of the draw. Gus had disappeared into a grove of pine and mountain catclaw. Just as quickly he reappeared, waving his arm. They went to him. The tracks were clean in the soft soil. One horse. One rider. And judging from the direction of the tracks, the rider was heading back down the mountain the same direction the trio had come up. Odds favored those tracks were heading straight back to San Lacita.

Eddie turned to Curt, "That varmint is heading back to town. Let's finish off the old man and get moving."

"Leave him!"

"Whatta ya mean, leave him? You gonna leave him to die like that?"

Curt's eyes flashed anger. "Leave him, I said. Don't waste your ammunition. Now let's ride."

Eddie stood his ground a moment. He might be an outlaw tagging behind an older brother, but he sure as hell had a heart. He couldn't stomach leaving any man to die like that. It didn't ruffle Curt's feathers, but it did Eddie's. He trained his revolver at the miner's skull. The man's eyes opened again. They were looking directly at Eddie. He couldn't do it.

Then the sound of hoof beats jogged him back to his senses. The other two were leaving. He ran to his pinto, leaping to saddle. As he rode off, he could feel the evil and strangeness of that place closing in behind him.

The old miner had laid sprawled in the depression for a long time. He knew he was dying. If not from the gunshot wound then his back. *It must be broken,* he thought, *my legs won't respond.* The sky above was growing darker. *Dusk!* He had been in the pit for a long time. For just how long, he couldn't be sure. Time was not a part of his reality.

He had been lapsing in and out of consciousness all day. *My mind must be playing tricks on me,* he thought. There had been voices. A shadow crossed over his eyes. Inky blackness swept everything away. He could not see. He could barely hear. He became aware of someone talking, whispering close to his face. The numbing pain grew more intense in his chest. He could feel blood choking him inside. He wanted to scream out in anger and pain.

But the words wouldn't come.

Dickson had shot him! Yes, now the man remembered. Dickson caught the old man as he was coming off the mountain trail. He'd held him at bay until the old timer revealed where the map was, and then Dickson had shot him twice and laughed as he smashed backwards into the pit. His friend Dickson was a killer!

Stabs of pain swept up through his chest again. Breathing grew more and more difficult. Blood...he could feel it slowly running out the corner of his mouth. He became aware of sounds - familiar sounds. Hoof beats moving away from the cabin, crossing the creek and heading down the slope. There must have been people there; he must not have imagined it! There had been someone talking to him moments ago. It wasn't a dream.

Then another sound brushed against his ears. Even as the hoof beats were dying away, the sound of footsteps on dried leaves arose. The sound was coming up quickly behind him. The old man tried to lift his head. He wanted to see more. They hadn't left him. He would be saved. But his head wouldn't move. He was paralyzed. Silence came down hard on him again.

The sound came back; closer still ... deliberate. Apaches! It must be Apaches. Oh, God. Let them do me quickly. Please, Lord!

A face appeared in front of him. The face was Indian but the clothing was that of a white man. The Indian carried a blanket which he laid gently over the miner's broken body. He cushioned the head. He was trying to stop the bleeding. He must be a friend. At last, a friend had come.

The old miner tried to say something. His lips trembled. Blood bubbled up again. He gathered his strength to speak, then a shutter ran through his body and he went slack in the stranger's arms. He was dead.

The miner was buried where he lay. A blanket covered his body. It took Ree Bannon an hour to fill in the grave sufficiently to keep wolves and cats from digging up the remains. As he worked, Bannon considered the conversation he'd overheard between the miner and bandit trio. There was the map he wanted and he had to get it before those outlaws did. Ree had been not more than fifteen feet behind the cabin when they discovered the miner. He'd overheard everything.

When he finished, the half breed removed his tattered hat and brushed his brow. The night breeze blew his black hair across his stone cold face. The intense eyes were unblinking, gazing off in the direction of San Lacita. He turned and moved quietly on desert boots to his mustang quartered a hundred yards back in the woods. San Lacita was his destination and a man who had taken his map.

Chapter Five

The saloons had filled up early on Friday night. Miners with their
in hand, cowhands and vaqueros off neighboring spreads and the usu.
of drifters had all wandered into town. All of them attracted by the boo.
sour-eyed pieces of womanhood lacing the crap and faro tables. The air w.
thick with the aroma of whiskey, sawdust, body sweat and oil lamp smoke.

Jud Courtough was on his corner throne. His gun belt was hung low for the
crowd; more for show than purpose. A half empty bottle rested in his grasp.
His shot glass was full.

The sheriff sat staring out across the room at nothing in particular.

Since his abbreviated conversation with Claire earlier in the day, Courtough had
been thinking and thinking hard. The woman and the gold were paramount on
his mind. *She is something fine,* he thought. A woman he'd be rightly proud to
have at his side … or own, as he would put it. He had never been hitched, and
never intended to be - but to have a woman like that was something that
appealed to him. Nearly as appealing as the gold that Curt and Eddie would
bring back to him. It should be enough for the four of them to have one hell of a
fine time in old Mexico, he mused.

By eight, the cantina was choked with people. Jud remained in his cocoon,
oblivious to the cursing, laughing and shouting all around him. He could sense
trouble if and when it came, he needn't watch for it. And besides, he had that
gold to think about. The barkeep palmed Jud's bottle to pour himself a drink.
Jud looked up from a vacant stare.

"Sketch, you ever been married?" he asked.

The fat man scratched his shiny dome, shaking his head. "Nope, I got enough
troubles running this damn place and paying my bills. Don't need no woman to
complicate things more than that."

"You ever get lonely?"

"I got things for that."

Jud cut a sneer. "I'll bet you do, what's your fancy, a heifer or a lamb?"

"Go to hell!" Sketch said, with an appropriate gesture. He stuffed the bottle
back in Jud's palm and turned away. He was just in time to see a young man in
store-bought clothes slip inside the crowded room and quickly move through the
pack. He edged up to the bar and motioned two fingers for a rye. Sketch eyed

ɔment, trying to figure out where someone in city clothes would
out of nowhere. *That boy didn't ride into town like that, fresh*
.d all, he thought. *And he wasn't on this morning's shot up Black*
.age. The introspection was interrupted as a gold eagle landed in
s open hand and the young man muttered, "Keep it."

ɪff Courtough had also noticed the youngster. He wasn't one of the regular
ɪmen working the mines. Jud could spot one of those slicks a block away.
nd he hadn't come in on the stage today. If it hadn't been for the clothes, Jud
would never have noticed him. Store-bought duds out in the middle of New
Mexico territory, especially a dump like San Lacita, didn't make sense. *Who*
cares? Jud reasoned, *he's not bothering anyone.* If the dude is dumb enough to
wear those clothes around here, let him. Jud emptied the shot glass, refilled it
and drained it again.

Dickson had made it!

The young man found an empty stool by one of the blackjack tables and settled
in, leaning against the rough cut walls. He had two hours to kill and he'd be on
his way. A Santa Fe ticket, punched and paid for, was snug in his breast pocket.
In his back pocket was a map that would make him richer than everyone in the
room combined.

Patrick C. Dickson, last of St. Louis and points east, was a baby-faced adult.
Even the bushy mustache camouflaging his mouth, couldn't hide that fact. He
was slight of build and tall. He wore fine cut trousers, a tailored jacket and a
matching vest. His chief weakness and greatest vanity were his clothes. He
couldn't stand the dirty crude garments he'd worn back at the mine even if they
were a necessity out in the wilds. P.C. Dickson was a city bred man and proud
of it. Those old rags had done him well until he had gotten the map. Now he
was dressed properly again. The thief knew that his clothes did stand out in the
unruly crowd. What matter, he reasoned, I'll be out of here soon enough. Still,
Dickson pondered, perhaps he should not have let vanity get in the way of his
cautious plan of escape. It had worked so well thus far, it just couldn't go wrong
from here on.

Dickson had come out of the hills, east of Bald Mountain Pass, just before dusk
that same evening. A dying sun was still throwing harsh yellow hues against
canted rocks and jagged crevasses in the stony hills. He worked his gelding well
into a pine filled draw and waited in the deepening shadows. As he waited, he
was very active. The horse he stole was unsaddled and hobbled near a patch of
grama grass. The saddle, blanket and bridle were jammed into a cut in the
rocks. Stones were rolled over the opening. No one would find that gear unless
deliberately looking for it. He sat down, lit an expensive Eastern cigar, and
waited.

The smell of heat, suffocating and rank, was beginning to lift off the baked rocks. Yet even as a night breeze began to blow, Dickson could feel his new clothes getting sticky with sweat. In his hurry to change, the Easterner had discarded his rags and donned new clothes without waiting for it to cool off. Now his new clothes were sweaty too. Damn, everything had been going so well. He hated this heat and the rank odor it laid on his body. Especially what it did to clothes. Perhaps he should have waited to change. No matter, he would be in town shortly.

Once satisfied it was quiet enough to enter town without being seen, Dickson unhobbled his mount and led him away. In his right hand he carried a little satchel. In it were his basic toiletries and a little derringer. All he needed to get to the next town before purchasing supplies and then finding the gold mine.

Dickson had entered San Lacita by a foot trail. He quietly moved toward a dry wash bordering the town. The washout angled past the northeast rear corner of a complex of low mud wall sheds and offices of the Santa Fe stage lines. Dickson walked the length of the arroyo and cautiously came out only fifty yards from the repair sheds and a large livery barn. He stood for some time, letting his scent float over the work stock. Once satisfied they would not stir when he approached, Dickson let his gelding inside the poled corral. He quickly slid the gate back in place, moved around the corral and past the barn.

There, it had been done, he congratulated himself. His gelding would not be discovered until next morning at the earliest. No chance of it arousing any suspicion until then. And by the time the law found who it belonged to, Dickson would be far away. Everything was working out according to plan.

"Hey, Mister," a voice called out from the barn.

The thief froze in his tracks afraid to turn and face his caller.

"You lost or somethin'?" Dickson heard it clearer that time. It was a youngster's voice. He turned to face a young boy, not over ten, walking out to meet him.

P.C. Dickson breathed a sigh of relief and scratched his head to begin the act. "Hello, son," he said, acting confused. "Maybe you could help me. I came in on the stage this morning and I've been sort of wandering around town waiting for the stage to leave tonight. Well, I guess I just wandered too far outta town. I seem to have gotten lost. What time might it be?"

The barn boy looked at Dickson strangely. "Gosh, anyone knows sundown comes around eight Mister; you aren't from around here, are you?"

"No son, just traveling through like I said."

"Say, was that you moving down in the wash a little while ago?" The boy's voice betrayed again his innocence and his lack of suspicion.

Dickson ran his hand over the boy's tousle of rumpled hair. "No, that wasn't me, boy, you been imagining things. Thanks for your help." He turned quickly away and was gone before the boy could throw out another compromising question. As he stomped down the packed earth toward the lights of town, Dickson cursed himself. *Almost caught, damnit, and by a snotty nosed shit shoveler! First the clothes wrinkled in the heat and now the boy. I have got to be more careful. This close to the gold. Got to be careful.*

The boy wandered back into the barn to clean stalls. From a far corner, an old man groaned and lifted one arm.

"Boy, I got me a desperate need again."

Billy Joe dug out a fresh bottle from under a pile of straw and gave it to the old whiskered gentleman. "Mister Montgomery, you drove the stage in this morning, didn't you? I mean you and Mister Dunn."

"Yeah, boy, what if we did," John Montgomery slurred.

"Well, didn't you say that your passengers got all shot up? All exceptin' for a girl. Isn't that what you said to me?"

The weather-beaten guard upended the new bottle, took a long deep swig and coughed up a loud belch of satisfaction. He sleeved his lips and lay back in the fresh hay. One eye cracked open at the boy kneeling a few feet away. Billy Joe's eyes pleaded for an answer.

"That I did, boy, that I did. Now why do you ask?"

The youngster threw a fleeting look out at the moonlight framed between the open barn doors. "Well, a finely dressed fella waiting to board the stage just came by and he said he was on that morning stage, but he wasn't at all. He was acting all kind of nervous, I think. Do you…"

Montgomery's loud, grinding snore cut the boy's stammer short as he drifted off. Billy looked down on a soul lost to the world. John Montgomery began dreaming of green pastures, rolling hills and the Kentucky home he knew he'd never see again.

The barn boy got up off his knees and moved back out to the stock. They didn't answer his many questions but at least they paid more attention to him than his loosely adopted friend did.

Two more straight up shots put Dickson into the right frame of mind. He had pulled off a neat clean job. The runty barn spy and barkeep's curious stare hadn't done much to help him relax, but the booze had. *It won't be long now*, he thought.

Then someone stuck a head inside the smoke filled room and managed a shout over the din of loud noise. "Stage leaves in ten minutes. All ticketed passengers board in five minutes."

The face was gone as quickly as it appeared and noise swept over the room again. Dickson wormed up to the bar, had two quick down-the-gullet shots and squeezed out the batwings to the ramada. The cool night air felt clean and refreshing to his sticky, smoke filled clothes. He leaned against a porch brace and lit a cigar. His time to leave had arrived.

A Concord was parked across the street. The livery barn youngster was there with its driver. They exchanged words and the man sent the runt off. The shotgun guard was already seated on top. Dickson stepped off the porch and crossed the street. He approached the driver who was adjusting the team's harnesses.

His voice was authoritative. "Here's my ticket," he announced.

The old man snapped his head in surprise and emitted a low guttural growl. Without turning, he spoke slowly, "Didn't anyone ever tell you about sneaking up on folks like that? You're likely to get your head blown off next time!"

"Sorry, I..."

"You got a ticket?"

"Well, yes..."

"Then get in and be quiet! You'll spook the horses with all your sneaking about. He turned to check the wippletree attachments, chains and leather straps. As Dickson climbed inside the cab, Montgomery watched from above.

The runt was right, the guard thought. *That one hasn't been on the stage before. And where did he come from in those clothes? Sure as hell didn't ride into San Lacita that clean and spiffy.* Something didn't fit right. The guard shrugged his shoulders and started to doze off again.

A shuffling of feet on the hotel porch brought up Montgomery's eyes. Claire and his partner, the driver, were leading a small group of passengers toward the coach. The guard cocked his head. *Eli is still trying to shine up to the girl.* Montgomery didn't understand his partner. Eli was old enough to be her grandfather. *What the hell is he trying to prove?*

Claire settled in first followed by the others. A full cab of paying customers brought a smile to the guard's face. Even with a load shot up this morning, when men want to move, they want to move - period! *So why do I think they're crazy?* Montgomery thought, *What the hell am I doing here?*

Eli swung into the driver's box and gathered up his reins. He dug out a wad of chewing tobacco, gnawed off a piece and settled it behind his cheek. "Here we go again," he muttered. He let out a snarl and snapped his wrists. The horses hit their breastbands. The coach lurched, settled back on its thoroughbraces, and was off into the darkness at the end of town - Santa Fe bound with a beautiful woman and horse thief safely aboard.

Chapter Six

Above the din of barroom noise, Courtough could hear Eli's loud voice and the coach leaving. Injun trouble or not, Santa Fe Stage lines kept to their schedule. *Fools!* Jud thought. *While they're risking their lives, I'll be counting gold nuggets on my way to Mexico.* The sound of pounding hooves was quickly swallowed up by the cantina's drunken commotion.

The hours passed by. It was a gut-twitching wait for the sheriff who was growing impatient. Sketch noticed it and commented. Jud brushed his inquiry aside with a noncommittal grunt. The bar crowd grew larger as a second shift of miners descended upon the cantina. The air was thick with smoke and the rank odor of working men. Sweat trickled down Jud's back and settled around his waist. He couldn't take much more of the waiting.

After what seemed an interminably long time, the wall clock struck midnight. No one noticed it but the lawman whose eyes had been riveted there for the last hour. *The Lanker brothers should be back soon,* Jud thought. *Time to get on with the business at hand.* He slipped off the stool and was gone before Sketch could collect for the liqour.

San Lacita's rarified mountain air was cool and sharp after the cantina's stifling layer of heat. For a moment, Courtough stood and sucked in his gut, drinking in the night breeze. It even bested the rye whiskey sloshing inside him. Jud dropped off the planked porch and scuffed up a back street toward the edge of town. The street was deserted and quiet. Several carretas, two-wheeled Mexican carts, were parked next to the feed store. Dark shadows lay over the street. The buildings were closed up tight. Still to be on the safe side, Jud kept to one side back in the shadows.

The flickering stub of a candle danced shadows inside the livery barn. Jud approached it on silent feet. He looked around cautiously. The barn boy had gone home. Sliding the heavy wooden doors closed, the lawman snuffed out the candle. One quick look-see to make certain he was alone then Jud traversed the length of the barn and went out its back door.

In back of the barn, the night seemed darker. A breeze was rolling off the mountains. Several horses stirred in the corral at his sudden presence then relaxed. The low wail of a coyote echoed in the distance then died away. There was a hushed stillness about the land broken only by the common nocturnal sounds. The trio should be waiting in the wash behind the barn, Jud calculated. It's goodbye San Lacita, hello Mexico.

Jud palmed his .44 Colt percussion and slipped into the wash. His boots made soft crunching sounds as they moved over the sandy bottoms. At one point, his boot came down on a pile of chamizo someone had gathered there for kindling. The report seemed loud within the high walled confines of the draw. He froze in place, gun hand ready. A gust of wind kicked sand at his feet. It carried particles swirling up around his leg. Yet there was nothing else. *No sound above that of the wind moaning softly,* he thought. Jud stepped out again.

Bordering the wash were clumps of grama grass and sage. As sheriff Courtough crept by the foliage he failed to notice a difference in the brush. Molded into the blackness was an unnatural lump. It lay at the base of the sage and stirred when the lawman was past. As Jud's footfalls moved away, the black lump became a head. Piercing eyes trailed the sheriff's every step. The black form, wrapped in shadows, arose. It raised itself off the ground and slipped silently to the edge of a lateral wash; a safe, soundless distance behind the sheriff. The stalking had begun.

"Hold it," a low muffled voice cut the air.

Courtough stopped, hand on the Colt, fingering its trigger. "It's me," he whispered at the recognized voice. His legs were tense, ready to spring should it be a trap.

"Right, boss," the voice returned. A man appeared around a sharp bend in the wash. It was Curt Lanker with his Smith and Wesson leveled at the lawman. Two other men appeared behind him.

"What the hell are the guns for?" Jud demanded to know.

"We're a little edgy, boss. It was spooky up at that cabin. Varmints or Injuns must have been watching us the whole time."

"Forget that," Jud snarled. "What about the gold? You got it?"

Curt holstered his piece and dug out the makings of a cigarette. "It sure wasn't like you said, boss. He didn't have any gold around that place of his. We scrounged around and searched the cabin high and low. He had nothing. Except a map, he claims. Anyway, he's dead now. Someone else got there first and plugged him."

"What!" Jud exclaimed.

"That's why we were playing it careful with you. Could be the same joker that plugged the miner and hightailed it back to town."

"You followed him here to San Lacita?" Jud asked, trying to calm his anger at the trio's failure.

"That's right! We followed his tracks all the way. He camped out half a mile back. Chucked his old clothes and all his gear in some rocks. Must have set his horse free and changed clothes. We found this under the rocks with his old gear." Curt held up a handful of brown wrapping paper.

"That's what they wrap new duds in," Eddie offered, "I seen them in St. Louis once. We figure our man's got himself decked out in new fancy duds, alright."

"Sonofabitch," Jud snorted, "I saw him tonight!"

"You saw him? Where is he now?"

"On a stage heading for Santa Fe."

A groan arose from the three bandits.

Jud's eyes shot up, determined and firm. "What about the map? What did the old man say about it?"

Curt answered. "Not much. Just that this fancy dresser took his map. Claims he had no gold, only a map. I don't know if he was telling the truth or not."

"The bushwhacker believed him."

"Yeah," Lanker agreed. "But did he get a map from the old man or not I don't know."

The sheriff's eyes were alive again, his mind filling with calculations. "He must have! Otherwise why would this guy hide his clothes, ditch his horse, and light outta here on a stage. And dressed like a courting sage hen at that!"

Eddie scratched his thinning hair. "Yeah, I guess that does make sense."

"Damn right, it makes sense! You guys will have to get him before he reaches Santa Fe. I want that map!"

"Oh. Christ, boss, why don't we forget about that map? Whether it exists or not, we ain't no miners!" Eddie threw the words out but refused to look directly into Courtough's anxious face. He was tired and saddle sore and a little fed up with the sheriff's wild ideas of lost gold and easy money.

Jud ignored him. He produced a flask from his back pocket and motioned the trio to sit down. As they hunched down around him, the sheriff told about the man in new clothes and his sudden appearance in the cantina. He had no visible gear except a satchel which he clutched tightly. Without traveling gear, he couldn't go very far. Not on the frontier. So he was probably going no farther than Santa Fe. There he could resupply and disappear into the hills and seek out the gold mine.

"If it exists," Eddie threw in.

The cold eye of the sheriff silenced the younger Lanker and Jud carried on with his rambling analysis of the situation.

As the four bandits squatted down to share Jud's bottle, none were aware of a fifth pair of eyes watching them intently less than twenty feet away. The breed lay nestled under a collection of boulders. His body lay flat and still, perfectly melded into the contour of the rough ground. Ree's face leaned against an upthrust sheet of rock, so perfectly molded into the darkness that someone standing a yard away would not have seen him lying there. His hand gripped a knife, like a seasoned fighter waiting for action. Ree was easily within earshot of the bandits' conversation. From his nest near the draw's bend and purposeful location downwind, neither horses nor bandits had any idea of his presence.

Ree had caught up with the trio an hour after burying the miner. Once he was certain they would pass along the arroyo behind the town, he hid there. He had seen the horse thief's cache. Now he overheard what Jud had seen in the saloon.

The bandit's conversation was dragging on, getting hotter by the minute. Curt and Eddie were arguing against shagging that Santa Fe-bound stage when they had no proof the man Courtough had seen in the saloon had their map. Eddie was more adamant than his brother, grumbling about the division of labor that made them do all the dirty work and Jud collect his share just the same.

Jud heard them out and then cursed their laziness. He knew he was right about the miner finding gold. His Apache spy was reliable. And he, for one, was convinced that the young tenderfoot in the cantina had that map when he left on the stage.

"And what the hell are you gonna do while we're busting our ass, trying to break that stage?" Eddie demanded to know.

"My job!"

But that didn't satisfy young Lanker. He took a long draw off the bottle and muttered, "Your job is with us, if you want some of that gold."

"Mind your mouth, boy," Jud snarled.

But Eddie was feeling no pain, the tiring ride and liquor having numbed his reasoning. He was tired and fed up and feeling gutsy enough to say so. "No, by damn, I won't. We do all the robbing and killing and you take most of the money. And for what, nothing! Just so's we can get laid up in this pig hollow and not worry about being bushwhacked in bed. It may be your town, Courtough, but we aren't your darkies anymore!"

The .44 Colt percussion, hair-trigger cocked, was out of Jud's holster and pressed against Eddie's pug nose before the boy could close his rambling mouth. Lanker looked, cross-eyed, down the long black barrel to Courtough's narrow cut eye slits. They were fuming. Sweat beads sprang up across Eddie's shiny forehead.

"You got a job to do, darkie…and you aren't finished yet! Now I want that map. And you're going to get it for me. Right now! Or else stand and fight like the man you'll never be. What's it going to be?

Eddie gulped weakly, trying to think his way out of a situation the long day and too much whiskey had put him in. He knew Courtough was one of the best gunfighters in the territory - if not the best. He hadn't a chance against him straight up. Overworked or not, Eddie didn't want to die just because of his big mouth.

Curt Lanker cut the silence with a weak laugh. "Come on, Jud, Eddie don't mean nothing. Kid's just shooting off his mouth. Of course, we'll go after that stage. Just as soon as we get some rest."

Jud's taut finger eased back on the trigger. The cold steel broke contact with Eddie's nose. A crooked grin returned to the sheriff's face. "Forget the rest," he said. "You'll move out now. That stage has got a four or five hour head start. You'll have to stop it while it's still in the clear. Once it gets to the relay station or beyond, there may be Army patrols. All you got to do is rob the passengers and make sure you get the map." Then Jud cut narrow, mean eyes at Curt. He spoke deliberately. "And leave the girl on board alone. I got plans for her myself."

"What girl?" Curt asked with great interest.

"The one you aren't going to touch," Jud stated firmly. "I'll follow you in a day. We'll meet by the waterhole this side of the Rio Grande at its narrowest point. We've been there before. I got other plans for us once we get that map."

"Something to do with this here girl, Jud?" Curt asked with a grin.

"That's right," Jud snapped, "and don't forget what I said about leaving her alone." He rose off his haunches and stretched his legs. The night air felt good for all the booze he'd drunk all day. Overhead the sky was dotted with thousands of tiny pinpricks of stars.

Eddie arose slowly, still fuming inside at his humiliation at the hands of the sheriff. His eyes were downcast and full of hate.

A half mile away, a moon-washed gray figure lead his mount, rein-thrown, out of cut rock. He angled up a narrow deer trail alongside the mountain. He moved easily through treacherous switchbacks and narrow rock strewn paths. Below him, unseen, the trio was just walking out of the wash and sheriff Courtough leaving them for a saloon stool. Ree moved quickly, topping the saddle of the ridgeline as the trio mounted for their ascent of the worn roadway through the mountains. The half-breed took a gander back at the few lights of the buildings huddled together at the mountains base, then he was gone as quickly and silently as he had come.

Bannon was familiar with the Santa Fe stage route. He knew he'd have to avoid Camp Puerco on the Rio Puerco River and its cavalry patrols. Indian trouble notwithstanding, there was not an Army patrol alive that would ask Bannon questions first before shooting. Ranchers and bluecoats were the same. Ree's dark hair and Indian features marked him suspect immediately. He'd have to avoid all contact with the Army and other whites. His only chance to get the map was to meet up with the stage somewhere between the Rio Puerco and the relay station in the Placitas.

Chapter Seven

The Santa Fe stage line followed an unmarked trail crossing the territory. A route first walked out by wandering tribes hundreds of years before, then perhaps the first conquistadors searching for gold and finally nomadic Navajo and Apache family bands. At times it followed the most logical pathway. Other times it seemed to twist and turn needlessly. It was the only trail through that part of the territory. There was no other sure way to go…and Eli Dunn knew it by heart.

After leaving San Lacita, the trail wound its way around White Oak Mesa and through a narrow cut canyon up to Cabaña Plateau. Upon crossing those windswept high plains, the trail dropped again down to barren desert.

Claire LeFonte tried to sleep but couldn't. The Apache ambush that morning and the dying cowboy laid heavily on her mind. She'd seen killings before, been attacked by Indians before but never with the savagery and intensity of that morning's attack. For a time, she was certain she'd never see her father again. She had lived and the shock of death subsided, but she remained shaken.

Now she was back in the same setting with a new set of passengers and the same enemy lurking outside. Back in her favorite corner, Claire tried to relax and go with the bouncing and swaying of the cab. The Concord seemed to be hitting every dip and rut in the rough cut roadway. The leather curtains kept out very little dust. It soon coated everyone a pale gray. Even in the darkness behind drawn curtains, Claire recognized the same motley lot of passengers. They differed little from the first group; two miners instead of three and two ranch hands instead of one. The last passenger was a young man dressed in new store cut trousers, vest and jacket. All he seemed to lack was a pair of spats and paper collar. He could have been plucked right off a main street in New York or Philadelphia. *He looks like a model out of a mail order catalog,* Claire thought.

Except for the young man, the other passengers were no different from those Claire had encountered all of her young life. They dressed the same, smelled the same and made the same guttural sounds as they slept. Claire nestled in tighter to her corner and stared at the vast emptiness outside. There was nothing but sage and rock for miles and miles. The young nattily dressed passenger would occasionally raise his head, pass an eye over Claire, then drop down again. Claire was alone with her thoughts.

The stage teams were beginning to tire when Eli hauled back on the reins and stopped them for a blow. Inside the cab, he could hear a murmur of voices and leather curtains being drawn up. "Ten minute stretch," he said and swung off the driver's box. John Montgomery kept his place and rolled a cigarrito.

The assorted crew of traveling humanity disgorged itself out of the cab and milled around aimlessly. Claire followed them out. She stretched her arms wide and arched her back with a straining yawn. Her muscles were cramped and sore from the long jerking ride.

John Montgomery was watching her out of the corner of his eye. *She doesn't belong out here in the middle of nowhere all by her lonesome. Not a proper kind of lady like that. She needs an escort - a gentleman friend.* A wrinkle crossed the guard's cheeks. *If only I were half again her age,* he thought. "It's a fine kind of night, Miss."

Claire looked up, her teeth gleaming in the moonlight. She swept her hair back with a flip of her wrist and smiled. "Yes, I believe it is, she said. Gazing out across the endless blanket of gray darkness, she asked, "How long until we reach Camp Puerco?"

"If all goes well, we should be there before dawn," Eli answered from up front with the leaders.

John Montgomery threw a cross stare at the driver then turned back to Claire. "Would you like to climb up here, Miss, you can get a right nice view of the land."

Claire looked up with a warm smile. "Yes, I believe I'd like that, thank you." Before Montgomery could unlap his scattergun, the girl had stretched on tiptoes to grasp the brake handle. She quickly climbed onto the deck seat. Locking her feet on the foot brace, Claire stood up tall, drinking in the surrounding land.

"It really is beautiful, isn't it?" she said, "even in the middle of the day when it's so terribly hot, I still think this is a beautiful place. There's something about the sky and the largeness of everything. I can't explain it ... do you understand what I mean?"

Montgomery tipped his hat. "Ma'am, with all due respect, I guess I'd say there's something powerful strong about this part of the country. I wouldn't call it beautiful. The Rockies, now they're beautiful ... but this, this is a hard land. Mean on a man. You can burn up alive in the desert and in winter, in the high country, a man could freeze up as hard as flint. Only one that seems to like it here is the Apache and they've been here forever. I don't reckon I can call this a nice place ... I surely do respect it. I do that."

Claire smiled unconsciously at Montgomery's response. Her father said much the same thing - harsh land, a tough land, but his land. The smell of sage and mesquite drifted past Claire. A night breeze was just picking up. She sat back down. The guard climbed off the bench at Eli's request for help. Claire could hear the other passengers moving back inside the cab. It was time to press on again - first Camp Puerco, then the relay station, then home to Santa Fe. She was growing restless.

Eli finished with the harness gear and returned with Montgomery to the coach. Claire climbed down off the box, thanking both driver and guard in the same breath. She got an instant dual 'you're welcome' and missed the angry stares they gave one another.

After all the passengers were boarded and the stage was off again, Montgomery began to needle Dunn about his overt friendliness with Claire, but Eli wasn't about to be needled easily.

"Montgomery, you haven't the sense of a jackrabbit caught in a briar patch," the driver countered. "I've got no intentions other than to be a little friendly with our passengers - always have been. I consider it a part of my job. That young lady is no different from anyone else, 'ceptin maybe she's a bit younger and prettier than most. Anyway, it don't hurt to be pleasant."

"Dunn?" John Montgomery replied.

"What?"

"Bullshit!"

And that ended their conversation for the moment.

The moon hung like a bright Chinese lantern directly overhead. The night air had warmed since they dropped to the desert flats. Still it was cooler than during the day. The dust remained, thick and penetrating. The miles stretched out ahead of them for as far as the eye could see. Over the level pull of the flatlands, they made good time. By the time Eli drew his teams to a canter, the stage was well within the foothills of the Puerco Mountain chain.

Claire was getting tired. Her eyelids were weighted down with fatigue. The horsehair headrest came up to meet her neck. The roll and sway of the cab were working their hypnotic effect. Her head rolled to one side and she slept … fitfully, but she slept.

In the corner opposite Claire, Patrick Dickson was still counting his good fortune. Everything was working out right. From the miner to the stable boy to the bar keep; he had bluffed his way through San Lacita. No one was any the wiser for it. By the time they found the miner, he'd be only bones. No one talking there! And by the time they discovered an extra horse in the stage line corral, he'd be in Santa Fe. His back trail was covered and the roadway ahead wide open. There was nothing to stop Dickson now. That wasn't bad for an inexperienced Eastern hustler come west three short months before.

The miner, Ben Torrance, had been a stroke of luck for Dickson. He'd met him in a bar two weeks earlier in Cerro Verde, San Lacita's neighboring town. The old man took a shine to the young Eastern kid and did some long serious drinking with him. The more Torrance got liquored up, the more he talked of his good fortune, a place in the mountains and the treasure he was seeking. Young Dickson was listening more intently than the old man gave him credit for. He was reading between Ben's words, wondering if he hadn't indeed already struck gold. By the time Torrance was ready to leave, Dickson had convinced himself there was gold in those hills and that Torrance would lead him right to it. It was worth a try, Dickson reasoned, if not for the gold already accumulated there than for whatever else he could rob Torrance of.

When old man Torrance left to go back to his claim, he had a silent partner trailing behind him. It took two days of hard tracking but Dickson didn't mind. He had gold on his brain. Once he reached the general vicinity of the cabin, he camped out and kept Torrance under constant surveillance. The miner came and went but never carrying anything besides his tools. He worked the stream most of the time. There didn't seem to be any mine around. So far, it had been just as Ben described his operation back at the bar. After three days, Dickson's patience wore thin. He decided to make his move.

Torrance was coming off the mountain along a narrow goat trail when Dickson confronted him. The miner claimed he was kidding about the gold. He laughed and called Dickson a foolish city slicker for believing all his talk when he was liquored up, but Dickson wasn't buying it. He leveled his gun at the man and made his demand once again. Torrance realized the kid wasn't joking. He meant to take his secret map. Torrance went for his old cap and ball Colt. Dickson shot him twice and laughed as he tumbled off the ledge into the hole. Thinking him dead, Dickson sauntered away to rifle the cabin.

His search was short. He found the map under the bedding first thing. It was crudely scratched on a piece of doe skin, the lines made solid with dye. Dickson could not recognize any of the symbols but that didn't bother him. There were always Injuns around town, any town, who could translate it for a bottle of rye - but the map alone would not put whiskey in his belly. He needed cash for that - gold or greenbacks; and there was none to be found around the cabin.

He hurried back to the miner and found him still alive. Laying his revolver against the old man's head, Dickson demanded to know where the gold was. Torrance insisted there was no gold, just the map. He pleaded with the youth to help him or kill him but not to let him lie there in such pain. The thief turned a deaf ear to the man's pleading. He rode away angry at his failure and confused about the map. By the time he was halfway back down the mountain, he'd made up his mind. He would go back to town, dispose of the horse and catch the next stage out of San Lacita. Once in Santa Fe, he could find a translator for the map. It didn't matter when he got to the gold mine; a week's delay wouldn't hurt. He could use it to get acquainted with the area, and then perhaps a short job at Fort Marcy for some grub money and he'd be on his way; everything still clean as a penny whistle.

Miles behind the stage, the three bandits worked their way down a terraced series of foothills toward the far stretch of desert bordering the Rio Puerco. They had been riding steadily for three hours. The hills were cool and the air clear. Among the trio, however, heated words still flew. The Lankers were still embroiled in their snarling argument. Eddie was spitting mad at Jud for threatening him and Curt for not backing his own flesh and blood. Curt tried to calm his brother to no avail. It was a stupid plan, Eddie announced with an acid tone. They shouldn't have taken it.

"But what if there is a map and it does lead to a gold mine?" Curt countered, "What would you say to that?"

"I'm not complaining about the gold for us. If it's there I say we take it and head for Mexico - but I don't hanker on letting that cow dung sheriff in on the take. He's tried to run our lives for too damn long. It's time we do some thinking for ourselves."

Curt shook his head. "We wouldn't stand a chance. He'd hunt us down like animals. You know Courtough as well as I do. There is nothing he hates worse than someone who tries to double-cross him. He'd shag our trail all the way to Mexico and beyond. With that Apache varmint he's got for a spy, we'd never shake them."

Gus raised his double barreled shotgun out of its scabbard. "You know what I think? I think we should give him a taste of this doorknocker. That's what I think!"

"Right, Gus," Curt interrupted, "But I think…"

"No, I mean it," Gus persisted, "and we don't have to worry about them passengers talking. Not if they're dead!"

Curt's eyes shot up. Gus was serious. His leering glare was back again. His simple mind was delighting in the anticipation of a killing. His eyes showed it. The drooling lips fluttered as he spoke. "No witnesses and no one to say who done it!"

"Forget it, Gus," Curt cautioned. "Courtough would know…and that's all that matters. He's still the law in or out of San Lacita and he's still better with a gun than any of us."

Eddie reined back, twisting in the saddle. "Wait a minute, Curt; if we split up in three different directions it just might work. He can't follow all three of us at once. And he won't have his Injun friend with him at first. That means he's either got to double back for him or follow us himself. He's good but he can't follow three separate trails at one time."

Curt wasn't sold on the idea. "The heat's got to you both today, you're both loco."

"Yeah, but …"

Curt snapped his head around. "But what, Gus?"

The simpleminded man merely smiled. "Even if there ain't no gold or map, that stage has got paying passengers. If we jump them, we can at least get whatever money they've got. The sheriff did mention some girl, didn't he?"

Curt let the conversation die there. The elder Lanker mulled over the options and came up short every time. If there was a map, there might be gold. If not, the passengers would have some cash on them ... but to double-cross Jud Courtough was something else. A plan he'd let cross his mind only fleetingly, but never to stay.

Eventually, Curt agreed to the plan. "Alright then, we take the stage and try to find the gold for ourselves. If there is no map, we'll have to do with whatever we can get off the passengers. We leave no witnesses. If we disappear, Jud might wonder about the map but he still won't know for sure if we double-crossed him."

Camp that night was a shallow depression that had been wind-worn in the sand. The horses were hobbled on grass nearby and hot coffee was the evening meal. The trio huddled around the small fire, their bones cramped and sore from the day's long ride.

Curt rolled a cigarette. "We'll hit the stage at the relay station. It'll stop at Camp Puerco for a blow and should be at the station day after next."

"You wouldn't want to go back and rob that Army paymaster again, would you, brother?" Eddie asked with a wide grin. Camp Puerco had been their last job.

Curt grinned back. "Not on your life. And you'd better keep a sharp lookout for Army patrols. They're still out looking for us because of that job. I don't want a flock of Army blues on my tail."

"Did you mean it about not leaving any witnesses on that stage?" Gus asked with a stupid grin on his face.

"That's right!"

"And the girl?" Eddie asked.

Curt eyed his brother and smiled. "After me, brother, she's all yours. That satisfy you?"

Eddie just smiled.

Chapter Eight

Camp Puerco could only be called an army installation if military presence alone determined its status among the frontier establishments. From its drab, shabby appearance, it was obvious little money had been allocated for the garrison facilities there. Compared to the regular army forts dotting the Southwestern frontier, Puerco looked like a summer bivouac of cattle drovers.

It had no artillery pieces. No protecting walls. No permanent barracks save one and no watch towers. It was, quite simply, a tent town held together only by the continuing need for another garrison between Fort Defiance to the west and Fort Marcy in the east. The Rio Puerco River was a central, if desolate, location between those installations.

When Eli Dunn crested the last foothill and started his descent to the camp, he saw little to offer him encouragement or reason for relaxation. The army was there but only on a marginal existence.

Symbolic in its lifelessness, the flag hung limp against its pole. Below it, men were filing out of tents, dragging rumpled uniforms on for roll call. Eli recognized them as infantry. Doughboys they were called, in their brown canvas clothes. They always looked a bit queer to the driver with their pantaloons tucked and wrinkled in their service boots. Just what the devil those infantry would do in the desert, Eli didn't know. One thing was certain, against mounted Apache warriors; they would stand little chance of surviving. *What the hell, does the Army ever make any sense?* Eli thought not.

Dawn was still an hour away but already the men were forming into squad formations. Marching and drilling had to be done before midmorning. After that all strenuous activity would slow to a snail's pace. In front of the milling men, a sprinkling cart was crossing the parade ground; it dampened the dust and left a steamy smell behind.

Behind the orderly row of tents, several buildings stood half finished. A smile crossed Eli's lips as he drew closer. The buildings were being constructed by men who obviously weren't carpenters. Jerry-built to be sure. Unseasoned, unhewn, unbarked pine logs were being placed upright in some buildings and horizontally in others. The pattern was haphazard and uncoordinated.

Bordering the buildings on one side, the Rio Puerco river lay like a muddy brown road, its current barely noticeable. Strands of grass, sage and a few willows lined its banks. The river was shallowest at that point. It was the lifeblood of the garrison. Without the river, there could be no camp, no garrison, no central military force for the army in that part of the territory.

Inside the Concord, all eyes were peering out, taking in the early morning activity. Claire noticed at once the starkness and isolation of the camp. There was no hay bag row - no women anywhere. Not so much as a sudsville; no singing or laundry hanging in the sun. Instead she saw a motley collection of troopers, young and old. Most of them adorned with mustaches, burnsides and imperials. They were a wild looking lot, as tough as the desert itself.

Past the quadrangle the stage rolled until Eli came to the only permanent structure in the garrison. It was a long building made of adobe and hand hewn limestone. The building served as barracks at night and resting place for Santa Fe stage line passengers when the stage was in.

The passengers filed out slowly, stretching aching muscles and yawning. The girl was the last one out. She stood under the brush ramada and watched a line of gray begin to outline the horizon. Claire turned to gaze across the river and saw alkali draws dotted with lanky pitahaya stretching toward the mountainous horizon. Dingy green sagebrush lay everywhere. It was a wild and desolate place, unforgiving and uncaring. It made her a little depressed to think about the soldiers that had to stay there.

Captain Johnson, commanding officer of Camp Puerco, met them at the doorway. He led them to a table already prepared with breakfast. The passengers were the first non military faces he'd seen in three weeks. He quickly began to ply them with questions about the outside world.

Breakfast was slow and relaxed despite the growing heat outside and the captain's persistent questions. The rest stop was for the teams as much as for the paying passengers. After breakfast, the Captain extended an invitation to tour the camp and enjoy a second cup of coffee by the river. The tour was mercifully short and the group found themselves in a comfortable spot under the sheltering shade of a group of cottonwoods.

Captain Johnson explained he had been at Camp Puerco for over a year with little chance of being transferred for another year or more. "We're a feeder station," he explained. "Any military operation leaving either Fort Defiance or Fort Union can draw on these infantrymen as their support troops. Our central location makes us a pivotal point from which military campaigns can operate. In addition to that, our cavalry troop patrol regularly to keep the stage lines open between Albuquerque and old Fort Wingate. It's not a pleasant life here, but it's a job that has to be done."

Eli had heard the same stories before. They bored him. Every trip brought forth the tour invitation and concluded at the very same river spot. The Captain's tale of hardship for the glory of the United States Army was as predictable as the summer weather. Eli had more serious business on his mind. "We had some trouble with Apaches a couple of days back," he interrupted the Captain, "Have you had any reports of them warring again?"

"We did, but they've moved south now. In fact, that's where my cavalry troop, along with one from Fort Union, is right now. They're tracking a heavy concentration of hostiles heading for the border. Three or four bands it looks like. We've had reports it's the hesh-ke that got them all stirred up and wanting to jump the reservation. Those hotheads are going to start another war if something isn't done about them."

John Montgomery looked up from his pipe. "When did the first one end?" he asked blandly.

The captain eyed the old guard with a reserved expression and let the comment die unanswered. "Lieutenant Dunville has got a patrol due east of here. You might run into him the other side of your relay station. He's checking for any sign of trouble."

"What about the garrison in Santa Fe?" Claire inquired.

"Fort Marcy and Post Santa Fe still cannot be depended upon to garrison anything more than a token force. They're of no help to us in hunting down hostiles."

"I thought you weren't expecting trouble up here?" Dickson broke in, standing up. "You said all the Apache had moved south" All eyes turned to the young man who nervously ran a handkerchief across his forehead.

Captain's Johnson's eyes showed temperance and patience. "Young man, it's obvious you're new to the territory. The only sure thing anyone can say about the Apache is that they're totally unpredictable. The problem with fighting Apaches is trying to figure out what they're gonna do next. Once you've figured that one out, you've got a fighting chance."

Dickson wasn't satisfied with his answer. "Something should be done about the Apache, I hate those red devils!" he sputtered, to no one in particular. He kicked a flat stone which skipped over the brown water.

The officer looked up at the excited youth, his face calm and fatherly. "Don't waste your time hating the Apaches. That would be like hating this camp because it's barren and lifeless. It'll get you nowhere. Only make you more edgy. Learn to fear the Apache as you would getting stuck out here without water. That'll keep you alive much longer."

Dickson turned and stalked down to the river's edge mumbling. The girl looked past the others to the sky. It was losing its blueness under a wafting yellow sun. The heat was growing, even in their shade. It would be another scorcher.

Claire turned back to the Captain. "Captain, you sound like you've been around the Apaches for a long time. I have as well, but I still don't understand them. I was raised here. We have some Apaches who work on my father's spread. We don't make war on them, so why won't they live in peace with us?"

The officer shook his head, "I don't know. I doubt if anyone but an Apache really does understand them. That's just the way they are. It's part of their nature. They torture their victims to take away their power. The more their victims suffer, the greater the power of the Apache. It's savage and cruel. I don't think any white man can understand that kind of logic. It's beyond our comprehension."

Both the driver and guard were growing tired of the Captains philosophizing. "That patrol you've got riding east of here," Eli began, "wouldn't be hunting hesh-ke now would it?"

The officer was unruffled by the question. "Mister, I've got a patrol riding the north loop and another riding the south loop. Been there for a week. Now if they had reported any trouble or signs of Apaches, believe me your stage wouldn't be free to leave this camp. That satisfy you?"

Eli sensed bristling skin. One thing he didn't need was an overzealous officer holding him back from a scheduled run. So he tried to shift topics. "You said the hesh-ke had the tribes stirred up. You know that for a fact?"

"I do! Those bronco Apaches ambushed a small wagon train and several patrols before we caught them in Bruce canyon. Killed a dozen or so but the rest slipped away. Our scouts identified them as hesh-ke. They carried the same markings."

"Hesh ... ke? What does it mean?" one of the miners asked.

"It's an Apache word that means rage to kill - literally!" the captain answered, "and rather appropriate at that. The hesh-ke are an Apache sect. Their secret lodge brotherhood is dedicated to only one thing - killing white men. Old red sleeves, Mangus Coloradas, was purported to have been one of them. They're cultists. Fanatics! There is no logic or rationality to their actions. They just want to kill. Apaches are independent cusses. Never see their chiefs with a band of dog soldiers like the Cheyenne. Hesh-ke are the only band like that. If I knew they were still around these parts, believe me, that stage of yours wouldn't roll an inch into the Rio Puerco today!"

After an hour in the slowly diminishing shade, the group broke up and drifted back to the main building. The teams had been rubbed down, watered, fed and rested. Now Eli and Montgomery worked slowly in the blinding sun to harness them again. The passengers boarded the already hot and stuffy coach and Eli set out through the muddy waters and toward Santa Fe. Captain Johnson watched the Concord grow smaller in the distance; a little envious, a little concerned. He turned and walked away humming softly. "What Shall the Harvest be…"

The outlaws were four hours in the saddle when they crossed the unshod pony tracks. The trio had broken camp before dawn, leaving their tiny rock-seep waterhole at a canter. A midday desert crossing was courting death. They had to be across before the sun rose too high and the heat began. After four hours and two thirds the way across, they cut the Apaches' trail. The tracks were less than a day old. They led away in a southwesterly direction with at least a dozen riders moving at a fast pace.

Curt swung low and studied the tracks without dismounting. His eyes followed the impressions until they blended into the beige foreground and disappeared. The earth around them was a powdery dust studded with sagebrush and cactus. In the distance, purple serrations of low-lying mountains stood out against the horizon. In those mountains, at least fourteen hours away, was the relay station and the map they wanted.

"Well, what do you think, Curt," his brother asked, gazing off in the distance.

Curt shrugged his shoulders and kicked his mount into a trot. "Apaches, alright. We better get out of this sand and all that dust we're leaving behind us."

As they rode off Gus looked back. A trail of powdery dust was rising up behind them. As innocent and short-lived as the gray cloud might look, even Gus knew a keen Apache child could spot it from miles away.

It took another two hours before the three left the expanse of sand. They began traversing rocky ground chiseled with wandering arroyos and deep coulees. Dull yellow soil lay bare in many spots. The sun had begun to burn, rippling the air into gelatin waves. The men were soaked with sweat and riding slower. They couldn't chance a stone bruise or quarter-crack out there.

"Hey, boss, lets pull up awhile," Gus complained, "I gotta take a break."

Curt looked up briefly. "We will in a little while. Once we can find some shade. Let's keep on moving."

"How long to the relay station?" Eddie asked. "I judged it was closer this way."

The elder Lanker drew his Stetson farther down over his face, casting a little more shade there. "I figured half a day from here, but in this heat we had better find a place to sit out the afternoon and start again at dusk. We can catch the stage before it leaves the station at midmorning."

"You sure?" Eddie persisted.

"No, damn it! I'm not sure," Curt rasped, irritated by the heat and his brother's eternal pessimism. "But have you got any other brilliant ideas? We can't last much longer in this heat. If we follow the stage route we'd be running the risk of meeting cavalry patrols all the way. Stop your complaining and save your energy. We'll still get to the station in plenty of time."

Eddie was not satisfied but he let the matter drop.

They rode for another hour in the blazing sun before hitting higher ground. A comb-like ridge stretched across their path. Curt dug out a pair of army field glasses from his saddle bags and studied the rocky wall.

After some time, running the glasses back and forth, he announced, "There's a saddle off to the right and some kind of trail. It comes off the saddle and snakes back and forth a couple of times. It drops down over there." His arm stretched out toward some unseen point off to their right. "Let's go. We can rest on the other side."

They found the goat's trail after ten minutes and began the ascent. On a last stretch near the top, they dismounted to lead their horses up a steep slope to the switchback. Following the twisting pathway, the trio moved slowly and cautiously. The trail was very narrow. Footing was treacherous for the unsteady animals. Up there, the sun was hotter and more punishing. It bounced off huge canted rocks and sharp cliff sides. The heat seemed to roll in wave after wave over the men.

"Look!" Eddie exclaimed.

Curt looked up, eyes closed to a slit, He spotted the dark smudge of a cave on the ridgeline just below the saddle. It was barely visible in the sage along the sandstone. A second look indicated it wide enough to admit horses and men. "That's it," Curt said. "We'll stay in there until it gets dark."

The cave's mouth closed down quickly to only a few feet high less than a dozen yards in to the stone. Still it was enough to get the horses out of the sun and cool them a little. The air was dry but cooler up against the far wall. The three men huddled up against the cool sandstone and began to doze off.

Curt awoke after a few hours and moved to the cave's entrance. The horses stood still, their heads hung, tails twitching spasmodically. Outside the cave, the brightness temporarily blinded the bandit.

Grabbing his field glasses, Lanker moved down the saddle and studied the land they had yet to cross. He squatted against a rock. It was country much like that they had just crossed. Arroyos stood out like jagged scars on the land. The dark spots would be deep ravines and gulches. Curt studied the terrain carefully but it told him nothing he didn't already know. It would be easier at night but still it would be a hard stretch to cover in good time. He was about to lower the glasses when he saw something that made him freeze in place, keeping his lenses on a dark line that bordered a coulee.

Something about the shade and the clump of cactus lining its edge wasn't right. Focusing more closely, he saw the shade was really the brown flank of a horse. No, several horses! Painted Apache horses waiting out the sun in that same ravine. They must have been there for some time. Curt had no idea how long. He studied their encampment. It was an ideal spot, nearly undetectable.

Curt's surveillance was cut short as the war party began moving out, riding at an angle parallel to the ridgeline. There were six in all, carrying rifles and bows. Curt watched them disappear into the haze that covered the distant horizon to his right until they were gone.

Curt moved back to the cave and roused the others. He considered telling them of the incident but decided against it. They didn't need Apaches on the brain along with reaching the relay station. They ate hard tack and drank warm coffee and waited. Sundown was long in coming. When the trio finally moved off the ridge and into broken country again, Curt could not help gazing off to the right, wondering where those Apaches were heading - and what they were hunting.

Chapter Nine

After leaving sheriff Courtough and his scheming companions, Ree Bannon had ridden steadily for three hours. The night was alive with nocturnal sounds. Darkness was a veil which muted the landscape into indistinguishable shapes. As he rode, Ree's trained ear could raise no sound of trouble. He rode rifle across pommel, with a caution born years before fighting night-brave Comanches. The risk of meeting San Lacita-bound traffic was too great to tag along the stage route itself. Since the bandits would most likely chose a short cut straight across the desert, Ree's choice was narrowed down to one; a march over the mountains instead of around them. That route, although the least desirable, would skirt the army camp on the Rio Puerco and drop Ree back on the stage route where it reached the relay station. It was the most dangerous way to go. The mountains were high, sharp-out, and could, for all possibilities, be crawling with Apaches. Yet there was no choice. It was the only way to make good time.

The nonstop ride back from the mine had badly worn Ree's mustang. He had been twelve solid hours in the saddle before reaching the mine, now he was riding again. The desert bred pony was beginning to step short, hitting hock-high sage. Bannon knew it would go until its heart gave out. Mustangs were built that way. But Ree was no Apache. His mount would have to last a long time. He could not waste him as an Apache would. Besides, the route he had chosen was the straightest and most direct. The Santa Fe coach would stop at the army camp for rest and feed. If the sun were its usual scorching self, the driver would have to draw several stops after that before he reached the relay station for its change of teams. The breed had time to rest. This was his country. He knew its rules. It was a game he had played all his life.

Bannon made dry camp in the rocky folds lying between two mesas. He did not sleep. The rest was for his pony, not himself. He hobbled the mustang. There was good grama grass for it amid fissures and cracks in the stone. The night air was cool and sharp. A strong breeze played sand over his boots and licked particles up against his face where he lay. A faint circle glowed where the moon was trying to poke through a layer of clouds.

As Bannon looked up at the stars, images began to form. He imagined the old miner there, talking to him with his bony, arthritic fingers. Ree understood what he must do, but the old man was not satisfied. His age-gnawed joints would not stop. They clawed onto Ree's hand and clamped shut. Ree understood the urgency in the old man's eyes. His tongue need not speak; his eyes were saying it all. His fingers went slack. Ree laid the old man down again and began his death chant. It was a long painful ritual for him even for this man who had left his uncle for dead. Ree knelt over the old man for a long time. When he got back on the trail following that Santa Fe stage, he was keeping a promise made for the old man and his father.

Ree awoke with a start, one hand instinctively across his revolver. Nothing stirred around him. All seemed well. He realized he had dozed off - a foolish thing to do in the mountains. He must have been more tired than he anticipated. The mustang was still grazing, having moved farther off. He arose, slid his colt back in its holster, and to saddle. He paused long enough to slack his thirst from his canteen then nudged the horse down the mesa.

The night had grown darker with a heavy layer of clouds overhead. The night wind blew. Cool, refreshing air. Somewhere off in the distance, a bachelor coyote was baying. Ree felt very much alone. He rode at a canter for a long time, past dawn, far into the morning. The route he had chosen would avoid all the known Apache gathering places. Though he was not of Apache rearing - Navajo didn't know them all.

After seven hours in the saddle, Ree left the mountainous terrain for the level but broiling salt flats. It was a sandblasted stretch of land dotted with greasewood scrub and a few cacti. He crossed the Rio Puerco far above the army camp and continued on into the desert. Up ahead he could see the hazy serrations of mountains.

The wind grew, whipping up stinging clouds of alkali powder that burned Ree's eyes and nostrils. No matter now. He could not stop. The desert afforded no refuge for man or beast.

Ree kept up a steady pace, refusing to stop his sweating mount. Three more hours of steady riding brought the rider to higher ground.

Dismounting, Ree led his pony up the rough incline, sidestepping loose rock and slick sheets of shale. Sunlight blasted the bare mountain side, throwing blinding reflections back in Ree's face. He kept his head down and marched on. Crossing the mountains spine, Ree worked his way gingerly down the other side and up a second series of intermingled hills.

Unexpectedly, the sound of gunfire rolled past him. Bannon froze. Silence returned. The gunfire stopped just as unexpectedly as it had begun. *Where did it come from?* Mountains carry sounds great distances. This might be close or a long ways off. He cocked his ear into the wind, hearing no other sounds. After a few moments, Ree relaxed his taut body. He stepped out again with his Winchester in one hand. Except for the sound of iron hoofs scraping rock all was still and peaceful.

Ree found the source of the gunfire less than an hour later. Coming out of a narrow pass, he came upon an ambushed army patrol. Four horses lay sprawled in the sand where they had been cut down by crossfire. Three of the troopers were lying among surrounding rocks where they had sought shelter. None had made it. Their naked bodies lay glistening in the harsh sunlight. Ree's stomach tightened when he saw what the Apaches had done to the bodies. *Better they should never be found at all, than to be seen like that with no semblance of manhood left.*

There were four big army grays dead in the blood-soaked sand but only three troopers. One of the patrol was missing. A quick search of the surrounding rocks revealed nothing. He must have been taken prisoner! Apaches took prisoners for only two reasons; to make slaves of them or for torture - and Apaches didn't make slaves of soldiers. They meant to kill him!

Ree's shoulders went slack, as if a great weight had been placed on them. The trooper would die if he wasn't dead already. That was a fact. Ree was the only one who could do something about it - if he acted swiftly. He had a promise to keep. If he kept to his trek, he'd catch the stage before it reached the relay station. That meant he couldn't stop now. Not for the trooper. Not for anyone. Any delay meant less chance of getting the map. And that was the oath he'd made to his father.

Something would not let Ree Bannon leave that spot. The army meant nothing to him. Not after Canyon de Chelly. Not after the Long Walk. No, he owed the United States Army nothing, but he could not leave a man captured by the Apache just to die.

Ree found the rocky enclosure where the ramada had been held back out of sight. As the tracks led out, he noticed two mounts stepping heavy. But wait! Those were the boot marks of the trooper walking alongside the horses. Did the Apaches have other prisoners? Were some of their party wounded and riding double? The party was small, only four warriors. Why would they bother with prisoners? It didn't make sense! A smile crossed his lips. That was white man's thinking. Four broncos might do anything. They were Apaches.

Ree found their camp less than an hour later. It was good he stopped when he did. The heat was beginning to boil his brain. His head felt lighter and his eyes watered. Ree left the mustang back among a pile of rocks, tied down. He slithered up through a clump of mesquite and trained his worn eyes on the camp several hundred yards away.

Two of the war party were resting by a fire, talking and passing a jug back and forth. A cruel smile cut the breed's face. Tiswin. Dollar to a dime, they were getting drunk before beginning their little game of torture.

The prisoner! Ree cut slant-eyes across the camp. He spotted the trooper amid a jumble of rocks that formed one side of the encampment. The soldier lay naked but for his shorts. He was staked out, spread-eagled and cut badly. Two Apaches had just finished running their lances back and forth across his chest. Even as they left him for the tiswin, blowflies began to gather like black crust on the bloodied flesh. The man lay motionless. Only the heaving of his muscular chest showed him to be still alive.

Searching the encampment again, Ree's eyes stopped opposite the huddled braves. Two figures lay nestled by the side of a large boulder - an old man and a woman. Navajo by their clothes; his own people. The war party seemed to ignore them for the most part. Apaches were the enemies of the Navajo and had been for many years. The only reason these young bucks would bother with an old couple like that would be for barter or sale. This was an ambitious lot. Knocking off an army patrol and collecting two Navajos along the way. They were all young warriors, but that didn't make them any easier to outguess or attack.

The pony herd was in a natural bowl of rocks a half dozen yards away. It was a tight camp with little room for maneuvering. Ree knew he'd have one chance to get in there and get out … not very good odds. This midday camp wouldn't last long. Even if they did get drunk, the Apaches would never stay all night in one place. He'd have to hit them soon!

Wriggling like a snake, Ree wormed back into the thicket. Once off the skyline, he rose to a stoop and catfooted down the ridge. He circled back to where he had left the mustang. Resting on his saddle were both the Sharps buffalo rifle and the new Winchester. The Sharps was a cannon at close range, but the Winchester held seventeen shots. Ree chose the latter.

His plan of action was simple. Wait until the hostiles were drunk then try to catch them by surprise. Cut them down before they could kill their prisoners. The odds were not favorable at four to one. He just could not turn away at this point. Not for the troopers or the two Navajos.

Taking another gulp of lukewarm water, Ree turned to the task at hand. He chose to make his attack by a different route than his scouting one. The wind had shifted. He had to stay downwind of the pony herd. Checking his load one more time, Ree dropped his hat on the pommel and moved out. He quickly scaled a shallow ridge. By using a clutter of boulders and brush mottes, he avoided being skylined as he slid over the crest. By keeping every possible obstruction between himself and the camp, Ree kept out of sight during the advance. It was very slow going. The sun overhead had baked the rocks until they were impossible to touch. Ree found a tiny pathway, thick with mesquite that angled around the rocks on one side of the Apacheria. Following it, he kept downwind and out of sight.

Bannon worked in as near to camp as he dare. He drew up through a natural cut in the boulders close to the Navajo couple. At least he might be able to cover them when the shooting started. Rising off his haunches, he raised himself by inches until he could sight down into the camp.

Two of the raiders had moved back to their prisoner. Still drinking, they were standing over him, arguing. Ree knew enough Apache to understand them. One wanted to torture the soldier right then. The other objected. Both carried lances which shot off flashes of sunlight. Ree would have to act fast; their camp would be breaking up soon.

Quickly running his eyes over the camp, he sized up the situation once more. The Navajo stood a chance of escaping. The horses might bolt if frightened. Two braves still sat by the fire while the remaining two stood over the trooper. Ree's odds hadn't improved any.

Ree slid his Winchester up into the notch of rocks. He laid cheek against smooth stock, lining up on the Apache closest the prisoner. The argument had ended. They were dropping their lances, calling the others over for the fun.

A crack of rifle fire shattered the camp stillness. One Apache pitched over, a scream dying on his open lips. Echoes bounced off rocks, rolling over the hills. For a split second, the other Apaches were motionless, caught completely off guard. Again the Winchester barked and a second lancer stumbled backwards, his chest increasingly scarlet. He jerked his lance up, and before another shot was fired, plunged the shaft deep into the trooper. Ree fired again. The Apache doubled over, crumbling to the ground.

The camp broke apart like a whirlwind. Ponies shuffled and whinnied, nervously jerking at their restraining lines. The two remaining Apaches lunged for cover and disappeared into tall brush.

Two down, two left. The trooper was not moving. The lance hung slack in his body. Off to one side, the Navajos were stumbling toward the ponies. A shot rang out, one dropped to the ground. The woman was hit. Her companion gathered her about the arms and dragged her into the brush for cover.

Good. They should be safe for the moment. He guessed the soldier was dead or would be if and when he ever got to him. Ree's attention was focused on the remaining two Apaches. He knew their tactics. They'd have guessed from the location of his shots that only one man was out there. That meant they'd be circling around, trying to flank the source of those shots.

Laying his rifle over an elbow, Ree snaked away in the general direction of the two Navajo. It was an entirely different game now - one of cat and mouse. The hunter was becoming the hunted. One thing certain, he'd not be a stationary target for them. If they wanted him, they'd have to come to him. Ree didn't mean to make it a one-man stand - not with the Navajo still alive to help him.

He squirmed along the sand, digging elbows into the ground for more speed. Overhead an encircling canopy of scrub brush and mesquite made strange patterns of light on the ground. Pressed against the earth, Ree could feel the heat at its worst. Sweat trickled down his cheeks and into his eyes. Not a breath of air moved down among the brush.

When Ree reached the approximate location where the Navajo had ducked into the brush, he angled in. The thick scrub and mesquite blocked all clear views ahead. It must be the clearing, the campsite. There were still no signs of the pair or hints of movement off to his left where the Apaches should be flanking.

He toyed with the idea of whispering for the pair, trying to let them know he was a friend. No good. It would certainly alert the Apaches as to his exact location. His eyes crossed back and forth, trying to spot a sign of the couple, something to indicate where they might be hiding. He didn't have much time left. The Apaches had to be closing in rapidly now. They would be on him very soon.

There! Something off to the right made a slight movement; something was out of place. Yes, it was the woman. Ree dug his elbow into the sand, propelling himself forward.

Ree saw the knife a scant second before it arched up over his head. Throwing his weight to one side, Ree dodged the blade by inches as it sliced past his face. He jerked his piece up into the wrinkled face of the old Navajo man. The face was fearless, waiting for death. Behind the old man, his woman huddled by a tangle of catclaw, nursing a bloodied arm.

"Wait, old one!" Bannon spoke in fluent Navajo, touching left hand fingertips to his brow. "I come to kill Apaches, not Navajo. The two that remain mean to kill us both. Will you help me?"

The old man tilted his head slightly to acknowledge the stranger's sign of respect for elders. He understood this was a friend. When he looked up again, Ree saw the old Navajo had few teeth left. Still his smile came through warm and genuine. A skinny burnt copper arm came out, pointing at Ree's revolver.

"Here," the breed said, handing over his colt. "We must be quick ... and careful."

The air was alive with insects buzzing about their faces. The ramada had grown nervous by the smell of death and outburst of gunfire. The skittish ponies were sidestepping and yanking on their restraining line, ready to break away at any moment.

Bannon motioned over toward the herd. The Navajo, gripping the heavy piece with unfamiliar fingers, moved off in that direction. He paused by his woman for a moment and made his way into the brush.

Ree rubbed sweaty palms against his shirt front and sleeved his forehead. It did little good. The salty sweat still stung his eyes. Intense heat and lack of air was getting to him, Ree felt dizzy and lightheaded. The sand was hot to touch, burning through his shirt to the elbow. The Apaches were flanking right now, but where or how close he could only guess.

Something clicked in the hunter's brain. A sound he hadn't heard on a conscious level, an instinctive reaction to some sixth sense, born of years in the desert. It had come from close by - between himself and the old woman. She acknowledged the sound. It was an alien sound Ree couldn't identify. Yet it had to be … yes, Apaches.

Leveling his Winchester, Ree quickly sized up the brush to his right. It was thick, entangling, blocking out a clear view within a few yards. The sand was pocketed with slight depressions like the one he laid stretched out in right then.

Ree fired straightaway, spacing his shots, swinging in a half circle. He heard a groan, then nothing. Silence returned to the brush.

A slight thump scraped against his ear. He turned in time to see the second Apache leap out of tall brush and race toward the ramada. The brave waved his arms frantically. The wiry ponies started to whirl up and backwards, snapping lines. They broke out of the enclosure, and stampeded across the campgrounds. Ree leveled his rifle but the herd cut off his line of fire. The Apache was hidden behind a cloud of dust.

"Amigo."

Ree spun around, alerted by the old woman. The first Apache, his arm shattered and hanging, was racing toward him. In his good hand, he wielded a large hunting knife. His calico shirt was torn and stained with blood. Yet he leapt over brush with the agility of an antelope, screaming a high-pitched yipping. Ree fired once, catching him in the leg. He went down, struggling to arise. Ree fired again. The Apache staggered back, arching his good arm to throw the knife. The Winchester barked for a third time. The Indian collapsed backwards, sprawling into the brush, and then slowly sinking down to the blood-soaked sand.

Sweat drenched Bannon's face, stinging his eyes closed. He sleeved away the dirt and grime. He felt tired and sore and very thirsty. A shot cracked the air behind him. Pitching forward, he rolled over just in time to see the last Apache rolling off the last pony in the herd. The old Navajo lowered the smoking colt and jogged over to his wife.

Ree dragged himself up, leaning heavily against his rifle. Even the act of standing was an effort. Once up, he realized a change in temperature from the ground to his feet. He could breathe little better, The Navajo was moving to him. He palmed back the colt, returning it with another toothless smile.

Ree turned to the trooper still staked out. The soldier was making soft, barely audible sounds. It was neither a moan nor a sound of pain. Rather it was an animal whimper of one in great agony and the last throes before death. He was a muscular man, strongly built about the chest and neck. His white flesh had begun to turn pink in the harsh sunlight. Rawhide strips, strung tight, had squeezed the life out of his hands and feet. They were puffed up like balloons. The lance which impaled him was hanging limp to one side, still deep enough not to be removed. The man's lips fluttered but no sound came forth.

"Water," Ree called back in Navajo. The old man left his wife for the campfire and found a greasy intestine amid the Apache booty. Ree untied one end and let the precious liquid run down the man's mouth. No reaction. The trooper wasn't swallowing it. It ran back out over his lips. Ree felt the man's pulse. No beat. He was gone.

Gripping the lance pole, Bannon yanked it out and broke it in half. He flung the wood off to one side.

Ree buried the trooper in a shallow grave, piling rocks on top to keep away the scavengers. He turned his attention to the old couple. The woman was not badly hurt, a clean flesh wound that her husband had already bound tightly with the shirt of an Apache. Ree came down on his heels and offered them the intestine. They accepted the water and used it sparingly.

"You know the sign of respect for my people," the old Navajo said, returning the tube. "It is the sign for many tribes, not just Navajo,"

"Yes, I know it," Ree said.

"You are one of us then. How is it that you wear the clothes of a white man and talk his language?"

"I am not full blood. My Mother was white. I lived among the Navajo a long time, but no more. Now I live among the white man and by myself. I am a white man but I am also of the Diné. Can you understand this?"

The toothless smile appeared once again. "It is not for one as old as I to understand why the white eyes and Indian act as they do. When I was young we lived in peace. We wanted it that way. It was the Apaches that were always at war. They wanted the glory, the trophies of war. So they got all of it. Now my people are scattered and broken - by the white men and by the Apaches. I am sorry, my friend. I do not understand a man who is both white and Navajo. I can see two separate mountains and not a trail in between them. I am sorry."

Before Ree could reply, the old woman's age spots tightened in disbelief. She shook her head. She could not understand either one of them. White or not, the stranger was a friend. Had he not saved their lives? Why this foolish talk when there was food among these devil Apache and their savior, white or not, had the look of one who had not eaten for a long time. Would he share some fresh horse meat with them?

"You are kind to a stranger," Ree smiled, "I will not refuse your offer."

The woman hobbled over to the raiders' booty and dug out a meager ration of mesquite beans and fresh cuts of horse flesh. The three ate it with relish. When they were finished with the strong black coffee, Ree moved back to get his horse. He returned in a couple of minutes with the mustang. He dug three cheroots out of his saddle bag and passed one to each of them. Their faces lit up. A white man's smoke ... was no finer tobacco made. Much better than the

Mexican rope they used to trade for or that which their own people tried to grow. The trio smoked in silence, blowing blue smoke and marveling at the wondrous taste.

The old man took up the conversation again. "By what name do you go?" he asked.

"Ree Bannon."

"You are traveling across bad country. Apache country. You do not scout for the pony soldiers? Is this not true?"

Ree nodded. It was true.

Curiosity had a firm grip on the old man. "Then why do you come here? I am old and foolish; the manners of a fresh mind do not bar this curiosity as it should. Forgive my lack of silence."

Ree waved the apology aside. "It is no secret I need keep from you. I have traveled for several days now. I am following the Santa Fe stage that left San Lacita one night ago. I have business with a man on that stage."

The old Navajo's face tightened up. "You may not have much time," he warned. "The hesh-ke are out. These four Apaches were not of the cult but they were going to join them very soon. We were to be an offering to the clan from them. There will be a lot of trouble for all white men and peaceful Navajo very soon. The hesh-ke meant this to be a war to the death against everything white that crossed their path."

Bannon's shoulders sagged a little. He seemed to be carrying a heavy weight about him.

The old man noticed this but made no comment.

"Where were you traveling to when the Apaches jumped you?" Ree inquired.

"Dinétah."

The word tripped an avalanche of memories in Bannon's mind. They were going to the ancestral Navajo home. Dinétah. It meant old Navajo land - an enormous stretch of mountains, deserts, plateaus and grass lands. All located in the upper Northwestern corner of the territory. Land was given to the Navajo by the United States government after the tribe's infamous Long Walk to Fort Sumner and subsequent release. From where the three sat, it was a long journey, at least 150 miles away. Sizing up the two oldsters, Ree felt certain they would make it. He thought of his father dying or dead in a tiny canyon hideaway many miles to the south, never to see Dinétah. The need to continue his journey pressed harder against Ree's conscience.

Bannon arose. They followed him up.

"I must go now," he said, pointing toward the ponies that grazed a few hundred yards away, "They will not run. You have Yosen with you. May your journey be swift and safe." Again he made the sign of respect and mounted. He tipped his hat and was gone, riding away at an easy canter.

Gathering up their few belongings, the couple kicked sand over the ashes of the fire. Mounting two of the strongest ponies, they turned toward the sun and an arduous journey that would bring them atlas to their real home.

The delay had cost Bannon time and energy. He felt drained. The sky was beginning to lose its brassy texture when he drew rein in a rocky fissure by the side of a butte. The area was well sprinkled with juniper and piñon trees for shade and cover. He built a small fire under a piñon so that little smoke would rise up out of the branches. He made coffee, ate a little jerky and hardtack and lay back against his saddle. The Winchester lay warm across his stomach and the colt at his side. Behind him, the pony stood in the shade and contented itself with a cool bed of grass.

The rest was short-lived. He moved out as the skyline blazed sharply against the deepening indigo of nightfall. He rode for an hour then drew rein on the back side of a shallow saddle of a low lying ridgeline. He jogged to the edge of the spine and surveyed the moonlit landscape. In the distance he could see the vague outlines of a group of mountains. They lay murky along the horizon. Those would be the Placitas. Within those mountainous folds, lying just inside its perimeter would be the relay station. There was no chance he could catch the stage out in the open now. He'd have to chance it at the station.

By well past midnight Ree was already within the confines of the mountainous folds. He moved rapidly, yet with caution, up a steep slope toward a saddle in the limestone ridge.

The mustang stiffened and turned its head to the wind. Its ears were up and he was looking to the north, nostrils flaring for scent. Ree couldn't see or hear a sound, but the pony had. Ree slipped out of the saddle and moved swiftly off the trail, leading the mount behind him. Trail-tempered caution dictated he act quickly. Something or someone was farther up ahead, near the far side of the ridgeline. There was a depression off the main trail which wound around and dropped behind a jumble of boulders. Ree and his mount slid down the gravel sides to the wash. There, surrounded by boulders and upthrust sheets of mountain rock, the man held his hand on the pony's bridle and waited, quietly, for whatever was approaching.

They came like ghosts in the night. No sound came from their painted ponies or themselves as they topped the saddle, paused momentarily, skylined against the lighter shade of darkness, then as quickly slipped over and down the same trail Bannon had been on only moments before. They moved swiftly, carrying rifle and lance at ready. The wind stirred and Ree sucked in his gut, fearing it might shift and alert the mounts with his scent. The wind held and as quickly as they appeared, the Apaches were gone - all ten of them; down into the well of darkness that was the desert floor below.

Ree waited a long time before moving out again. There were precious hours left to reach the relay station before the coach was gone again. He had to catch it there rather than on the road. Already the three outlaws would be closing in on the station, and the hesh-ke were prowling in its vicinity.

Chapter Ten

A hushed stillness of predawn lay over the land. The Santa Fe-bound Concord had drawn into a spill of ancient lava which marked the entrance through the foothills that lay ahead. Past those slopes and ridgelines lay the relay station at the base of the Placitas.

John Montgomery was apprehensive and admitting it. "Too quiet," he muttered to himself in a hushed tone. His finger curled around the shotgun on his lap. He nestled it in closer. Below the brim of his slouched hat, Montgomery's eyes darted back and forth, digging into the darkness for any hint of trouble. "By damn, Montgomery, you're getting mighty jumpy for an old timer," Eli chuckled.

"Mind your driving! I'll mind the looking." He drew back both triggers on the scattergun.

Eli would not let it go. "What are you all lit up for, John? Either they've been there and gone, or they ain't been there at all!"

"Or they're still waiting!"

Eli shook his head. "Not before dawn. Even hesh-ke aren't so blood-hungry they'd risk a fight in the dark. We're still going in. We got no choice."

The stage rolled past a large sweep of rocks and then they could see the station off in the distance. The compound had been constructed with protection from an attack paramount in mind. The main building was situated well away from surrounding hills. Approach from any direction could be sighted a fair distance away. The main stone stock corral was attached to the building on one side. A well lay only a few feet from the front door. The station itself was not very large but built of stone and adobe with narrow gun slits for windows.

"Something's wrong!" Montgomery spat out the instant they rolled into view.

"Yeah," Dunn admitted slowly, teeth clenched. "No horses."

Where there should have been a dozen or more team horses, not one mare occupied the corral. Yet there was no sign of trouble. No fires. No visible damage to either the main building or the half dozen out buildings lying across from the corral. There was no sign of life anywhere.

"Old Jacob would be waitin' for us other times," Eli said as he realized that no matter what had happened to the station master, they'd be in serious trouble if there weren't fresh teams available. To attempt Santa Fe with the same hock-worn team was courting trouble - and left little room to maneuver. Yet there in front of him he saw it. No horses and to make matters worse, no sign of Old Jacob.

Dunn drew back the reins. The Concord rolled to a quick stop. Heads appeared out of the cab windows. "You men, climb out now," the driver ordered, "you're walking in." John Montgomery climbed down to lead the advance.

"What about me?" Claire called up.

Eli looked down at the pretty face staring up, her eyes wide in the moonlight. He motioned back inside the cab. "You stay put, Ma'am. Probably no trouble up there but we got to make sure. Sit tight. It'll be over in a minute or so."

John Montgomery, cradling his piece at hip height, led the advance. The buildings stood silent and forlorn. The main station house thatched roof stood out against the horizon that was just beginning to fray with the first sign of dawn.

They covered the ground to the compound at a fast walk. Dunn followed up behind with rein-checked caution. The men spread out, searching each of the wooden out buildings. Montgomery exited the main house after a minute and moved into the corral. He waved Dunn over.

"They've been here," he said flatly.

"How long ago?" one of the miners asked.

Eli joined his partner on the ground and answered after a moment's inspection. "More than a day, I'd say. These tracks are old and dried up. At least three of them run off the stock. It looks like they herded them up into those hills. The driver's forehead furrowed. "Where the hell is old Jacob? That son-of-a-coyote is mostly Injun himself. How'd they get the jump on him?"

Dunn's question was answered a moment later by the slight tinkling of a bell. It came from off in the hills. Driver and guard were off their haunches and circling the corral before the others could locate the direction of the sound. Behind the main building, the teamsters could make out the shadowy form of a man and small animal moving down a slope toward them. Neither one made a sound but for the soft tinkling in the cool morning stillness.

The man came out of a depression, up onto the slope directly in front of Eli and John Montgomery. Behind the stagehands, the passengers gathered in a loose body, watching the stranger's approach. Driver and guard were relaxed, their weapons holstered. The others followed suit, except for Dickson who stood next to Claire. Dickson edged to the back of the group then casually moved away. Claire watched him out of the corner of her eye as he moved back around the corral and out of sight. *He's acting a bit strange*, she thought.

Eli was first to break the self-imposed silence. "Where the hell you been, Jacob?" he called out.

Old Jacob waved aside the remark and resumed his casual approach in silence. His mule followed obediently behind. When Jacob got in front of the crowd, he stopped. His bushy eyebrows furrowed as he inspected the group. His dark eyes stopped at Claire for a moment then returned to his old friends.

"Dunn," he said in a voice so light the others could scarcely hear, "For once you was lucky you weren't on time. I told you jerk lines was your style. You just missed a heap of trouble - Apache-style."

There was a gale of laughter as the three men broke into backslapping, hand-yanking greetings. Eli pulled the old man's sombrero down over his eyes and gave Jacob a brotherly kick to the rump. When the laughter died down, the three ambled back toward the station. The passengers stood transfixed by the welcoming outburst. They followed the trio back to the station house, the mule coming up the rear. The soft bell followed them back to camp, tinkling softly all the way.

Old Jacob led the group into his adobe fortress and lit one of the wall oil lamps. Dickson was already in the room, seated behind a large wooden table in one corner. No one took notice of him as the crowd streamed in. Jacob chucked several pieces of wood into a potbellied stove. A tea kettle was set on top. The skinner settled down behind the table as the others moved in around him. With a talent for storytelling long his strongest trait, Jacob began his tale of a narrow escape.

He was alive, Jacob announced, only because of that bent-eared, stubborn, motherless jackass of a mule who awakened him early yesterday morning with an earful of braying. Jacob could feel the Apache's presence even before he'd set foot out the door. There was nothing to indicate trouble, but old Jacob hadn't spent the last ten years in Apacheria without learning a thing or two about those savages. Stepping back inside, he quickly slipped on his clothes and grabbed a handful of jerky and two canteens. With rifle ready, he edged along the corral and led his charge away. He towed the mule down into a dry wash behind the stone enclosure and through the depression until he could angle up into the hills and cover. By the time the first line of gray began to outline the horizon, Jacob and his burro were safely nestled into a cut of rooks high above the station.

They came at dawn. There were more than two dozen warriors in the party, all dressed for war. Vermillion strips adorned their faces and mounts. They streamed out of the hills from three different directions, armed with rifle, bow and lance. After searching the buildings and finding nothing, they circled the corral and picked up Jacob's tracks. They followed the man and mule until the rocks above the depression then lost track of them. Careful investigation brought no results. The man and mule had vanished. Old Jacob paused his story long enough to light his pipe… Old Jacob hadn't hunted and trapped with Jim Bridger and Jed Smith for near on to thirty years without picking up a trick or two. And when it came down to it, Blackfeet weren't much different from Apaches except maybe they smelt a little worse.

The audience sat in amused silence. Jacob had their complete attention; except Dickson, who had grown visibly impatient during the long oration. When the old keeper paused again to relight his pipe, Dickson left the table and ambled out the door. Old Jacob ignored him and kept on with his story.

Well, the Apaches went back to the compound and seemed to argue for a long time. It was obvious some of the younger braves wanted to hunt for Jacob's trail. They kept pointing toward the hills with their arms in angry gestures. In the end, the others won out. One old station keeper wasn't worth their time. So they took most of the food stuffs, rifled the buildings for supplies and then rode off. Jacob stayed put the rest of that day. He satisfied his thirst with the canteen and spent most of his time arguing with the mule.

Jacob was debating whether to return to the compound when he heard the Santa Fe Concord below. When he was certain the stage wasn't a trick, he climbed out of the rocks and came down to see his friends.

"You waited for us to smoke them Injuns out, did you?" John Montgomery said laughing. "I believe you are part Injun yourself, like Dunn said."

"And still alive because of it," Jacob replied with a wiry grin.

A shrill whistle turned all eyes to the iron stove. Coffee was ready. Claire moved to the stove and poured out the steaming dark liquid into several tins lined up in nest order. The aroma of bean coffee was thick in the cool, close air of the station room.

"Thank you, Ma'am," Jacob said, "I ain't been served to since I was huntin' with the Pawnees and up and married the chief's daughter."

"And run off to hunt with two old drunkards a week later," John Montgomery cut in.

"You should know," Eli said, "You old drunk."

All three broke into laughter again.

For his new captive audience, Jacob proceeded with his rambling dissertation on the Apache and his being stuck in the Placitas with no one for company except an ornery ex army mule. Eli and Montgomery had heard that story many times before. They went outside to feed and water the stock. If the team had to pull the coach all the way to Santa Fe, a long rest was essential.

Claire was not listening to the skinner. His words were drifting by but her attention was traveling around the room. She arose and stopped here and there to examine the curiosities an old man collects out of boredom and loneliness.

"Hey, what are you doing with those trunks?" a voice broke through Jacob's drifting monologue.

Claire stepped to the doorway in time to see Dunn approach Dickson who was by the lee of the Concord. He had drawn up the boot cover and was removing one of the girl's heavy trunks. The top looked ajar. Montgomery followed Dunn out of the corral to investigate.

Claire could hear Dickson explaining with casual ease. "Just reckoned I'd help you fellas get this heavy stuff off the coach while it's still cool out. I'm just trying to help!"

"Thanks," Eli said dryly, "but that's our job. You paid to ride, not to work! If there's any baggage to be moved, we'll do it."

Dickson shrugged his shoulders and pushed the trunk back. He moved toward the corral, stopped and then changed directions for the stone building. Claire moved past him and went toward the stage.

"Mister Dunn, I'd like to help if there's anything I can do. Perhaps breakfast."

"Yes, Ma'am, that would be something nice. It really would," John Montgomery said quickly before Eli could open his mouth. The driver's eyebrows rose up.

"Montgomery, you aren't in charge here," Eli snapped. "No thank you, Ma'am. Its mighty kind of you to offer but you shouldn't trouble yourself on our account. Cooking for this lot would be a lot of work and with little thanks."

Claire would not be put off that easily. She persisted, adding a smile when she sensed that might help. "I insist. I'm not helpless. It's silly to expect that old station keeper to make enough food for everyone here. I can cook as well as or perhaps better than he can. I insist on helping." With that, she spun around and entered the station, her hair flying behind her. By the time the two coachmen finished their chores, Claire had another pot of coffee brewing and the bacon frying.

Dawn came and went with no sign of the Apaches. If anyone was worried about them, it didn't show. Driver and guard waited by the gun ports until the sun was over the horizon then quit their posts. The Concord was parked alongside the building out of the main line of fire. The teams had been fed and watered. Now it was only a matter of time until the hottest part of the day was over. They could proceed again in the coolness of evening. If he had to use the same teams, Eli knew he'd have to slow his pace. It would cost the company money, but that was cheaper than buying new stock. Mainly it was the passengers on his mind. The idea of traveling on foot because of lame horses sent a shiver down his spine.

The passengers stayed inside after breakfast. A deck of cards appeared and a game began. Outside, a blood orange sun was beginning its ascent into the still blue sky. Tall saguaro cactus cast long shadows across the sand. A rag tag bunch of clouds lay overhead, offering little protection from the promised heat.

In their corral, the team horses moved with the approaching sunlight, turning their faces toward the fiery ball in the sky.

Dickson appeared in the doorway, adjusting his suspenders and hanging a jacket over one shoulder. Cards again, he muttered to himself. Didn't they have anything else to do besides play cards all day? He could earn more in five minutes than those idiots could in a whole month. Frontiersmen indeed! Lazy, complaining, ignorant itinerants was a much better definition for them. What this territory needed were men with ambition, intelligence and the wiliness to take a chance on making something profitable there. Those miners and cowboys certainly weren't of a mind to do that, but Dickson was. He meant to make something of himself. Of course that gold, whenever he got his hands on it, wouldn't hurt his situation either. They were saying that girl's father had some money. A large spread, they said, just outside Santa Fe. He'd have to remember that. It wouldn't hurt to renew acquaintances once he was in the money himself. He might be able to work something out. Perhaps a little romance and maybe a marriage was in the cards. With that gold it was all possible - that and more.

The young man walked over to the well. Running thin fingers through his unruly hair, he crudely combed the toss of brown curls into some semblance of order. Scooping water from a wooden bucket, he splashed his face and sucked in the clear, cool liquid. Leaning against the stone, he lit a cigarette. He gazed out at the bleached land in the direction of Two Man's Corners, unseen to the northwest. That was the spot the driver had said would be their next resting spot.

It won't be long now, Dickson thought. With his secret well hidden and no sign of marauding Apaches, the young man felt relaxed and secure. He was very proud of himself. Fantasies were filling his mind when a stir by the corral pulled him back to reality. The horses were moving about nervously. He studied the enclosure but saw nothing out of the ordinary. Still, that was something that should be investigated. He was on the frontier, he reminded himself. Any man would check into it right away. And he was as much a man and more than any of those foul smelling whiskered ruffians inside. As Dickson approached the corral, the team pricked friendly ears and several of them muffled snuffling sounds. The boy could see nothing out of the ordinary. The horses were calmed down again. Whatever it was was gone. Dickson sighed a deep breath of relief and turned around.

A long blue gun barrel met him at eye level. Behind it, a man stood, feet spread, grinning. Dickson had never seen him before. He wore a day-old beard and rumpled clothes which smelt of many trail hours. From the stone corral's far side, two other men popped up, equally unshaven and dangerous looking. They came quickly and quietly, one carrying a rifle, the other a shotgun. As they rounded the stock pen, Dickson noticed their revolvers hung low - gunfighter style. The young man felt his body tensing up; his stomach knotting as the others bandits crowded him.

"Look's what we got here," one of them said, his mouth curling at the corner. "Should we leave now and let the others go?" the second man asked.

The man holding a gun on Dickson spat out a lump of tobacco. It splattered over the dude's new shoes. The outlaw's face grew red with anger but his voice never changed an octave. "Listen, you saddlesore complainers, we agreed to take them all. Not just junior here. Now I mean to do just that. The money inside is a certainty. What junior's got is a chance."

"You don't mean me, do you?" Dickson interrupted in a low voice.

Curt Lanker poked his gun barrel into Dickson's nose, pressing it flat against his face. Holding it there, he cocked the trigger and watched the youngster's eyes widen in terror.

"You see someone else here that could go by that name?" he snarled.

Dickson turned his head slowly back and forth, eyes riveted on Lanker's pistol.

"We know you snatched a map off that miner you plugged. He told us about it before he died," Curt paused, releasing the pressure off Dickson's nose. "And we want it. So you think real hard where you put it. I ain't gonna waste my time with you once we get inside. Think about that!"

"Let's go then," Eddie Lanker interrupted his brother. Dickson was shoved ahead of the trio and warned that one bit of noise and he'd be blasted on the spot. He concurred numbly. Eddie and Gus swiftly crossed the yard and positioned themselves on either side of the door. They waited only a moment then burst through the open entrance. There was a crash of gunfire, a body hit the ground, chairs were upset and then silence.

"Move!" Curt rasped in Dickson's ear and shoved him through the doorway.

A scan about the smoke-filled room told Dickson what he feared. The passengers and crew had been taken completely by surprise. In the middle of the room a cowboy lay dead. His chest had been opened by both blasts of Gus's scattergun. The others stood back, their hands grasping air. The girl was still next to the kitchen basin and stove. The aroma of fresh coffee was still thick in the room. On either side of the entrance, a bandit stood training his piece on the crowd. No one said a word as Dickson was shoved into their midst.

"Gus," Curt commanded, "Get rid of that!" He pointed toward the fallen figure on the bloodstained earth. "The rest of you folks hand over them pieces. Right slowly now...or Gus here will have some more target practice."

They complied cautiously without a sound. Claire stood her place, eyeing the three outlaws with distain and anger.

"Now sit down, all of you. Hands on top of the table. Everybody just relax. No one's gonna get hurt if you listen to what I got to say. Any funny business and..." Curt raised his .44 Smith and Wesson straight at Eli, cocking it. The gun exploded in his hand, drilling a neat hole in the wall beside Eli's right ear. The driver winced, his eyes never leaving the bandit. Curt broke into laughter and Gus joined him with a stomach-churning snicker.

"What do you want from us?"

Curt Lanker turned to the girl. He was surprised she'd speak out like that. A smile crossed his face followed by a sneer again. He stepped toward Claire. The girl moved back until she was pressed up against the wooden stand holding the olla and tin basin. Lanker's hand swung up, locked onto Claire's chin and jerked it back. When the girl brought her hands up in defense, the outlaw tightened his grip, distorting her mouth and cheeks. There was movement behind him.

"One of you folks move and you'll all die!" Gus growled.

Curt's face was inches from Claire's, his breath nauseating. He spoke in a soft voice but loud enough for everyone to hear. "Shut your yap, Miss. I got plans for you. Stay out of the way and be still!" Then he shoved her back into the olla and turned to his partners. "Eddie, go check the stage. See what kind of goodies they're carrying this time. Check the front boot and floor boards too."

"If its bullion or gold from the mines you're after, you'll not find it onboard that stage. This is strictly passengers only." Eli declared in a controlled voice.

"Shut up!"

Curt holstered his gun and pointed toward Dickson. "You come on," he said, motioning toward the doorway. "Gus, keep them quiet. Anyone tries anything, you know what to do." Lanker shoved the frightened man out the door, threw an evil glint back at Claire, and disappeared into the bright sunlight.

Dickson was visibly shaking now. His hands were wringing wet and perspiration soaked his back. He could feel sweat trickling down his cheeks. He tasted salt on his lips. The bandit pushed him toward the tool shed.

"You're shaking, tenderfoot, what's the matter?"

Dickson swallowed hard.

When they reached the weathered lean-to, Curt pushed the young man through the door and into one of the stalls. Lanker's toughened face hadn't changed expressions since leaving the others. The outlaw thumbed his gun belt and spread his legs apart. His stance was that of a victor, a conqueror. It towered over Dickson's cowering humble figure sprawled in the dirt.

"Junior, I'm not gonna waste any time. You got a map and I want it. Now you either tell me where it is or I'm gonna kill you - straight and clean, just like that."

Dickson did something he didn't think himself capable of. "You'll never get the map if I'm dead," he said. The youngster couldn't believe he'd actually said it. It was true, he wasn't afraid. "Anyway, I don't have the map anymore," he said, "I got rid of it back in San Lacita. I'll take you there. You can have whatever you find. Just promise to let me go."

The elder Lanker didn't reply. His boot did it for him. It abruptly broke off the ground, swung up and buried itself into Dickson's groin.

The horse thief gasped out for air, doubled over and buckled to the ground. His pleading eyes looked up in time to see a fist come crashing across his face. A wave of nauseating darkness swept over him. He collapsed to the ground, flat out. The youth lay unconscious for a minute or so until he slowly began to stir.

Lanker's mouth was inches from Dickson's blurred watery eyes. "I said I ain't wasting my time on you. Now where is the map?"

Dickson was on his hands and knees, his stomach pumping in and out, gasping in air. He shook his spinning head, trying to clear away the pain and nausea that was crawling up his throat, threatening to pour out. Before he could utter a word, another stab of pain sent him crashing to the ground, doubled over, pleading for mercy.

"Please," he muttered, "Please don't kill me." His eyes watered freely. "I am telling the truth."

Cold steel pressed against Dickson's temple, pinning his head to the dirt. Lanker's mouth was again by his eyes, blackened teeth between parched lips. The bandit was not speaking, his hand forcing the gun barrel down tighter against the horse thief's head. A cruel smile passed over the mouth of the bandit and stayed.

Then Curt Lanker spoke and Dickson's eyes opened wide in terror.

"You ever been skinned, boy, inch by inch? Apaches do a good job of it. Picked up the trick myself."

"All right, all right!" Dickson gasped, "I'll tell you where it is."

Curt got to his feet, towering over the figure huddled in a fetal position below him. He aimed his .44 at Dickson's face. "Talk."

The sharp pistol report snapped Eddie's head over toward the tool shed. Moments later his brother appeared in the doorway, his revolver still curling smoke from its barrel. He stood there for a moment, looking through Eddie, out into the desert beyond the compound. He slowly leathered his piece and moved toward the main station house.

"What happened?" Eddie demanded to know as his brother approached.

Curt shrugged his shoulders. "The dumb bastard tried to jump me. I had to shoot him."

"Is he dead?"

"Do you know anyone I shot that isn't?"

"For Christ's sake, Curt, "how the hell are we gonna find that map without him?"

"Relax, I know where the map is. It's not going anywhere."

Eddie's face lit up. "Well, where is it then?"

Curt's mind was someplace else. He moved past his brother. Eddie reached out to grab his elbow but Curt jerked it away. "Look through the luggage if you're in such a damn rush," he snarled. He walked away toward the station house.

Eddie watched his brother amble into the adobe building. Big shot, always acting superior in front of him. It burned at Eddie's guts. Gus was at the doorway, watching them both. Curt always acted that way if the idiot was watching. The smell of coffee curled the boy's nose. Breakfast! The promise of warm food in his belly after three solid traveling days made his stomach knot up in pleasure. Home cookin' by a fancy-class woman, no less. Now that was more than worth a break in his search for the map. If Curt said the map was in the luggage then that's where it must be. He could start his search after breakfast. Heaving a trunk back into the boot, Eddie slapped his dusty hat against his leg, and stepped out for the station house and breakfast.

Eddie knew the other passengers had guessed Dickson's fate by their eyes as he entered. They were scared. They were not shaking like the tenderfoot but alarmed none the less. Gus was over by the girl, still cradling his shotgun at ready. The girl was holding back tears but just barely.

"Aren't you gonna look for the map?" Curt greeted Eddie with a cruel grin. "Stuff it," Eddie hissed back.

Curt slipped behind the end of the table and called for coffee. Claire came over with a fresh pot and poured it. For a moment, the bandit saw the girl tense up, her arm stiff. Lanker read her mind. "One wrong move with that coffee, Miss, and you'll end up worse than junior did. Now fix us some grub and be quick about it."

Gus guarded the prisoners while Curt and Eddie ate their fill, then Eddie stood guard while simpleminded Gus ate. Curt wandered outside and looked over the Concord. When Eddie peered outside, he saw Curt back by the boot, rummaging through one of the trunks.

"Wait for me, Curt," Eddie called out.

The elder bandit waved him back "No rush."

By the time Gus finished stuffing himself and Eddie moved outside, Curt was finished with his inspection. He was leaning against the stage, smoking a cheroot. Both the girl's trunks lay open at his feet. Her clothes and personal effects were scattered about. Blue smoke curled up past the bandit's nose. He didn't inhale it, instead letting the butt hang between his clenched teeth. His thoughts were a long ways off.

"Find it?" Eddie asked, still wiping crumbs off his face.

"Can't understand it," Curt muttered to himself. Eddie stepped up in front of him. "Hey, I asked if you found it." Curt looked up through the smoke, his eyes squinting. "Bastard must have been lying to me. As scared as he was, he still lied to me! I…"

Eddie was beside himself. "You're kidding me, brother. You got to be…"

"Nope!"

"You killed him … our only chance to get that map. For Christ's sake Curt, get the girl!"

Eddie's eyebrows furrowed. His brother was acting stranger than a man lost in the desert for months.

"Whadya want?"

"Bring her here, damnit!" Curt commanded, his teeth biting the cigar more or less in half. His eyes came alive, drilling into Eddie's own. Young Lanker held the stare for only a moment then spun around and stormed into the main house. Curt could hear his voice booming, shouting commands.

Claire walked reluctantly toward the outlaw. Her face was more composed now. She carried a look of determination like nothing the bandit did or said was going to scare her. She had passed any point of pretending they would leave without more killing. She was a woman. Her widowed father hadn't spoken to her of such things as rape, but she knew of it. Comancheros and Comanches were the worst - this kind of trash a close second. She knew what they did to women, especially young ones like herself. She knew she'd die before they did it to her. It showed in her eyes.

She took in the mess about her feet. Curt noticed and remarked, "You've got some pretty clothes there. Cooperate with me and I'll see to it you get a chance to wear them again. Try anything funny and you can forget about living. Do you understand?"

The girl said nothing; her eyes registered only hate and restrained anger.

Curt liked that in a woman; life, strength, vitality. Like some of those Comanche squaws he and Eddie had caught just last month down on the Pecos by Red Bluff Lake. Plenty of spirit there - made for one hell of a time in the sack, they did. This one looked like she'd be just as good or even better. Spanish blood. Fine breeding. She had it all, and Curt was a tester of fine womanhood from way back.

Claire couldn't mistake that look in the bandit's eyes. His brooding leer started on her face, lingered on her swelling bosom, then fell to her waist. She knew what was on his mind and it turned her stomach.

Then Lanker's expression changed. A smile replaced the leer. His look had changed to one of forced friendliness. His voice was calmer and easier going.

"Hey, look, I'm sorry I scared you in there. I had to do it. It's my brother, Eddie, he gets a little crazy sometimes. I have to act like that to keep him in line. You know what I mean?"

No response.

Curt's voice dropped even lower, forcing assurance with every word. "We don't want to hurt you folks, but we're gonna have to if I don't find that map."

The girl's eyebrows furrowed in surprise. Curt quickly explained, "We know that dude had a map. It belongs to us. He stole it. He claimed he gave it to you … said he put it in your luggage. It isn't there. So where is it?"

Claire kept quiet, staring at the bandit with her placid eyes, revealing nothing.

Lanker's act was running out of steam. He didn't like playacting or pretending. He was more used to blasting his way out of a situation or problem. The girl presented another kind of problem - one he didn't know how to handle. It made him ill at ease.

"Look, I'm not going to hurt you. But, damn it, I want that map."

No response.

Curt's big paw flashed across Claire's face, snapping it sideways. She cupped a beet red cheek and blinked away tears. Her teeth were clenched, but she said nothing.

Lanker's temper was on a short fuse and about to burst. His hand gripped Claire's shoulder tightly. "If you won't talk, Miss, I'm going to do you right here. You understand? Right in front of all them people. Think about that. Think what they'll think of you in Santa Fe … a girl like you." The bandit's hand moved to Claire's neck band. He curled his fingers around it. Fabric began to tear apart. Claire was rigid, tense with fear.

A scuffling from the station house caught his attention. Voices were coming from inside, fighting and arguing. It was Eddie and Gus.

As Curt reached the doorway, Claire in tow, Gus had just sent a chair crashing up against a wall, splintering it to pieces.

"What the hell's going on in here?"

Gus was fuming mad, his voice cracking and sputtering as he tried to get all the words out at once. "It's that damn brother of yours again," he hissed. "He called me a fool. I told him not to call me that. I told him…"

"Well, damnit; you are a simpleminded old fool!" Eddie chorused.

"No, I'm not!" Gus screamed and let loose with the shotgun into the ceiling. A deafening roar filled the room, acid smoke and wood splinters everywhere.

Curt lowered his palm to his gun butt, resting it there. "Gus, put that gun away. Eddie don't mean nothing. He's just…"

"Oh, yes I did!"

"Eddie, damn you, shut up or I'll plug you myself," Curt spat out.

Eddie stomped out the room, pausing long enough to kick one of the chairs through the doorway and clean into the yard.

Curt threw a few words of reassurance at the simpleminded man to calm him down. When Gus began to bicker about Eddie and the map, Curt cut him short. There was more money than gold here, he argued. Gus would get his share, if he just stayed calm and didn't let Eddie get to him. When the third partner was calmed down, Curt told him to watch the others. He had a job to do outside.

"Now it's your turn," he said to Claire. "Let's go!" He grabbed her by an arm and propelled her outside. Curt spied Eddie by the Concord and called him over. "Stay by the doorway and lay off Gus. I'll be back in a little while."

Eddie's eyes narrowed, glaring at the girl's heaving bosom. "Where you taking the senorita?"

Curt smiled back. "For a little talk. You want to question her after me?"

Eddie laughed out loud and slapped his hat to knee. "Alright! Now you're talkin' sense! Hurry up about it."

Claire doubled her hands into tight fists. "I won't go!" she rasped for the first time.

The Smith & Wesson came out in one fluid motion. Curt pointed it straight into the girl's strained face. He slowly pulled back on the trigger. "Start walkin'," he whispered. Claire took a step back. "Move," he shouted. She turned about, facing the rocks. "That way," he commanded, shoving her toward an outcropping of boulders opposite the corral.

Eddie watched them disappear behind the rocks. He licked his lips in anticipation of his turn with the girl.

Upon reaching the upthrust of rocks and lava formations, Lanker grabbed Claire by an elbow and drew her close. He leaned over, his breath foul and nauseating. When the girl resisted, he yanked back her hair and pulled the pale face toward his own. He smiled, yellow teeth showing. Claire forced her face to one side, fighting with all her strength. Curt cuffed her hard.

"So you want to play hard to get, ah? You and your fancy fine new clothes. You ain't good but for one thing … and you know what that is." He forced the girl closer and kissed her hard on the lips. His tongue pried at her clenched teeth. His powerful arms crushed her shapely body tightly against his.

Claire tried to push him away but couldn't. Muffled sounds came from her throat. She tried to squirm out of his hold, but Curt was too strong, too menacing. His rough, calloused hand slipped from her shoulder and found the softness of her breast.

Summing up her fast-fading strength, Claire jerked out of Lanker's grip. Her fingers came down hard against the bandit's face, raking the skin, drawing blood.

Curt roared in anger and backhanded the girl. Claire staggered back, whimpering and gasping for air. Her eyes were wide with terror. She knew Curt would kill her if she resisted but she had to.

The aroused bandit, angered by Claire's resistance, moved in again. Thin lines of blood ran down both sides of his face. His eyes were wide and bloodshot. Claire retreated against a boulder. When Curt drew closer, she kicked out a leg, smashing it into his groin. The outlaw gasped in pain, staggering back. Claire saw her chance. She leapt forward, trying to pass the reeling bandit. Unfortunately, Curt Lanker was a grizzly fighter from Montana. As Claire dashed by, he clipped her with a solid right upper cut that sent her sprawling. She flew into a ledge of rock and crumbled to the ground.

Lanker reared up, like a wounded grizzly sow. "You bitch," he screamed in anger,

"I'll kill you for that. I'll kill you."

Before Claire could arise, Curt was on top of her. His eager hands tore savagely at her dress, ripping off a sleeve in one jerk. One powerful paw clamped down hard on her neck, pinning her against the sand. He was straddling her struggling body with obvious pleasure. When she tried to knock him off, Curt sent an open-palmed hand smashing against her cheek, drawing blood from split lips.

Deliberately, the bandit ran his dirty paw down the girl's throat to the opening in her blouse. One finger wrapped around a button and tore it off, followed by another with a sick tearing sound. Milky white flesh was opened to bright sunlight. The outlaw's eyes dropped to the round firm mounds being exposed. His dark face widened in pleasure. He grinned, yellow teeth again. His arm locked onto the front of the blouse. He tensed his arm to rip it open.

A quail whistled.

Curt Lanker froze. Tension gripped his body. His head jerked up. The sound was close. It seemed to be directly behind him. He felt his senses keen and alert. The girl was sobbing now. He ignored her. He leapt up and spun around. His hand dropped to his holster, drawing out the .44 with lightning speed ... but too late.

The knife hit him square on, plunging through his breastbone, burying itself up to the hilt. Curt gasped out for air, empty eyes wide in terror. His revolver exploded into the ground. He stumbled back, swaying on rubbery legs.

Claire wanted to scream but couldn't. Her throat tightened and made her choke for air.

The bandit staggered back several steps, his foggy eyes locked onto a shadowy figure less than ten yards away. He tried to negotiate a turn but collapsed instead, burying his face in the sand.

The discharge of Curt Lanker's Smith & Wesson made Eddie nervous. Curt wasn't a woman killer, not his brother. And besides he had promised Eddie the girl when he was finished. Something was wrong! Maybe she got his gun and shot him. Maybe it was Apaches. Eddie's mind spun around with a whirl of threatening scenarios closing in. He spied Gus standing in the doorway, curious about the shots too. Eddie called him over. "Gus, go on out there and see if Curt needs you," he commanded him. "I'll watch the others." Gus' bushy eyebrows furrowed in suspicion. "Go on," Eddie egged him, "Curt might need you."

Still suspicious but hungry for action, Gus leveled his heavy shotgun and started a sprint toward the rocks. Eddie watched him and backed up to the adobe building, hustling the passengers back inside.

Gus' mind was whirling as he dashed around the pile of large boulders. Now he'd show that punk Eddie just what he was worth. He and Curt could take care of whatever needed handling - just him and his boss. He stumbled over something. He peered down. Lanker lay sprawled in the dirt, a knife buried in his chest. The girl was still up against the rocks, clutching her blouse tightly about her.

Instinctively Gus swung his shotgun down at the girl then stopped. She was unarmed. Whoever killed Curt was still around. Gus spun around. He saw nothing unusual or suspicious. His brooding eyes darted back and forth, examining rocks, scrub brush, tangled weeds, everything. Nothing

A quail called softly off to his left.

Gus spun around. He fired; first one barrel, then the second.

The shots reverberated off the mountainside, their echoes rolling back and beyond. Leaves fluttered off the blasted mesquite trees. Loading quickly, Gus fired again. Nothing moved. There was nothing to fire at. The mottled foliage of green and beige melted into a montage of light and dark shapes; forms and abstractions. The trees were thick in spots, and when laced with brush, were virtually impenetrable.

Sweat beads popped out on the outlaw's balding forehead. He licked his lips unconsciously. Fingers stiffened on the triggers. He wanted to fire again; to avenge his partner and boss. His eyes peered into the brush. They crossed over dark lines and green leaves. Wait! That dark line ... and there, the hues of skin and eyes... He was looking right at a man - right down a rifle barrel.

Gus brought his shotgun to shoulder. He fired the same instant the dark line exploded in his face. The blast lifted Gus off his feet. He cartwheeled backwards, spraying blood everywhere. His shotgun spun off in one direction, his hat another. He hit the ground, did another tumble and crumpled into a bloody heap.

Still gripped with fear, Claire looked up at the shadow... but he was gone, out of the trees, reloading a buffalo rifle as he jogged by. He disappeared into a clump of mesquite without indicating he'd even seen the girl.

Standing in the doorway, Eddie Lanker couldn't miss the distinct roar of a Sharps bull gun. He knew where that placed the odds. Eddie had to act fast. Some person...several persons were out there. Maybe it was Apaches. With two partners probably dead and himself left, Eddie felt fear for the first time. A slight movement behind him sent Eddie swinging around, firing as he did toward the house. Passengers tumbled back inside. The outlaw sprinted toward the corral. There was someone behind the rocks where Gus had gone. Eddie snapfired three rounds. Slugs splintered rock into flying chips. The blurred figure was gone as swiftly as it had appeared. Leaping on the first available mare, Eddie wrapped arms around the mane and kicked its flanks. The horse burst out of the corral and galloped past the station. Eddie threw out two more shots and sent passengers flying back inside.

Eli Dunn was the first one back outside. What he saw made him lock heels. A man approached the relay station, coming at an easy lope. A pace well suited to running quite some distance. He carried a long Sharps buffalo rifle. His revolver hung low on his thigh. Reaching the station, the stranger paused long enough to study the fast disappearing rider.

Eddie's mare was still kicking up great clods of earth, taking the bandit straight for open desert. The youngest Lanker was hung low over the horse, making for a very small target.

That didn't seem to bother the stranger. With an easy leap, he grasped the overhanging beams of the mud-packed adobe building. Sharps slung over his back, the man hoisted himself up onto the roof as passengers gathered below. Shouldering the big rifle, Ree Bannon quickly sighted in on the rider. The commotion below was not noticed. He sized up the desert, judging wind speed and direction. He steadied the Sharp's needle-eye sights on the small target. He sucked in deeply, held it, and slowly squeezed the trigger.

The rifle exploded. All eyes swung to the bandit now a tiny figure far out in the sun-bleached desert wastes. Horse and rider seemed motionless for a moment. The man rolled off the horse's back. A puff of dust arose where he hit dirt. A shout of approval went up below Bannon.

As quickly and gracefully as he had gone up, the rifleman came down. Landing on cat's feet, Ree turned a back to the crowd and stepped quickly toward Claire who was stumbling into view. In all the commotion of Eddie's escape, no one had attended to finding the girl.

Claire was near exhaustion, totally spent from her fight with Lanker. Ree caught her as she started to collapse. He held her loosely in his arms, as a man does something he fears might break. Claire managed to roll her eyes up momentarily, catching sight of the stranger's intense and sullen face. She noticed the dark leathery skin and startlingly blue eyes, then everything went black and she fainted.

Old Jacob was the first to reach Bannon. The stranger cradled the girl's limp form and thrust it into the old man's arms. "Take her," he said in a commanding voice. Before Jacob could say a word, the man was gone, past the outcropping, moving at a swift pace.

A minute later, he rode out from the rocks at a canter. He moved toward a tiny dot that was Eddie Lanker. Eli, John Montgomery and the others stood their ground and watched him go. No one said a word.

Minutes later a shot rang out and rolled back across the station yard. All heads turned. The stranger was coming back, leading Lanker's mare.

When Ree Bannon rode back into the station yard, Claire was again on her feet. Upon his return, she had a chance to study him close up. What she saw made her feel uneasy.

It was his face and eyes. The face was that of an intense man. It was burnt leather brown and taut like he had been chiseled out of stone. Jet black hair hung over his ears and curled down his neck, brushing his frazzled collar. His eyes were narrow slits, conditioned to squinting against the sun's harsh glare. Even more surprising, they were blue, not black like most Indians and they didn't just look at things. They stared unflinchingly straight into a person. They were not the eyes of a man at peace.

Ree quickly skimmed Claire's figure. She felt as if he were looking past her brave facade and straight into her soul. The eyes might be a white man's, but the stare was pure native. The rider turned away as quickly as he looked over.

Old Jacob studied the man as he dismounted, facing them and unsaddled his mount. Jacob didn't look at Bannon the same way Claire did. He saw the stranger quite differently. It was Ree's movement at first. The breed didn't move, he flowed. A smooth calculated step off the pony and forceful stride into the corral presented the walk of a hunter stalking. A gunfighter at least, a killer no doubt. Jacob was sure of it.

Jacob's tired but intense hunter's eyes examined Bannon closer. He wore faded jeans with a buckskin shirt which hung low - hunting clothes. A walnut handled .44 colt revolver hung loose on one hip. On his saddle were two rifles. He recognized one as the Sharps, .50 caliber or more. The other one he didn't recognize until Ree slipped it out of the scabbard. It was a short barreled Winchester; a new model with seventeen shells to a load - a deadly weapon in anyone's hands.

His mount was a mustang: short, wiry and tough. It was clearly bred for desert riding and totally self-sufficient. It could match whatever the Apache had. In the harsh, unforgiving environment of a desert, it was the best kind of horseflesh around.

As the man turned back to unsaddle Eddie's horse, old Jacob caught sight of a knife, neatly tucked in back of his gun belt. It was an Indian hunting knife. He'd seen them before; well-balanced, tooled and finely honed to a razor sharp edge. It rested in a beaded Indian's sheath. This was no stranger just happened upon the scene, Jacob was quick to grasp. He was a bounty hunter or tracker of some sort. Certainly he had a purpose for being there. He wasn't going to be stopped easily. *Not by that bandit trio. Nor,* Jacob mused to himself, *by the Apaches either.* That kind of man spelled trouble - for himself and those around him. They sought trouble and it always seemed to find them in turn. Jacob looked up at the hills, burnt sun bright in the midmorning heat. They seemed empty, serene. They were deceiving. The hills could bring trouble for Jacob and the others, but especially for this new man now in their midst.

Chapter Eleven

"Mister, I'd be obliged if I could shake your hand."

Bannon extended a strong arm out to meet Eli's calloused paw. John Montgomery stepped up and extended his hand also. Eli dug out a freshly rolled cigarette from behind his ear then offered the stranger a tiny bag of tobacco. Ree took it from the driver and rolled his own. "What might your name be, stranger?" Eli inquired.

"Name's Ree Bannon."

"It's lucky for us you showed up when you did. Those no good varmints would have done the little lady some harm if you hadn't been there."

Ree removed his battered Stetson and sleeved his dirt-caked forehead. "Would have been here sooner but some 'paches decided to cross the same set of hills I was passing through."

"You were heading here on purpose?" Eli asked.

"Yep."

Dunn wanted to ask more but he held off, warned by some inner sense that Bannon wasn't the type to take kindly to a lot of questioning.

"Was there a couple of dozen, leading good stock animals?" John Montgomery piped in.

Bannon shook his head. "No, only about ten in a war party. No extra stock."

The guard scratched his whiskers. "Musta been a different bunch then," he offered. "Old Jacob said a large party came here last night and stole all his stock. I figure they're reservation bucks out trying to raise a little hell. Maybe count a few coup before the troopers push them back onto the reservation."

"You're right," Bannon said, "and you're wrong. I've cut their signs ever since leaving the Salt. They're out in force, alright. I don't reckon they mean to go back to the reservation. I ran across an old Navajo couple. They said about the same thing. Those aren't ordinary wild-eyed bucks. They're hesh-ke ... white killers. They aren't going to turn tail and run. They'll hide alright; and they'll fight ... from ambush ... at night ... whenever and wherever the odds are in their favor. They mean to kill as many whites as possible before they're cornered and stopped.

Eli and John Montgomery exchanged solemn stares. "When we were at Camp Puerco, the captain there said just about the same thing. Only he was sure the hesh-ke were all south of here. Said he had patrols out and they reported nothing."

"That's army logic," Ree remarked, "only it doesn't work on Apaches. Never has. Never will."

"We were jumped a couple of days back over the other side of San Lacita. You figure that was hesh-kes too?" Eli asked.

"Probably."

Montgomery was surprised. "They cut off the attack when they might have wiped us all out. That doesn't make sense."

Ree smiled. "It does if you're an Indian," he answered. "If they'd wiped you out then all stage traffic … traffic of any kind, in fact, would have been stopped outside of town until the army had the hostiles put away."

Driver and guard gave a lame nod.

"This way, they cut you up or let you go and then wait to cut you up again farther down the road. They can count on killing more whites every time. If the captain hasn't heard from his patrols, they might have run into an ambush. I came across a four man patrol about fifty miles back in the mountains. Hesh-ke recruits had ambushed them. You can guess your chances are pretty good of getting hit before you reach Santa Fe. They'll find out soon enough that you're here and where you're heading. All they've got to do is wait someplace up ahead."

"Just like that." Eli said dryly.

Ree responded with a nod.

Driver and guard didn't try to hide their apprehension. Ree moved off to rub down his mount and store his gear with the others at the end of the stone corral. In the rocky basin, where the relay station lay situated, the noonday heat hit one hundred and kept climbing. The air hung heavy and stifling. Not a breath of air moved the dust. Everyone and everything moved at half pace.

Claire called everyone indoors for lunch. The air was still cooler inside than out.

It was heavy with the smell of freshly brewed coffee. They ate bacon, beans and venison Jacob had mysteriously produced out of his hidden cellar. The station keeper was absent most of the meal. He reappeared after twenty minutes.

As the others finished their meal, Jacob sat in a corner, plate on lap and looked over at the stranger. Ree had settled into a chair against the wall, placing himself in direct line with the doorway. He could see more outdoors than anyone else. That intrigued old Jacob. That and the intuition that he had seen this man before. Ree Bannon's turquoise gun belt had triggered that connection. The same kind of metal work was on a band around the worn, sweat-stained brim of his hat. Jacob had seen similar turquoise ornamentation on other men. There was nothing unusual about it. Seeing the gear on this particular stranger, it made a difference. It made him different.

It kept nagging at the old muleskinner. He couldn't remember where or when but Jacob was convinced he'd seen this strange man before ... and it wasn't over breakfast coffee either.

After a second cup of coffee, Bannon leaned back, tipping the chair against the cool mud wall. He fished out a cheroot and slipped it into the corner of his mouth. He touched tip to table candle and blew out a perfect smoke circle.

The conversation began to wane. Ree let the others talk amongst themselves. His eyes traveled the room, noticed the station keeper's stares, and ignored them. He studied the girl who was busily pouring more coffee and beginning to gather plates. She was a pretty girl. No, pretty wasn't the right word... Handsome, perhaps. She had strong blood lines. Spanish features, he guessed. She could be called striking by some people. She had a full figure and dark intense eyes. There was strength about her. Something he had seen in Navajo women but never in a white woman. It intrigued him.

Eli fished out another cigarette from behind his ear, lit it and leaned over to Bannon. "You seem pretty certain those 'paches will be up ahead. Got any ideas where they might be laid up, waitin? I ain't ashamed to say 'paches make me more nervous than a young squirt in the hay with some dark-eyed filly for the first time."

John Montgomery joined in, his eyes never leaving Bannon's, "I got a feeling this man's got a plan, Eli."

"Then let him tell it!"

"I've got a proposal," Ree said. "It's no more than that. There is another way of reaching Santa Fe. Your stage could make it but it'd be rough. The Apaches aren't likely to split whatever force they've gathered to cover two different routes. They'll expect you to stick to the road. This trail will go around them. By the time they've figured out your route, you should be safe. Should be...I guarantee nothing."

"What kind of route is it?" Dunn asked, "and how do you know about it when none of us has ever heard of another route to Santa Fe?"

"It's an old Navajo trail," Ree explained. "They've used it for centuries, leading their stock to winter feeding grounds. Most whites, except for a few gold seekers and hunters, don't know about it. Most Apaches do but they avoid it. Apaches fought some big battles with the Navajo on it. They call it a dead place. They keep their distance because of evil spirits. That trail should be a lot safer than the regular route and not much longer. Like I said, it's your choice."

"Yeah," Eli muttered, "I get the point."

"If you're smart, Dunn, you'll take the strangers advice," old Jacob announced from his corner of the room.

Eli Dunn was a cautious man. Born and bred to trust no one else when his life or responsibility was at stake. That went double when it was a half-breed suggesting a route he'd never heard of - or even knew existed for that matter. "How do you know so much about this here trail? I've made this run hundreds of times and never heard of no such thing."

Ree threw a smirk at the prospector. "I first heard of it from an old Navajo a long time ago."

"Have you ever been on it?"

"I haven't," Ree admitted with a tone of finality to his voice.

Eli realized that was it. The statement made and nothing else offered. The meaning was clear. This stranger was offering them another route around possible trouble - Apache trouble. They didn't have to take it if they didn't want to. Indian logic was that simple. Never a stand or command. Just a suggestion they could take or forget. Ree stood up, stretched his legs and walked outside. Eli watched him go with wary eyes.

"You think he's telling the truth about that other trail?" Montgomery asked.

Eli nodded affirmatively. "I figure he's telling the truth alright. The question is whether he's right about the Apaches not being up there. He isn't whole white you noticed. It's not unheard of for one of them breeds to side with the Apaches." The driver sucked in deeply on the remaining nub of his cigarette then crushed it with his fingertips. "I don't know. I got mixed feelings about this one."

"Well, he did save our lives."

"Alright he did! But maybe he's got something else planned for us. Something he didn't want those three varmints to interrupt. There's something about that man. Something he isn't letting out. He never said why he came here in the first place. It wasn't an accident, he said that. He'd planned to be here even earlier - but why?"

The guard shrugged shoulders and upended his coffee. Most of the others had already drifted outside,

Eli mulled over the stranger's puzzling nature but could draw no conclusion. This Bannon fellow had rescued them. He'd admit that. He had killed those three killers. Still, he was a breed! Bannon knew a lot more about the Apaches than even the captain back at Camp Puerco. And now he spoke of a secret trail to Santa Fe that few white men had ever seen and none ever talked about. Maybe it was his admitting he planned to come to the station and then not saying why? Maybe it was his metered confidence. Whatever it was about this

Bannon, Eli didn't like it. He didn't trust the man. Respect him, yes. Trust him … Dunn just wasn't sure.

Eli came out of his reflections in time to see Montgomery exiting the room. He finished his coffee and followed outside.

After the pair left, Claire moved over to clean the table. As she stacked the tins into a pile, Jacob eased himself out of his chair to leave.

"Mister Jacob, I couldn't help but overhear what the driver and guard were talking about. What do you think? Is that new man telling the truth about Apaches waiting up ahead?"

Old Jacob replied with confidence. "I heard them too. Right now I'd side with the breed. I think they're wrong about him. I have a feeling - a kind of mountain instinct about him. I think Bannon's leveling with us. Don't know what it is about that man, but I like it. I trust him."

"I think I do too," Clare said, surprising herself.

Jacob stood for a moment in the doorway, watching driver and guard remove the two lamps that had been shattered days before. They had the wippletree apart and were checking all its parts. The Concord wore a coating of dust which showed their fingerprints everywhere. They worked quietly and slowly, not bothered by the heat or lack of tools. Jacob turned back to the girl.

"One thing you've got to remember about Eli and Montgomery - they're not mountain men or traders. The only contact they've had with Injuns is at the point of an arrow. They don't like them or trust them. Bannon's a breed and that makes him the same as an Injun - full blood."

"Is that fair?"

"No, but it's a fact." He stepped outside into the heat.

The dishes took only a few minutes to clean and put away. Jacob had few utensils and cooking pans. Claire set them neatly back on a shelf fashioned out of cottonwood planks. She felt like taking a nap but the day was fast approaching its hottest part. She didn't relish the chore of wrestling with sleep in that blistering heat even inside the adobe walls. So instead she got her torn blouse from behind the curtain where she had changed. With one of Eli's rough needles and a little thread, she began sewing it pieces back together.

The sound of iron hitting iron drifted inside. Jacob was shoeing several of the team horses. Claire was pretty near finished with the blouse when a shadow filled the doorway. It caught her eye immediately. She looked up and saw the indian standing there, framed in the sunlight. He was inspecting her with his mysterious eyes under the battered Stetson.

"Any coffee left?"

"Yes, there is," Claire replied, quickly rising to fetch it.

Before Claire could go two steps, Ree was at the stove. He poured himself a cup then offered the pot to Claire.

"Don't trouble yourself, Ma'am," he said, "I've got it. Do you want some?"

Claire declined and returned to her sewing. She instantly felt anxious being alone in the same room with this strange man. Still she wanted to start a conversation. Her mind had already fantasized about his past; romantic and dangerous she was sure. Now with him standing just a few feet away, Claire was more than a little curious why he had appeared out of nowhere to save her life.

When she looked up to face him, Claire felt her stomach getting queasy. She couldn't bring herself to say a word. She retreated back to her sewing and kept her eyes down.

Bannon brought his tin back to the wall. He settled in a corner chair facing the doorway. Leaning back against the cool brick, the gunfighter seemed content with his thoughts.

Claire watched him out of the corner of her eye. He caught her staring once, held her eyes for a moment then looked back outside. Claire felt silly and embarrassed. *I'm a grown woman for heaven's sake! Surely I can talk to this man even if his presence causes me to feel flutters all over.* This was a kind of arousal she'd never felt before. She was scared of his actions and at the same time she was drawn to him as a person.

"Mister."

"Bannon, Ma'am, Ree Bannon"

Claire put on her nicest smile. "Mister Bannon, I want to thank you for what you did out there. I owe you my life. I don't know how to repay you."

Ree's sparkling eyes caught hers and held them again. Their blue hue stood out, contrasting with the darkness of his skin. They were like bright gems glowing in the night. He lowered his coffee tin, keeping his eyes on her, "You don't owe me anything, ma'am. It's something any man would have done. I'm sorry I didn't get here sooner."

"Nevertheless, it was a very brave thing to do … I happened to overhear you tell our driver about another route to Santa Fe. Do you really think it'll be that much safer?"

Ree lowered his eyes, searching for words. "Ma'am…"

"Claire, my name is Claire LeFonte Martinez … please call me Claire."

"Ma…Claire, it's like I told the driver and guard. I can't guarantee anything. I can assure you the Apaches aren't done with this stage … not by a long shot. They mean to destroy it and everyone on it. I am sure of that. Now, where or when they try it is anyone's guess."

"You don't think the Indians will be looking for a stage to go through the mountains?"

"That's right. That's the gamble."

Claire persisted. "It's still a gamble, though. I mean we can't be sure either way."

Bannon shook his head. "Life's a gamble - with nothing guaranteed!"

"Yes, but…"

"So is this … with nothing guaranteed."

"What brought you to this part of the territory?" Claire asked, anxious to change the subject but not let Ree walk away.

 Bannon's brow furrowed. He looked intense and strong. "That Eastern dude those three bandits killed…he had something of mine."

The bluntness of Bannon's reply took Claire by surprise. Before she could think clearly, she heard herself saying. "Then it's your map they were after." A gasp came from her lips when she realized what she had said.

Bannon shook his head, undisturbed by her frankness. "It's just an old Indian map. It'd be misunderstood by white men. That city slicker took it off a friend of mine after he'd killed him. It's my map and I mean to get it back…anyway I can."

"Why are you telling me all this?"

Ree looked directly at Claire. His eyes bore into her mercilessly. His stoic composure persisted. He didn't say a word.

Claire's hands were trembling. She gripped them together and hoped Ree wouldn't notice her brow beginning to bead or the catch in her throat. She had no idea what was happening to her. It was a fear that gripped her and yet made her feel safe and secure in the man's presence.

"I was wondering why…"

"Because I think I can trust you."

"You can…I won't…"

A smile wafted across Ree's brown face. He blinked. His eyes softened. "You and that old station keeper. You don't seem to hate Indians like the rest of them here."

"I don't … I never have … I…"

"So what can you tell me about the map?"

"I don't really know anything other than the fact that those outlaws seemed certain that that Easterner had it. They killed him and rifled through all my belongings but didn't find anything. Then you came and…"

"I was hoping he may have talked to you," Ree explained. "Perhaps given you some idea where he was heading?"

Claire shrugged her shoulders. "Really, I don't know anything about him. Those three bandits reasoned the same thing … that he would have told me something. Well, he didn't. We didn't say two words between us since leaving San Lacita. I have no idea where this so-called map is or even what it looks like. And that's the truth, believe me."

"I believe you," Bannon assured her, "But I had to ask."

"Now what are you going to do?" Claire asked.

"Stick with the stage until we get to Santa Fe, then see if anyone there knows something about that fellow."

"You're persistent, but I think you're wrong about him having the map. Like I said, those three outlaws searched through the stage and all our clothes trunks. They couldn't find a thing. I don't see where he could have hidden a map and them not finding it."

Ree arose and stepped toward the door. "No, Ma'am, I'm not wrong. He had that map and it's still around here someplace…or someone has gotten to it already. And if those Apaches don't find us first, I mean to find that map myself." With a slight nod of his hat brim, Ree was gone.

Claire didn't know what to think. Her mind was whirling in a thousand different directions. Her sewing became mechanical, it was a distraction. While her fingers were working, her mind was brooding over Bannon's words. He seemed so sure of the map. *He's so possessed with the idea of finding it at all costs. Perhaps the driver is right. Since Ree is a half breed, he might be in with the Apaches.* It may be, but she hoped not.

The hottest part of the day came and went. There was not a breath of air to stir the dust. The brassy sky offered no clouds, no relief from the punishing sun. Eli and John Montgomery finished with the coach and joined the others in a card game. They gathered under the scant shade of a cottonwood tree in the yard. Bannon was over in the corral, cleaning his rifles. He looked undisturbed by the sun and heat. His gear was still stored on the stone wall, within easy reach. He puffed on a cheroot and went about his business quietly. Occasionally the voices of Eli and the others drifted over. He paid them no mind, never changing the pace of his work.

Claire moved to the doorway. She leaned against the door jam and stared out at the mountains in the distance. A few cotton puffs for clouds had gathered overhead. There was not much color to the land. Gray, beige and brown made up most of it. The few Spanish dagger plants and huisache added something to the landscape colors but not enough to make a difference. It was a dried up, wind-blasted stretch of country. There was little color and scarcely any life there at all. After only a few minutes in the harsh sunlight, Claire could feel perspiration gathering along her forehead and down her back. She retreated back inside.

Old Jacob came up quietly behind her into the room.

Claire jumped a little when he greeted her. "Oh, you scared me," she said, clutching her chest.

The old skinner offered a little grin. "Sorry, I just come in to get a little nip for the boys," he explained. He went to the cupboard and pulled down a half bottle of rye from in back. Gathering up several tins in his free hand, he headed for the door.

Claire stepped in his way. "Mister Jacob, I was just talking to Ree Bannon. I think he's on our side, but..." She had so much she wanted to say, the words came tumbling out. "He said some pretty strange things. He's convinced that map does exist and that the Apaches are out there just waiting for us, yet he still intends to stick with us until Santa Fe ... and that's not all..."

"Wait a minute!"

Claire stopped, taken aback.

"You're talking mighty fast but not making a whole lot of sense," Jacob said. "Now I've been doing some powerful thinking myself, but for another reason. I know Bannon from someplace else. I don't know where, but I've run into him before."

"You know about his past then?" Claire asked.

"Said I did once, but not anymore. I'm getting old. My mind can't hold on to all them memories like it used to. Why, I once had a memory like a finely tuned clock. I could remember everything; people, places, everything. I'm getting' old like everything out here - old and forgotten."

The girl wanted to say something reassuring, to argue with the skinner. She realized it would be an empty argument. Jacob was an old jerk line teamster oddly out of place in the desert flats. He wanted to die in his beloved mountains and he knew he never would. That disturbed Claire but she knew there was nothing she could do about it. Jacob stood his ground, staring outside, his eyes wandering over the land.

"Well, enjoy your drinks. I guess I worry too much. What with the Apaches on the prowl, I guess I'm lucky just to still be alive."

Jacob spun around, his eyes wide with excitement. "That's it!"

"What are you talking about?" Claire asked.

Jacob eased himself into a chair, still holding the liquor and tins. "It was in the Lucky Lady Saloon that I first laid eyes on Ree Bannon. Lordy, has he grown up. He was no more than a pup back then - seventeen or eighteen at the most. I don't recollect much that far back but I sure do remember that gunfight. Our friend Bannon is a wanted man!"

"Wanted for what?"

Jacob's face was alight now. His eyes sparkled with a memory that was coming back out of a fog after all those years. "He's wanted for murder ... or so they say. He shot down Lane Fowler and his boys in the Lucky Lady Saloon that day. The marshal had posters of him up around town for a long time. Chances are those posters are still up around Spanish Wells and some neighboring towns."

"You mean he's a killer? Like those three outlaws that came here?" Claire asked, her throat catching on the words.

"No, Ma'am, not really. That's what the poster claims and most folks believe. It isn't so. I was there. I saw the whole thing." He looked toward the door, making certain no one was close by. His voice lowered to just above a whisper.

"But you've got to keep this a secret. Yours and mine. Eli and John Montgomery will never listen to Ree if they found out about that fight. They have little faith in him the way it stands right now. If they found out about this, they might try to collect the bounty themselves. I think Ree's our safest bet outta here. I don't want some fool gunning him down for a ten year old bounty."

"I won't say a word. I promise. You must tell me what happened back then. Why did he kill those men?" She leaned toward the old man, her clear eyes intently studying the old man's wrinkled, whiskered face.

Jacob moved over to the table, deposited whiskey and glasses on top, then pulled out an old pipe from his shirt pocket. Poking about the dying embers in the stove, he found a proper coal and popped it into his corncob. After sucking on it and producing a cloud of blue smoke, he felt ready to begin his story.

"Well before I begin telling you about Ree and his fight with the Fowler gang, there's something you got to understand about Spanish Wells. That's where it took place. Spanish Wells isn't a town. Not like you'd know one. It's a lair, a breeding place for cutthroats, bandits, no-good drifters and confederate sympathizers. They don't hanker to no one that isn't a rebel or wanted by the law. No injuns, no niggers, no yanks, and no greasers. They hate just about everyone outside their own kind. And by the way, they'd shoot up the town every night, I'd say most of them can't stand one another too much either."

Old Jacob, amused by his clear analysis, allowed himself another deep draw on the pipe. "Well, Bannon drifted into town one day. No one saw him coming. He just appeared in front of the saloon and went in. Before anyone had a chance to say anything or warn him. Just that quick, he was there at the bar, ordering a beer. Now the Lucky Lady is where most of the Fowler gang hung out. Of course, Lane Fowler's old lady didn't let that get out. Old man Fowler wasn't the kind to get his name in the papers. Pretending he was a respectable rancher and all. If a paper printed something he didn't like, he'd burnt it down. He was probably one of the biggest crooks in that part of the territory. Even the law, what there was of it, didn't fool around with the Fowlers too much. Not if they wanted to live, they didn't."

"Please," Claire said gently, "What happened then?"

"Sorry," Jacob said with a grin, "I get to wandering sometimes when I tell stories. Anyway…" a look of perplexity washed over him. " I … ah…"

"You said Ree had walked into the saloon," Claire reminded him.

"Yes. Yes, he was at the bar and I was in a corner. Sort of sleeping off a little of the dog's hair, if you know what I mean. Anyway I wasn't so bad off that I couldn't tell he was injun. Or at least part injun. Well, I hope to tell you I just about fell off my stool. No, come to think of it, I had already fallen off my stool. Or someone knocked me off."

"Please, continue."

"Sure, he was injun … I was drunk and sobering up fast. No Indian enters the Lucky Lady unless as a scalp on someone's belt. None ever walked in on their own two feet. Yet there he was off by himself near the end of the bar. Just drinking that beer slowly, minding no one else around him. He had these fancy boots, injun boots - and a colt tied to his leg.

Just like them fancy gunslingers that come in once in a while from Dodge City or west of Abilene or the saddle tramps Lane Fowler hired to do his dirty work sometimes. He … Ree, that is, he's got this gun and knife; an old Comanche hunting knife by the looks of it. I got off the floor slowly. Always move carefully around Indians. I move off into a corner, farther away. I don't want to miss the action, but I sure as hell don't want to be one of the casualties. No sir!"

"Then Mr. Fowler started the fight with Ree. Is that what happened?"

Jacob scratched his whiskered chin and puffed on his pipe. "Sort of. I can't remember exactly what was said. Old Lane, drunker than a skunk, comes up alongside Ree and tells him that he's a no good stinking Injun. Dirty siwash, he calls him. Fowler's foreman says they're going to string him up, right there, inside the bar. They're all laughing, swinging their guns around - but the boy doesn't move! He just takes a long swig of his beer and doesn't even look over at the old man breathing down his neck. Now that made old Lane madder than a grizzly separated from its pups and weaning. His face gets all red and he backs off. And as he moves, he's pushing back his jacket, like he's gonna draw on the boy at any second,

"What about Fowler 's men? What were they doing all that time?"

"They're circling Ree. Like vultures closing in on a kill. There were three of them. Everyone else just moved out of the way. No one was standing straight up except Fowler and his three...and Ree Bannon."

"And what did Ree do while they were moving around in back of him?"

"Nothin!" Jacob answered with a smile.

"Nothing?"

"That's right. Ree just stood his ground and finished that beer. Then, he's got the nerve to ask for another. I speculated old Lane was gonna let loose right then and there ... he didn't! He just stood his ground and cursed the boy, calling him all sorts of names. Ree, he isn't moving a muscle but I could see his face reflected in a mirror behind the bar. He ain't movin' but his eyes are. They're darting back and forth. Faster than any white man. He's got something planned. I could feel it in my bones. He isn't gonna wait much longer. Then just when I was *sure* Fowler was gonna plug him in the back and forget the fun, the boy turns to face all four of them. He's got his hands back against the bar at first and then he lets them slip down. Old Lane, he doesn't notice it. He's just jabbering a mile a minute, entertaining everyone with his insults. They're all laughin' at something the foreman called Bannon's parents when Lane lets go." Jacob paused; his eyes were intense but focused far away. He remembered that moment as clearly as ever.

Claire was nearly off her chair, leaning forward, "Please, I need to know what happened."

Jacob shook his head. "Miss, what happened next is kinda hard to explain. One moment old Lane Fowler is standing there, laughin' so hard he's holding his gut and the very next second he's going for his gun. Bannon reacted faster than any man I've ever seen. He threw his knife from out of nowhere. Lane hadn't cleared leather when suddenly he's gagging on a knife that's lodged in his throat. Ree threw himself to one side and blasted away at the others.

He cut down Fowler's eldest boy in the first shot...blew him right out the window. Lane's foreman hadn't cleared leather himself before Ree cut him down too. That left Fowler's youngest and he got off three shots. All went wild. Ree shot him once in the gut. When the boy tried to level his piece again, that breed let loose with the rest of his load. Two shots - both between the eyes. It was over in seconds and no one made a move as the smoke cleared. Ree got up. Yanked his knife outta old Fowler. Loaded his colt and lit out the back door. He didn't say a word. And no one there said anything to him. Nobody stuck his head out that back door for a full five minutes. We all just stood there looking at those four bodies and not believing a breed youngster could do all that."

"Then you never saw him after that?"

"No, Ma'am - not until this morning. They sent a posse after him but that's like trying to corner the wind. Couple of bounty hunters and the like tried to cut his trail but they couldn't. It was like he'd just disappeared into thin air. All those stories Fowler's wife started up after that are just lies. I was there ... I saw it all. Bannon was defending himself all along."

Claire leaned back in her chair. She felt relieved after hearing the skinner's tale. At the same time, she felt even more uncertain about the breed. That incident explained a lot; Bannon's quietness, the way he moved ever cautiously, trusting no one. Jacob said it happened over ten years ago. She wondered what he had done during those intervening years. *Has he killed anyone else?* He was a strange and frightening person to Claire, and a very fascinating one at that.

"Jacob!" A voice called from outside. "Something's heading this way!"

Claire and the old skinner rushed toward the door and collided at the entrance. There they saw a dust cloud small against the sky, coming in from the desert.

Chapter Twelve

The rider came alone under a merciless sun. He rode at an easy canter, pushing neither mount nor his luck in the desert's scarifying heat. A dust trail hung behind him. He was on a straight line for the compound.

"Fetch me them glasses inside," Eli called down to John Montgomery from atop the Concord. The guard threw up a pair of army field glasses. The driver focused in.

"Well, if it isn't that sonofabitch sheriff come from San Lacita. Now what do you suppose brought him way out here?" Dunn asked out loud.

His partner shrugged his shoulders, throwing a puzzled look over at the other passengers. "I don't know. Maybe he's looking for someone. Like the breed perhaps…" Eli turned around. "Speaking of that breed, where did he go?"

Montgomery looked toward the house. The girl and old Jacob were standing just outside the doorway. Bannon wasn't there. The guard went over to the corral. He returned in a rush. "Hey, Eli," he said, "his mares gone"

The mustang was gone; and with it, their rescuer. They had vanished into thin air. Driver and guard looked at one another in surprise. Only minutes before they had seen him by the corral, shining his rifle and colt. They had exchanged more small talk and Ree still insisted there were hesh-ke up ahead. Montgomery was uncertain. Eli remained adamant that they not take his advice. The talk ended in a stalemate, both sides firm in their opinions. Now the breed was gone and there'd be no more talk of trouble up ahead.

Sheriff Jud Courtough made a quick survey of the relay station and its inhabitants as he rode in. Four freshly dug graves behind the out buildings answered most of the questions paramount on his mind. The fancy dresser, the Lanker brothers, and that sidekick of theirs had been killed. He wondered who killed who, and in what order. Dunn and Montgomery were by the stage, bigger than life. It seemed incredible that those two old gaffers or any passengers could have taken Curt and Eddie and lived to tell about it, let alone crazy shotgun Gus besides. Who could have faced up to that shotgun? The stone ramada held only nine horses. Six were team mounts and those others were from the Lankers and Gus. The work stock was missing. Their absence could mean there had been a raid recently. Perhaps it was Apaches that jumped the trio. He truly only cared to have one question answered. *Did the Lankers find that map before they were killed?*

Swiftly checking over the low adobe building, Jud saw the girl and an old man standing in the doorway. The girl was wiping her hands on an apron. She registered neither surprise nor pleasure at seeing Jud. He'd have to change her mind about that... Jud spied one more fresh grave behind the pine-walled southern corner of the building. *Now who would that be?* he wondered.

"If you come to help, you're late," Eli announced.

"Again," John Montgomery piped in.

Jud threw a mean snarl down at the two and dismounted. He ignored both men and threw a question out at the gathered passengers. "Those three graves back there wouldn't be the Lanker brothers, now would it? Them and an idiot that rides with them? I've been following them nearly two days solid now."

The driver stepped in. "Now sheriff, they just might be the same. Fact is we didn't get any names. They rode in this morning and tried to rob us. Simple as that."

Courtough stood silently surveying the yard, staring at nothing in particular in deep contemplation. Neither Eli nor Montgomery trusted the lawman's stance. They felt he always knew more than he let on. He probably knew full well what the three outlaws were after.

"Besides your money, did they go for anything else?" Jud asked the two leathery teamsters.

"For the luvva Christ, Courtough, why don't you level with us?" Eli burst out, "If you've been following those varmints for two days, you know damn well what they were after. A map it was. They came after some fool map they were sure that one of the passengers had."

"And?"

Eli cocked an eyebrow. "And what?" he asked.

"And did they find it?" Jud snarled.

"No, they didn't find it. It probably doesn't even exist."

Jud was not convinced. "I wouldn't be so sure about that, that rumor was going strong around San Lacita," he lied. "Eastern dude was supposed to have killed a miner to get the map. He lit outta town on your coach."

"Well, he won't answer any of your questions," the driver said, "he was killed along with one of the other passengers. And by the way, why'd you follow those three outlaws just because of a map?"

"They were wanted for other things," Jud hissed. "Now you two back off ... unless you want some real trouble. And I'll make it all legal as hell. Don't forget I'm still the sheriff." He turned away and angrily stomped toward the main building.

Eli and John Montgomery watched him leave. They both knew how far the sheriff could be egged on. They realized they had crossed that point.

"Eli, I got me a sick feeling that sorry excuse for a lawman is planning to ride with us to Santa Fe."

"My friend, I do smell that same sorry wind."

Claire was over by the stove when Courtough entered the dark adobe building.

"Hello, Miss LeFonte," Jud said, removing his dust-coated hat, "I'm glad to see that you're alright. Those three bandits were very dangerous men."

Claire greeted him with a curtsy and pointed toward the table. "There's coffee here on the stove. Take a seat and I'll pour you some."

"The driver and guard weren't much help outside. Would you mind telling me what happened here?"

Claire touched fingers to the swollen, discolored lump on her cheek bone. "We were fortunate, I guess. It could have been a lot worse." She poured herself a tin of coffee and sat across from the sheriff. She began when the bandit's burst into the room and gunned down one of the cowboys. She told of Curt threatening her and then taking Dickson outside. They all heard the shot and Gus began laughing, saying that was just the beginning, that they were all going to die lest the map was found. They seemed incensed with the idea of the map and its importance. Old Jacob laughed at them and the younger brother, Eddie, got furious. She stopped then. Not wanting to talk about Curt's attempted rape. "Let's just say we would all probably be dead if that stranger hadn't shown up when he did."

"What stranger? Who are you talking about?"

Claire looked surprised. "Surely you saw him out there - the half breed. He was by the corral just a little while ago." She turned toward old Jacob. He was shaking his head. "What is it?" Claire asked.

"Ree's gone."

"What? But where?"

Jud interrupted. "Who is this Ree fellow? What was he doing here?"

Jacob ignored the question. "Don't know where he's gone," he told Claire.

Sheriff Courtough was plagued with confusion. Someone had killed his boys. Someone not on the stage. "You mean to say someone happened to come out of those hills in the nick of time and wiped out all three bandits? Why, that's quite a story!"

Claire's eyes widened in protest. "But sheriff, it's true. That mean one, Curt he was called; he dragged me behind some rocks. He was trying to ... he..." She stumbled over the words. " Ree Bannon came out of nowhere and saved me. It's no story! It's perfectly true!"

Jud's interest was aflame. A stranger had materialized, killed his partners, and then disappeared as soon as Jud arrived - someone called Ree Bannon, a half breed. What would bring a breed to the Santa Fe relay station? And why show up just when the trio was there? Unless he knew about that map and wanted it for himself! It seemed preposterous. How would he have found out about it? The Lankers killed the miner before they left his place. There were no other witnesses. It didn't make sense. Jud felt his body tightening up from the long ride and further tension at this discovery.

"Old man, have you got any whiskey?"

"I do."

"Pass it over, I got me a powerful thirst. Need something to relax before we leave for Santa Fe."

"We?" Claire inquired.

Jud nodded. "Yes, Ma'am. I mean to escort this stage all the way to Santa Fe. Apaches are raiding again. By the looks of your corral, I'd say they've been here already. That right, old man?"

"Jacob's the name, sheriff," the station keeper said, "Yeah; they've been here and gone. Took all my stock and most of my supplies."

Courtough shrugged his shoulders nonchalantly, "I just care about the stage and its passengers. And Miss LeFonte, that includes you too."

Claire returned his smile, though weakly. She went to the stove to chuck more wood for an evening meal.

Over by the Concord, Eli and Montgomery were tightening luggage in the rear boot. Both were lost in contemplation; each thinking about the mysterious breed that had vanished with the sheriff's appearance.

"Do you figure Bannon saw Courtough's dust and thought it was someone else?" John Montgomery asked Dunn.

The old driver shouldered the last piece of luggage. "Breeds are funny ... especially that one. Who knows what was going on in his mind."

The shotgun guard settled down under the back boot extension and lit his pipe. He puffed on the corn cob until it blew a long trail of blue smoke. "Eli," he said, "I'll just bet Ree knew it was Courtough all along. Don't ask me how, but I think that breed also knows what the sheriff is really after. That's why he lit outta here. Why, he's probably sitting in them hills right now, just watching our every move."

True to Montgomery's word, Ree Bannon was watching the two coachmen at that very moment. He lay not more than a thousand yards up a steep slope. He had left undetected when a faint trail of dust crept into the sky, a minute speck of gray against blue. Only Jacob had seen him as a fleeting shadow among the rocks when the skinner stepped outside with the girl. By second guessing the breed's intended destination, Jacob caught sight of him again as he crested the first series of hills.

Jacob didn't know the precise reason for Ree's strange disappearance. He didn't need to. After observing Bannon handle the three killers and then his gentleness with the girl, Jacob needed no more to know about Bannon. The breed must have had a good reason for leaving camp. Courtough may or may not have been that reason. At any rate, with Bannon now gone, Eli and Montgomery would not give his alternate route any consideration. That disturbed Jacob. He believed what Bannon had said about the hesh-ke. Claire would not be safe, neither would the other passengers. Sheriff Courtough riding escort made little difference. There was danger on the road ahead and Jacob knew they would find it now that Bannon was gone.

The stage was loaded and ready to roll. Eli and John Montgomery were stationed on top, chewing cut plug, spitting red juice and tapping toes for the last of the passengers to board. Sheriff Courtough situated himself in front of the coach. He was eager to ride. Old Jacob was the last to leave the compound, and the only reluctant one to go. He moved slowly to each window slit, swinging shutters in place, bolting them down and moving to the next ones. Once done with the window slits, he pulled the creaking oak door shut and applied an old skeleton key to its ancient lock. Jud yelled at him to move faster but the old skinner ignored his remarks.

Jud yelled again. "Come on, old man," he bawled. "If the Apaches want in, they'll get in. No amount of locks could secure anyplace against them. You're wasting time."

Jud was anxious to get moving. Darkness was upon them and the time was ripe for an Apache attack. Jud felt gut-tightening apprehension gnaw at his bones. It had rankled hairs along the nape of his neck. It always did. He hated dusk...as much as he hated dawn. The feeling of uneasiness arose whenever he got out of the safe confines of a town - any town. He could be top gun there. He was the best. Out in the desert, in Apacheria, that was where his skills lacked. He wasn't a superior force. He was only a white man in the red man's territory. And he hated it.

"Old man, you either hump it or I'll pitch you in that cab myself. Now move! We've got a lot of hard traveling to do tonight."

Jacob again ignored the threat. He finished securing the door and shuffled over to the stage. He carried an old carpet bag in one hand and a Sharps buffalo rifle in the other. As he climbed onboard, Eli let out a low guttural roar and the horses moved out.

Before the stage had moved out of the station yard, Ree was on the move. He dislodged himself from the cut on the hillside and scurried back over its crest. Minutes later he rode down the far side of the hill and toward the now abandoned relay station.

Ree Bannon had been watching the station party since Jud's sudden arrival. His Navajo-trained observations hadn't missed old Jacob's long winded, drawn out closing activities. The old keeper had given him enough clues to let Bannon know he'd left something there at the station. And Ree didn't have to look far to find it.

Sure enough, Bannon saw a bit of white as he squatted down, eye level with the key hole. Wedged in tightly into the hole was a piece of paper. Poking at it with a sliver of wood off the door, Ree managed to work it out in a matter of seconds.

The note was short, terse, and to the point. Ree had expected a warning about sheriff Courtough or perhaps some reference to the Apaches. Instead Bannon got a sentence that sent him shooting off his haunches, swinging around toward the darkness into which the stage had disappeared.

The note read: "The girl has got your map."

That was all. No explanation of how Jacob knew Bannon too was after the map or that he had dismissed Claire as a possible suspect. Ree was puzzled. How much did that old teamster know? Maybe he had known the miner? That seemed unlikely. Ree didn't know how much the bandit trio had said before he killed them. Perhaps they told the whole story of finding the miner and trailing Dickson back to San Lacita. Even if they did, that didn't explain how Jacob knew Ree was after the map also. It had to be a hunch.

An educated guess ... or else?

The options facing Ree Bannon were narrowed down to one. And there wasn't much safety in that one. He had to dog the stage, get the map from the girl and do it before they reached Santa Fe. Although neither teamster expressed an interest in the possibility of a map, Ree was convinced they meant to thoroughly search the coach the first chance they got. And that said nothing of sheriff Courtough and what he might have in mind. Hiding behind the guise of frontier justice and his tin star, Courtough could pull a lot of legalized weight in finding the map. If Claire had that map, Ree would have to get to her before Jud found out. He was certain she wouldn't be alive by Santa Fe if Jud found it first.

Putting spurs to his rested mustang, Ree moved out fast. The stage was gone and its dust had disappeared into the night sky. No matter, the breed knew its route and the lay of the land. He could cut it off within three hours. Ree knew he must bide his time, waiting for the opportune moment to try for the map. There would be a time and a place. He had to wait for it and plan his moves accordingly.

Sheriff Courtough's strategy was simple enough: ride all night, hole up during the day, and hope the hesh-ke weren't close by. He admitted the chances of meeting up with a wandering pack of hesh-ke wolves was real enough. So much so that Eli's suggestion of waiting out the night was accepted without an argument.

Both driver and guard had had their minds changed about the Apache hotheads after crossing pony tracks less than an hour out of the relay station. They lay across the roadway, clear as glass in the moonlit sand. There were seven of them, traveling fast, in a Westerly direction. Where they were going or why didn't matter. Their very presence gave creedence to the rumors that had spread through San Lacita. The area between the relay station and Santa Fe might, for all possibilities, be crawling with Apaches. Their only real chance of making Santa Fe without an attack was to drive at night and fort-up during the day. That, and a lot of prayers - and neither were a sure bet. Montgomery had suggested a ranch nearby. Ralph Barlow's spread. The roughneck rancher always had extra hands available for hire as escort. For a price, he'd do it himself. So the Concord swung toward the east and the possible help at the ranch.

The road followed the twisting spine of broken mountains for twenty miles before climbing a saddle between mesas and sweeping toward the Sandia Mountains. The roadway was more level, smooth, and firm-bedded. The Concord moved easily there, creaking and swaying on its leather thoroughbraces. A near full moon hung overhead, providing more than enough light to see the road up ahead and the landscape alongside. A light breeze provided just enough cool air to freshen their lungs and clear heat-dulled minds and eyes. Eli felt confident despite the sheriff's presence and the Apache tracks they had cut earlier. John Montgomery hummed a little ditty alongside him and he imagined what a nice sight it'd be to watch Jud Courtough hit a hole in the road. Luck was not with Eli's daydreaming. Courtough glided along up ahead, a small figure on horseback, just far enough ahead to be out of voice range but not out of sight. Say what he might into the wind, Jud wasn't about to leave Eli's stage, and the driver knew it.

The team kept Eli's reins taut and the ride a steady pull for over five hours. Mile after mile fell behind into darkness. Courtough kept his distance at the same pace, never varying one way or the other. He remained a distant figure, clothed in partial darkness, seemingly afloat up ahead. Once, when the roadway crested a low-lying ridgeline, driver and guard could see Jud, full-figured, for a moment when he reined back to check on their progress. Just as quickly he was gone, down the other side and out of sight.

They had covered, by Eli's reckoning, at least thirty or thirty-five miles when he hauled back on the reins for a half-hour rest. They were on Orlando mesa. Stretched below, the desert revealed no secrets. No sign of trouble.

The passengers emerged slowly out of the cab, stretching cramped limbs and wandering off into the surrounding darkness. All except Claire who moved around back of the coach and stared up at the stars. The breeze had died down, the air was still and clear. Off in the distance an unseen coyote lifted its head to the moon and a companion, still further off, answered his plaintiff howl.

Claire was still thinking of Ree Bannon, though she wasn't sure why. It couldn't have been their first and last encounter. That meeting had been short, structured and awkward. The words spoken had been more traditional pleasantries than words of friendliness. Only one thing intrigued Claire about that brief exchange. He had said he trusted her and old Jacob. *But why?* Surely Ree knew nothing about her before rescuing her from Curt Lanker. Why was he so certain Claire wouldn't tell the others that he too was seeking the map. He was a killer. Did that mean he would kill anyone on the stage right now who got in his way? Claire held her arms tightly against her breasts. She felt a chill even though the night was warm. It was the thought of Ree Bannon and his searching for the map that brought the tingling spine. And what he might do if he found it.

"Lovely evening, isn't it?" a voice commented behind Claire.

Jud Courtough appeared around the boot, lighting up a cigarrito in cupped hands. As the match flashed up against his face, Claire could read his eyes. Narrow and sharp, they were going over her figure. She wanted to turn away but didn't. He was like Bannon in only one sense. Courtough was also a very dangerous man.

"It is lovely. Too bad we're not in Santa Fe right now. I'd feel a little more like stargazing there."

Jud moved abreast of the girl, practically brushing elbows. The aroma of his cigarette drifted over to twitch the girl's nostrils. It was obvious he wanted to talk. For a second, Claire felt like turning her back to him. She remembered the many miles left to go and decided against it. Sheriff Courtough was too unpredictable and dangerous to have as an enemy out there in the middle of nowhere.

The sheriff took a deep drag on his cigarrito. "I wanted to ask you more about that man who rescued you from the Lanker brothers. You said he just came out of nowhere. Did he say where he was from? Or why he happened to be by the station when those three outlaws showed up?"

"No."

"But he must have told you something! I mean, he couldn't have just appeared, killed three men and then vanished into thin air. Not without saying something to someone."

Claire tried an understanding smile, a slight turn of the head. "Sheriff, you don't seem to understand. When he shot those outlaws, no one was about to throw a lot of questions at him - especially not me! I was grateful for what he did. I couldn't have analyzed his motives at that time. Nor would I have tried!"

"But you could now?"

Claire again donned the perfect smile and the understanding eyes. "If I were of a mind to, I guess I could."

"But you don't want to. Is that it?"

The answering smile disarmed Courtough. He wanted to snarl out a gut reaction but Claire's eyes wouldn't permit that. Feeling stifled and up against another wall, Jud wheeled about and dug in his heels, propelling himself away.

Claire heard him call to load up. Dunn growled back but obeyed. As Claire boarded the coach, she looked back. There was nothing to see but the dark and somber shapes of hills and rolling countryside wrapped in darkness. *Is Ree back there? Will he be waiting up ahead?* She knew the breed would return. One way or another, she would see him again.

The stage moved out, quickly picking a fast pace. The Barlow spread was hours away. It might have the help they needed. At the least, it would be other white faces to confer with. At the most, it might mean a safe journey to Santa Fe.

Chapter Thirteen

Squinting crow's-feet laden eyes against the dawn's harsh glare; the lieutenant trained his field glasses on a tiny enclave of buildings below him. He and his three squads were perched along the rim of a mesa, looking down on the ranch of Julius Ralph Barlow. Second Lieutenant Andrew Dunville III had purposely detoured his patrol on a hunch that the feisty, independent rancher might not heed the danger of hostilities with the Apaches off the reservation. As Dunville looked down on Barlow's spread, he feared his worries had materialized.

From where he stood, the lieutenant could see the whole layout plainly. He took in the weathered sheds, the poled corrals, the parked Democratic and the low, wind-scarred adobe house. All seemed peaceful and quiet, but that was precisely the problem. The corral was empty where work stock should have been saddled and ready. There was no one moving about the yard. No breakfast smoke curled out of the main house chimney. It was too still. To Dunville, it smelled of death.

The patrol was two weeks out of Camp Puerco with a week left to go. Their assigned duty was to ride the eastern loop of the camp's jurisdiction on scout for hesh-ke trouble. Although unshod pony tracks were plainly visible along several trails, the patrol had encountered no trouble. The men were growing restless waiting for something to happen. Dunville could feel it in the ranks. There was nothing he could do. This was a waiting game. The first to make a wrong move might be first to die.

The Apache exodus from their reservation had prompted the mission. Even before the first trooper rode out of the camp's perimeter they were too late. The Indian escape had been quick and thorough. Dunville and his troop found tracks of many women and children heading south - but no sign of the warriors.

Second lieutenant Dunville was at twenty-five, a veteran of three years in the Southwest. He had graduated from the academy in the spring of '73 just in time to join the Walsh expedition through the Montana high country. Upon completion of that seven month exhausting trek, he was transferred to Fort Wingate followed by Camp Puerco, as one of three junior officers assigned to Captain Johnson. It was a tiresome, dirty, sometimes languid assignment. One he accepted with quiet reservation. His father had been a Major General during the War Between the States. His brother, Lucas, was a Captain already. Andrew Dunville knew his time would come for better tours of duty. Until then, he had a job to do and do it he would.

The lieutenant turned to his second-in-command, Sergeant Flaherty; a beefy, solid chunk of soldier.

"What do you think, Sergeant?"

Flaherty scratched the stubble on his chin. "I think we may be too late for old Julius. Place looks deserted. It doesn't smell proper ... I'd be careful going in. Could be a trick." His sentences like his mannerisms were short and to the point. He was not a man to waste or mince words. With twenty-two years of military service behind him, the top sergeant was not interested in military flamboyancy. He trusted the Apache about as far as he could shoot one. Past that, he was a man of supreme caution.

Dunville rubbed a sweaty forehead. "We'll have to go down and check it out." Flaherty saluted. The lieutenant continued, "Assign two flankers for the column. Get three volunteers to ride point going in."

"I'd like to be one of those three, lieutenant," the non-com said.

"Like you said, it could be a trap."

"That's why I want to be there. Most of the men haven't skirmished in a while. They're too jumpy now. No telling what they might do if there's trouble."

Dunville tipped his campaign hat with a finger and dismissed the non-com. Flaherty moved out with the other men moments later. The lieutenant moved to mount and waited until the trio was halfway down the slope before moving his column out. The three ahead of him were veteran troopers: hardened, seasoned fighters. Though Dunville had to agree with Flaherty. They might be too anxious, too hungry for a fight to reason clearly. The non-com was a good tempering force there.

The column came down the rocky slope slowly. The sound of chafing leather and iron shoes hitting rock followed their descent. The air was growing noticeably dryer and hotter as they came down off the mesa. Already the sergeant and his two troopers were at the bottom, separating to make their approach.

Sergeant Flaherty was in the main yard when he reined back and dismounted without warning. Dunville slipped a hand to his pistol. He readied the column for a charge if there were gunshots. The point men circled the springboard wagon and dropped behind it. No sound came from the main house. The troopers cornered the light rig and ran up against the mud-walled structure. One poked his rifle through the window slit. The other moved inside. A moment later, he reappeared and waved for the column to come in.

The patrol rode into the ranch yard and swung down. A perimeter line was drawn and men dispersed to search the sheds and work area. Dunville found Sergeant Flaherty behind a cord of stacked elm. He was crouched over someone. The lieutenant could see a pair of legs sprawled out. As the officer moved around the non-com, his eyes fell upon the man who lay there.

Dunville's stomach took a flip when he saw the man's face. It had been burnt black. A nauseating smell lifted off the man. He was mumbling something incoherently. The sight and smell didn't seem to bother the sergeant. He gently cushioned the man's head with his own forge cap and let water drip from his canteen onto the man's crisp lips. The pitiful creature emitted a low moaning sound.

"How long ago, sergeant?" Dunville asked.

"Ten. Fifteen hours at the most."

"Has he said anything?"

"Can't ... they cut out his tongue."

Dunville felt nauseous again but swallowed hard and fought it away. He rose off his haunches and moved to the ranch house. Flaherty could take care of the poor soul. The ranch hand couldn't last much longer. Dunville still had a lot to learn, he realized. Not the least of which was a compassion for death. It was something he hadn't faced up to yet. Nor did he relish the task.

The ranch house was deserted as expected. The Apaches had rummaged through closets and kitchen in search of ammunition, coffee, and sugar. Finding their booty empty, they ripped out shelves, overturned beds and broke furniture. After pouring the little food scraps that remained on the floor, they departed.

It was not a large party. No more than four or five braves. The tracks leading out of the corral indicated they had captured only three or four horses. Barlow and his men must have taken the rest and left only the worn stock.

Sergeant Flaherty met Dunville outside the building. "He's dead," he announced as the officer exited the building.

"I wish he could have talked," Dunville commented.

"I figure he wouldn't have been able to tell us much anyway," Flaherty said. "From the looks of him I'd say he was a line rider. He probably missed a rendezvous with Barlow's men when they left this place. He must have ridden back right into these devils."

"Better bury him, sergeant, before it gets too hot."

"Being taken care of right now, sir," Flaherty remarked matter-of-factly. He pulled a partial cigar butt out of his breast pocket and stuck it in the corner of his mouth. "The men could use a break, lieutenant," The non-com said.

"Take fifteen minutes - and relieve the perimeter line first," Dunville replied. There was little need for rank courtesy on patrol. Dunville had an understanding with the sergeant. An unspoken agreement that formalities and some of the more banal regulations had their time and place inside the confines of a camp or fort, but not out in the middle of nowhere. It was a mutual respect and acceptance of each other's rank and position of authority. Never discussed, but understood perfectly.

"Lieutenant!"

A trooper was waving at them from a gully several hundred yards away. They jogged over.

The trooper pointed to wheel ruts in soft sand at the bottom of the gully. A stagecoach and a single rider accompanying it.

Flaherty squatted down, studying the tracks. Dunville followed him down. It was a stage loaded down. Footprints indicated several passengers and crew had approached the ranch yard but never entered it. The tracks were not old. They looked to be from the early morning hours.

"It has to be the stage for Santa Fe," Flaherty said. "But what's it doing here? It's far off its regular route.

Dunville thought out loud. "Tracks indicate they never got to the ranch house. It might be they don't know about the Apaches. They never found that poor sucker the Apaches caught." His face was somber. His eyes followed the tracks as they left the gully and disappeared into the beige distance. The Concord was traveling fast as it left. In those early morning hours it was still in the open, passing through hostile territory. If those raiders were any indication of what might lie ahead, that stage and its passengers could be in for some real trouble.

Flaherty followed the officer out of the bottoms. He sucked on his brown stub until its end grew red as a cherry. The aroma was strong and foul. The non-com removed his forge cap and mopped a brow of sweat-plastered hair. "Lieutenant, you figure they're gonna fort-up during the day?" he asked.

"Driver will if he's worth his salt. He must have guessed nothing short of real Apache trouble would drive Barlow to leave his spread. Yeah, I think that driver is holed up someplace."

"He might be in the Cintativos then. They're not far away."

"That's what worries me, sergeant," Dunville replied.

"Sir?"

The lieutenant's eyes widened a bit, his voice calm but forceful. "The Apaches might be thinking the same thing. That's what worries me."

Trailing the stage, Ree had sidelined the Barlow spread. He'd gotten close enough to read the signs the others hadn't. He knew Apaches had been there. They probably hadn't torched the place so as not to draw attention to their presence. Ree didn't know if the men onboard the stage were aware of the Apaches or not. Their tracks took them farther off the regular route. It became obvious to Bannon; they were searching for a place to fort-up for the day. Ree knew about drivers like Dunn. Eli might be a whiskey-rattled gaffer in town, but on the road he had more cunning than an empty-bellied wolf. The driver would not risk a daylight run with hesh-ke close on the prowl. He'd find a place to fort-up instead. The best possible place to hide a Concord would be in the Cintativos, northeast of the trail he was on.

There was a ghost town there. Ree vaguely remembered his people talking about it from time to time. They called it a dead place. Like the Apaches, the Navajo never bothered a place once they had killed it. With the white and Mexican inhabitants driven out by dried up mines and increasing Apache strangulation, that ghost town should prove a logical nest for the Santa Fe-bound coach.

Ree understood that spirits and ghost towns meant little to the hesh-ke. Those cultists were no ordinary Apaches burdened by the fears and superstitions of regular Apache custom. They were above that when it came to killing whites. They might not be afraid to enter the town. So even in that deserted remains of a town, Ree understood that Claire and the others might not be very safe.

He walked his mustang into a tangle of rock and creeping scrub brush and found a rounded stone tank containing a few scant inches of water. He let the pony dip its dark muzzle into the warm, murky water. He would wait himself. He was trained for that. Ebbing darkness would soon bring the hot sun. The Concord could not be more than an hour's hard ride away.

The pony had its fill and began chewing at strands of grama grass growing along the side of the tank. Ree slid out of the saddle and checked his rifle loads on both Sharps and Winchester. He dug a piece of hardtack out of his saddle bag and gnawed on it absentmindedly.

Darkness was fading rapidly. The sky was gray already, hiding the moon completely. There was not much time to locate and set up to watch the stage. As Bannon stepped to saddle, the thought of Claire crept into his mind. He rode with a natural caution, but his mind was not on the trail. He would be in the foothills soon. The town would not be hard to find. His mind drifted.

Claire was different from the others he'd known. She was soft and feminine with a toughness about her. Bannon remembered the way she had looked over at him that afternoon. Her face was emotionless but her eyes did a lot of talking. It was a curious stare; inquisitive yet probing. Longing for an answer but never daring the question. She was different from others who had been with Bannon. Women had tried to second-guess the breed before. His dark features, the white man's blue eyes. They were attracted to him, especially the honkytonkers. He took their favors and left with his money intact.

For all his wandering years, Ree had never before met a girl like Claire. From her clothes and posture, Ree guessed her to be the daughter of a Don - a wealthy one at that. The girl had breeding and confidence. She carried no aloofness about her. There was a sensitivity Ree admired. Their dark skin was alike, but the similarities ended there. He was still half white, half Indian. She was of Spanish decent. They were from two different worlds. She of Santa Fe aristocracy, he of nameless trails and forgotten camps.

Santa Fe... Ree had been there once before in the middle of winter. Only the noon hours in the sun-drenched plaza were warm. Down from the plaza, the Rio de Santa Fe flowed through the heart of town. Ree often sat on its banks for hours, stoning the river and passing the afternoon.

The town was a comfortable place. Snow crowned the high mountain peaks of the Sangre de Cristo and filled in its valleys and flanks. Santa Fe was in a bowl, sheltered from the murderous winds and savage snowfalls of the higher reaches. Only when his food supplies ran low, did Ree venture out of the comfortable confines of his lean-to to into the hills hunting for game.

That winter the town's ancient narrow streets were crowded with immigrants and the mixture of the town's inhabitants: Soldiers of Mexico, the Union and disbanded Confederacy, bullwhackers, pueblo Indians and dark-eyed Spanish women. They all mixed and mingled together, no man standing out among the rest. The bells of the church of El Cristo Rey drew many of the inhabitants together. Ree watched them move slowly into the tiny church. From a distance, the service intrigued him. He never got closer than the plaza bordering its front steps. There he stood, watching the fine young Spanish women clothed in black. It was a fine thing to do for a young man not yet twenty-one.

Ree had felt at home in Santa Fe until the first signs of spring began to appear. On a hunting trip, Ree saw the cottonwoods along the streams turning green. Restlessness began to gnaw at him and he knew he had to leave.

The images were gone. Ree was again alone with his reflections of the stage and its passengers. Ahead of him loomed the dark, rounded humps of the Cintativos, a shade darker against the horizon. It would take hours to reach them. If his hunch was right, he'd be looking down on the Concord within hours. If he was wrong about the crew forting-up, Ree wasn't sure what he'd do.

The long wait had begun. For the Santa Fe stage line passengers and Jud Courtough there would be no more traveling until the sun, now rising in the east, was gone again. The delay would mean a full day of stifling heat to contend with. There was little water and no food left. They could rest or play cards but could not move about. The risk of being seen from the hills was too great for anyone to move outside.

The party was holed up in the decaying ruins of a ghost town called Defiance. Once a mining town of some repute, Defiance's silver mines ran dry long before its neighboring towns and enclaves to the south. Now it was no more than a skeleton collection of weather-beaten, rundown shacks, sheds and a few free standing buildings. Along the ridgelines and mountainous slopes behind the town, placer holes were still visible through the sage and mesquite covering them. Everywhere was visible the pock marks of drift mines that laced the hillsides. The motley assortment of frail structures that made up the town of Defiance were nestled under the curving rim of Mantooth Ridge in the Cintativos foothills.

For Claire LeFonte and the others, Defiance was a relic of the past most wanted to forget. At present they accepted its dirt and decay as the only available protection from the ever watchful eyes of Apache war parties. If they could remain undetected for just one more day, a full night's ride would bring them to the Glorieta Mesa and then Santa Fe. It was worth the worry and frustration of waiting, Claire decided, for she had no illusions what their chances were on the open road in broad daylight.

Defiance was located off the main stage line route by several miles. The only trail leading to it was a washed out rut that shook and jarred both coach and passengers every inch of the way. Jud lead the advance on foot. Eli brought up the stage slowly behind.

The large iron wheels creaked and groaned as they hit and scraped over small rocks. The coach swayed back and forth drunkenly. Most passengers exited the cab for solid ground and walked the rest of the way.

John Montgomery brought up the rear, swishing the trail clear with a juniper branch. It would not fool any keen-eyed Apaches, he explained to Claire, but might not give them reason to suspect a party was holed up in Defiance. The town's abandonment was their only hope of little Apache interest in the ghost town. Their fort-up was a gamble, but it was their only choice.

Claire ran fingertips down a broken window frame and swept it clean of cobwebs and dust. She was nestled in the corner of a room, her back to the wall. From her vantage point she could look out on the storage sheds of the Defiance Mining Company next door. Through its ruptured side boards, she could see Courtough's big roan and some of the team stock. Eli and John Montgomery had elected to remain with the stock. Even now the girl could hear their arguing voices drift over in the stillness of early morning. Although half its roof had collapsed, the building would still afford more than enough shade for the animals during the blistering afternoon. Water was scarce for the mounts but there was enough for several more days. Unless! And that was a closed subject with both driver and guard. Neither one would openly discuss the alternatives if they were discovered by Apaches. They had shade for their animals. They were satisfied, for the moment at least.

The Concord had been parked behind the main street buildings. It was farther back inside the ruins of a feed shed where it would not show beyond the walls. Jud helped Eli maneuver the heavy coach inside before he disappeared among the other ruins. They watched him go without a word. His reputation as a gunfighter was reassuring with the Apache trouble present. However, no one was about to applaud his presence openly - especially the teamsters who both felt uneasy in his presence, and very suspicious.

Claire, along with Jacob and the others, were quartered inside the largest of the remaining buildings. A paint-peeling false front identified it as Laurel Belles. It had been one of the more popular watering spots outside of Santa Fe, Jacob announced with a knowing smile. Its dusty full-length bar still held a few glasses under a coat of spider's lace. Chairs and several tables remained piled up in one corner, giving the appearance that the bar might reopen someday. Its batwings creaked lazily on their rusted hinges to an early morning breeze.

Dispersing to all four cobweb-laced corners, the passengers tried to catch little sleep before the afternoon heat robbed them of that small comfort. Jacob and the girl were sitting together. The words between them were few. Jacob was smoking his pipe, content to whittle on a small piece of wood he had retrieved off the floor. Claire was looking over the town ruins outside the window.

After a while, Claire slumped back against the wall. She could feel herself growing fidgety and irritated. Any kind of movement would have been a relief. She realized she couldn't and that made it all the more frustrating. The station keeper was content with his block of wood. His knife moved effortlessly back and forth across the thick block. Shavings curled and dropped to the floor without a sound. The quiet, the waiting, the deathly atmosphere of Defiance eventually got to Claire. She got up, walked around the room several times before settling in again next to the skinner.

"Sheriff Courtough asked me about Ree. He was quite persistent. Do you think he knows anything about Ree's past?"

The question brought no more than a shrug of shoulders from the teamster.

"He was acting kind of suspicious. It was strange he wasn't the least bit interested in what Ree had done. He only wanted to know where Ree had come from and why he happened to show up at the station right after those bandits did."

"Figured he would."

Claire waited for more from Jacob.

"He's interested in more than saving our necks," Jacob said. "I wouldn't be surprised if he had something to do with those three that tried to rob us. He's a blackard, Miss. Don't forget that; and he's a killer. His tin badge don't change that one bit."

Now the old man was warming up. His knife and wood were on his lap. His eyes were mere slits, looking out into blinding sunlight off the surrounding mountain peaks. "I've seen dozens like him. Not many that become sheriffs; but man killers just the same. They prey on youngsters looking for a fight. Young pups that haven't felt the cold steel of a bullet tearing through their flesh.

They get a reputation first. They settle in one town and con the local merchants into paying their way. It works for a while. Until the man killer gets tired of little action and he starts to create some himself. No one will stand up to him, so the merchants have to hire another gunslinger to run the first one out of town - and the whole process starts all over again. I imagine that's what Courtough did in San Lacita. That's what he'll try to do someplace else."

Claire looked around at the other passengers. They were dozing or staring up at the ceiling, hoping for sleep. The girl's voice dropped low, guarded. "Why do you think the sheriff insisted on escorting the stage to Santa Fe? If it isn't for our safety then why is he doing it?"

Jacob gave the girl a smile of understanding, laced with patience. "Men like Jud Courtough only go out of their way for one reason; their own profit - directly or indirectly. I don't think this is any exception."

"But we have no mail or money onboard."

"The sheriff has it in his mind to do or get something, Whether it's to rob us before we get to Santa Fe or…"

Claire looked up into his eyes. She read his mind. "Or perhaps try to kidnap me, is that what you were going to say?"

"Not exactly," Jacob lied. "I was thinking maybe he has it in mind to hunt down that mysterious map. I don't rightly know, but mark my words; he's not doing it because he cares about us."

"Do you really think he is after that map?"

Jacob realized his folly as soon as he had opened his mouth. Of course, he couldn't fool the girl. She was too alert for that. "Only a hunch, but I'm probably wrong… Of course, we know that map probably doesn't exist in the first place. Even if it did, it's just a lot of trouble for all of us. They say that some maps are like gold mines: cursed. The persons holding them get nothing but trouble. Considering what happened to that Easterner onboard and then those three road agents, I'd say this so-called map would be one of those. Bad medicine for whoever is holding it."

Claire let the subject drop. Jacob didn't pursue it. Instead she took up on a subject even more paramount on her mind. Ree Bannon. They had seen no sign of the half breed since he disappeared upon Courtough's arrival. She felt certain he would come after them. She didn't know why. Nevertheless, Claire felt she would see him again.

"Do you think we'll ever see Ree again?" she asked with hesitation.

Again the same old shrug of shoulders, but this time with words. "Don't forget he's part Indian. That makes predicting what he'll do next nearly impossible."

"Yes, but do you think he'll come after us. I mean he did stop those bandits. Perhaps if there's trouble with the sheriff he might come around."

"Don't bet on it, Miss!"

Claire persisted. "Why not?"

Jacob turned his wandering eyes back to the girl. They were tired, bloodshot eyes, but still full of understanding. "Because there's Apaches out there too. Ree's good but he's not an Apache. If he decides to follow us, he'd best be holed up somewhere himself if he knows what's good for him. And I think he knows!"

Next door in the storage shed, Eli Dunn was not so positive about the breed. "Ten to one, that Injun is halfway back to his own kind. Why should he stick around here?"

John Montgomery, himself an old hand at judging people, didn't think so. "I'm telling you he knows something about the sheriff. He wouldn't have lit outta the station like that unless he had a good reason."

"Yeah," Eli interjected, "He was scared!"

"You're loco," his partner jaded him. "You've seen that kind before. They don't scare off. Not unless they're biding their time, setting up for something else. No Sir, I'll lay you odds Bannon is coming up here to Defiance. Don't know why or how. I just got it in my bones that's what he's gonna do."

Dunn waved off the notion and turned to check the stock. The driver and guard spoke - but now it came in disjointed sentences, letting the pull of heat slow them both down. The air was still and growing thicker inside the shed. No breeze stirred the bits of hay on the ground. The day gave all the promise of being another unseasonably hot one.

By noon that promise was fulfilled. It was miserable. Although out of direct sunlight, the team horses and the roan hung their heads like beaten dogs. They were panting slightly but not enough to worry either teamster.

The driver spat out the last of his cut plug and replaced it with a cigarrito. He looked out through the splintered front doors and stared up and down the sage-filled main street. The litter of buildings on the opposite side of the street cast short shadows across the ground. The sun was approaching its peak. It would be beating down directly into the storage shed shortly. Behind the buildings facing him, Eli looked up at the sun-scarred ridges of the mountains. He wondered if any young bucks were, at that very moment, staring back down at him. At the end of the street, sage rolled in the wind. There was no sign of life in the town. To anyone looking down on the deserted town, it was totally abandoned.

"Where the hell is Courtough?" The guard asked behind the driver.

Eli looked back. "Who cares?" he answered. But in the back of his mind, the old jerk line driver was thinking exactly the same thing. He moved around to the side of the shed. Through a boarded up shutter, he could see inside the

Laurel Belle. There was no sign of life there. He moved to the back section of the shed. Across the back street, the Concord's wagon tongue could be seen through cracks in the feed shed - but still no sign of the sheriff. Puzzled, Eli moved back to the guard and settled into his bundle of hay. The sweat ran freely down his face and chest. It felt sticky and uncomfortable but not because of the heat. He could bite into that and hold it. It was the waiting that knotted his stomach and troubled him. Too much of it could turn him into jelly. It could turn a steady gun hand shaky. And there were the Apaches. The ever present savage fighters were, at that very moment, hunting for prey such as themselves.

Chapter Fourteen

Sheriff Courtough made himself scarce after the big Concord was safely parked and the horses tucked away. It was still dark as the others kicked about the ruins of the storage shed and adjacent saloon before settling in. As they wandered, Jud unloaded his saddle, bedroll and saddle bags into a rear stall of the storage shed. He stepped outside in the dawning light for a smoke. When the coast was clear, he slipped back inside the shed to a corner feed stall. Drooping hat over face, he wiggled down in a corner nest of straw. Neither driver nor guard noticed him when they wandered by to settle up front with the stock.

Courtough had picked the corner stall for one main reason. There was a small hole in the wall just above ground level. He could slip out and in without detection from up front; nice ace card to have when he began his search for the map.

Except for Eli and John Montgomery, the passengers had all moved into the Laurel Belle, preferring its airy spaciousness to the shed's close confines and strong aroma of horseflesh. Jud didn't blame them. Normally he would have been first to pick the saloon over the stinking old shed, but not this time. He had a different rationale now. Jud felt certain the map still existed. Someone either had it or it was still hidden in the coach without anyone's knowledge. In either case, he meant to have his chance at the map. If he had to kill to get it, be that as it may. He'd still try for it.

In his corner pen, the air was thick and heavy. Flies buzzed loudly overhead. The shed smelled of rotting vegetation and decayed straw. Jud tried to sleep but couldn't. He rolled one way then the other. To make matters worse, the driver and guard were fencing with their usual verbal sparring. Unable to sleep, Jud tried to eavesdrop. After a while, the words just slipped by. *That pair could argue in the middle of nowhere with a hundred Injuns on their necks*, the sheriff thought, *why should this Godforsaken ghost town be any different?*

Time dragged by. Jud felt drained from the night's long tense ride. The stifling air of the shed didn't help. He let the insects explore his cheeks until they left. He had that map on the brain and it wouldn't let him go. Nor would the mystery of how the Lanker brothers had failed.

Curt and Eddie Lanker were good men, Jud reasoned, and they were reliable. So what happened to them back at the relay station? How did they manage to get themselves wiped out by one man? One mysterious stranger no one had seen before or since. More than that, Jud wanted to know why they hadn't found the map. Surely they would have searched both stagecoach and passengers thoroughly. The station keeper mentioned that Curt had taken Dickson out into one of the back sheds for questioning. There had been a shot, and later they found Dickson dead. Lanker had searched the cab and boot, rifled through the girl's trunks and the men's things. Curt was good, he would have found that map if it were there. He obviously had found nothing. After the trio was killed, the passengers had searched their bodies for identification. Someone would have found the map then, but they hadn't. If it wasn't on the passengers and not inside the cab, where could it have been?

The sheriff's eyes wandered over the rafters overhead. He tried to piece the puzzle together. It seemed to follow a logical pattern until that stranger showed up. Everyone had been searched, he was told. Dickson disappeared outside with Curt. Lanker took the girl back in the rocks, presumably to search her. And that was when the sense of it all ended. Curt and Gus were cut down by the stranger and Eddie blasted out of his saddle with one shot at a long distance. Damn, Jud muttered under breath, if the map wasn't on the passengers, or in the cab, or on the girl…

Jud's eyes stopped wandering. He was honing in on a theory.

What if Curt Lanker hadn't searched the girl? Yes, what if? It was presumed the older brother had. Jud knew Curt well enough. The man was always as horny as a stud mustang in springtime. Although Jud cast him as a half-baked playactor, Curt may have tried to take the girl first before searching her. That meant he couldn't have searched her! The girl admitted being rescued before anything happened. In short, Claire could still have the map! Dickson might have slipped it, knowingly or otherwise, to her before the trio showed up. Claire could be holding the map right then or she might have hidden it inside the cab during the previous night's ride.

Jud had planned to wait until midmorning to begin his search. It would be safer when the others were dozing off. Sleep was an impossibility with the bickering twins up front and the shed's oppressive heat. And now Jud had a definite target in mind: first the cab and if it wasn't there, the girl herself. It was time to move out. So the sheriff sat up, flopped on his Stetson and crawled through the ruptured wall.

The air hit him like a cold chill. It seemed at least thirty degrees cooler outside than in. He wiped a sweat-streaked brow and sat on his haunches for a moment, breathing in the sweet mountain nectar. An aroma of mesquite and juniper, carried by the breeze, added to the flavor.

Less than ten feet away and five feet off the ground was Claire's window. The sheriff could hear the girl talking to someone. Her voice came across sweet and pretty. Claire LeFonte had been on Jud's mind - not just for the map. The girl presented an interesting challenge to him. She had class where he was crude. She was intelligent where he was crafty. Interesting opposites, he mused. He was attracted to her more than any whore in any town north or south of the border - and for more than just one reason.

Jud examined the back street buildings. Most were on the verge of collapse or had crumbled into heaps of debris already. A slight breeze blowing down off the mountains pushed against their broken frames and oilpaper windows. *This is a hell of a place to fort up*, the lawman thought. *A readymade graveyard of buildings.* Now maybe the last stop for them too. He muttered out loud to reassure himself. In spite of himself, Courtough could still catch the drift of the two stage men arguing. His eyes searched out the coach. The feed shed was situated directly behind the saloon. It lay across a short stretch of back street. Large clumps of sage and pieces of wagon debris littered the ground there. Still it was no real cover. Once he stepped a foot out, he was an exposed man to both Apache eyes and arrows. He'd have to risk that.

Holding a fistful of hat, Courtough dug boot heels into dirt and sprinted across the open ground. Dashing alongside and behind the feed shed, Jud crouched down and waited. Nothing moved along the ridgeline bordering the back street. Nothing stirred but what was moved by the wind. The constant insects kept up a steady hum but all else remained quiet. Turning on his heels, Jud worked loose two bottom boards and wormed his way into the shed. The hulking coach loomed above him.

Bright streaks of light poked through cracks in the shed's ceiling. They painted the coach a strange mixture of light and dark shades. Jud noticed for the first time smeared oil stains off the broken running lamps; then the scratched and splintered letters 'U.S. Mail' on the door panels and a layer of gray dust coating everything. It looked more like a coffin than a stage coach.

Upon arrival, Eli had backed the coach into the shed, leaving tongue and gear up against the broken down front doors. That meant Jud could work with a maximum of cover at the rear of the shed.

Jud climbed inside the cab, swung into a corner and began to probe the interior with sensitive fingertips. He ran his hands up both sides of the leatherette window curtains. Nothing there. The horsehair upholstery was smooth, uncut. No openings to slip a piece of paper inside. The corner gaps of the bench seat were tiny. A finger inserted there revealed no stuffed paper or material.

Outside, the story was much the same. Luggage behind the drop-style leather boot came first. A quick search revealed the clothes trunks were still jumbled up inside. That made lifting each piece out and shaking it much easier - but still no map. The men's carpet bags produced the same results - nothing.

On top, the few pieces of luggage were easy to open and probe through. They gave up nothing out of the ordinary. Next Jud ran fingers over the leather thoroughbraces, around the many spokes of the big iron tires, and under the large oval body frame.

Courtough heard a sound from outside.

Jud froze in place, crouched over. Body tensed, the sheriff strained ears to pick up the sound. He heard it again: a footfall moving his way.

Jud stepped on cat's feet to the shed's far corner. Dropping to his knee, he peered out into blinding sunlight. He could see nothing, but the sound was coming closer. Someone was moving along his side of the building. Jud caught the fleeting tag of a shadow against the siding, blocking out sunlight for a second. Someone was by his entrance hole in back of the shed. The intruder stopped just outside the hole. A hand appeared. It gripped the bottom board with rough, callused hands and a flannel shirt around the wrist.

It was one of the miners.

The face was as ruddy as the hands: big, leather-tough, and mean. The miner looked up into Jud's .44 as he crawled inside.

"Howdy, sheriff," he said, "figured I might have found you here." No emotion showed on the miner's face. It was relaxed, unafraid. He stood up and scratched his bare chest as he looked about the tiny room.

Jud leathered his colt percussion. Reluctantly, he eased up off his knee. His body felt tense, keyed up. In the back of his mind, Jud realized he'd have to use his brain power this time. Not his gun hand. He didn't know if the miner had guessed why he was in the coach shed. It seemed reasonable he would have. That meant problems for sheriff Courtough … and the miner.

Jud dug a cigarrito out of his vest pocket and thrust it into his mouth. "What are you doing in here?" he asked.

"Same as you, sheriff," the miner replied, surprising him. "I think we got a few things to talk about."

"Meaning what?"

The miner cupped hands to light his own smoke. All the while, he kept wary eyes locked on the lawman. His speech was short and simple.

"I got it figured you're looking for that map. The same one those varmints were after. Well, I am too. That's why I came back here. I want in, Courtough."

"How did you know I was here?"

"Saw you sneaking along the side," the miner allowed himself a little smile.

Satisfied the sheriff wasn't going to blast his presence away by then, the miner stomached up a little more courage. "I figure you and me should have a kind of partnership over this thing. I see you haven't found the map yet. Even when you do, you'll have to get it outta here. That means taking your chances with the Apaches out there. Two guns are better than one."

"And you mean to help me find that map?"

"Exactly!" The miner was visibly relaxed, sagging against the side of the shed. He'd cornered his man and had made his point.

Jud laid a hand on the butt of his .44 "I could kill you right now, and call it self-defense."

"And blow your cover over one harmless old hillbilly? I doubt it! Courtough, I ain't asking much. Just a piece of whatever we find. I know you could gun me down anytime you want - but for what? I can help you! All that map can do is lead you to a hole in the ground someplace that you'll have to dig out. You'll need someone that knows mines and the mountains. I'm your man. I can dig out any mountain mine shaft around and I won't cross you. You need me."

Now it was the sheriff's turn to go limp. The coach leaned against his shoulder. Jud felt boxed in - and by words no less! The miner was right, Jud wasn't a miner. He didn't know the mines, nor did he trust his ability to negotiate any underground shaft if the map lead that way. Still, he couldn't be sure. The treasure might not be underground. It gnawed Jud to the quick to be cornered into any kind of deal. He wasn't used to taking orders from anyone else, especially not from a black-faced roughneck miner.

"Have you searched the cab and luggage?" The miner interrupted Jud's thoughts.

"Yeah, but I didn't find anything. It must be on one of the passengers."

"You got any idea which one?"

"I got an idea," Jud muttered. The miner was honing in for the big question. Jud felt sure he had no idea who might have it himself. Either that or he was carpet bagging the lawman like a vulture, closing in on the kill.

The miner gained confidence as Jud fell farther back into contemplation. "I figure you got more than just an idea. I mean, you were trailing those three varmints in the first place."

"They were wanted in San Lacita for breaking the law. I wasn't after them because of the map," Jud lied.

"Yeah, yeah," the miner waved off Jud's protest. "Come on, sheriff, you don't have to play your game with me. I seen you in San Lacita. I know your game."

"Got it all wrapped up, do you?" Jud said, teething his cigarrito tightly. "I find the map. You ride cover. And you get a cut of the gold or silver for your troubles."

"Don't forget the mine shaft, that's where you'll really need me," The miner smiled back.

Jud dropped the butt and crushed it underfoot. "We're wasting time here. Let's split up. I'll get to the girl before tonight. You stick tight. If I get it off her, we'll ride out of here right after dusk."

"What about the others?"

"We'll leave them but run off their stock. If anyone of them makes it back to Santa Fe, that'll be a miracle. Most likely they won't. So there'll be no witnesses to worry about."

"But what if you can't find the map? What if the girl ain't got it?" the miner asked.

"Then we rob everyone before the stage reaches Santa Fe and kidnap the girl. We can hold her for a ransom from her old man. There should be some good money in that."

An evil grin crossed the miner's weathered face. He turned to leave.

As the miner was bending over to exit the tiny hole, something occurred to Jud; something that would give him easy access to the girl. This plan would send everyone else, including the stage crew, far enough away for him to escape. He would do it with the miner's help. Or more correctly, the dead miners help.

"Wait, I'll leave first. You follow me."

Jud ducked down to the bottom boards and crawled out. Rising quickly, he extracted a long thin knife from his boot. He stood, flat-backed, against the shed wall. The knife remained out of sight. Seconds later, the miner crawled out after him on hands and knees.

As the roughneck miner started to rise, Jud grabbed a fistful of his shirt collar.

He slammed the miner back against the wall. Just as fast, he buried his skinning knife deep into the man's chest. The miner gasped out in shock. A spasm ran the length of his dying body. His huge paws gripped the sheriff's knife hand. Fading eyes rolled up to Courtough's stone face, pleading why?

Jud leaned over, his eyes hate-locked onto the miner's pale face. "No one tries to blackmail me," he snarled, "No one!" The dead man's lips fluttered but no sound came forth. His body went slack in Jud's grip. The miner slid back down the wall and crumbled to a heap on the bloodstained ground.

Satisfied, Jud slipped around the corner. Hesitating only a moment, he scurried back across the street and up to his escape hatch in the storage shed. Someone was moving near the rear of the building. Jud peered through wide gaps in the side boards. It was the driver. He glanced out the rear door absentmindedly then turned and moved back toward the front section. He looked hot and tired. Sweat ran freely down his face. A smile creased Jud's lean face. Both driver and guard would be ready for Jud's bait. He was even more certain of it now.

Once Dunn was past, Courtough slipped through the opening and into his corner stall. Nothing had been disturbed. Up in the shed's front section, he could hear driver and guard resuming their persistent tiff.

Lying back, Jud sucked in the hot, stifling air and plotted out his idea. The dead miner was only the start. Now Jud had to make sure that body was found and the passengers alerted for the Apaches. The ones he'd say were prowling around. Jud let the minutes slip by. He needed little time. He would put his plan into action.

"You two sure make a hell of a lot of noise"

Jud Courtough stepped out from behind the door leading to the shed's rear section. He stretched his arms wide. "A man can't even get a little sleep around here," he said with a well-acted yawn.

Eli and John Montgomery looked up from their fashioned nests of hay. Both were startled by Courtough's sudden appearance.

"What the hell you mean sneaking up on us like that?" Dunn hissed. He spat out his spent cigarette butt.

Jud put on his favorite sneer, satisfied he'd scared both of them. "Hell, I didn't sneak up. You two just weren't paying no attention. I've been trying to get some sleep in back. In this heat with you two jabbering, that's near impossible. Whadya say we play some cards?" He tried on another more normal smile. It didn't fit but it was the best he could do.

"Cards," Eli replied suspiciously.

"Yeah, cards. You've heard of them, little pieces of heavy paper. They've got numbers on them and…"

"Oh, shove it…"

"Well, what do you say? None of us can sleep. We can't leave here until nightfall. We might as well make some good use of the time."

Eli scratched his white whiskered chin, casting a wary eye at his partner. John Montgomery, long on wind, but short on reasoning, shrugged his shoulders in agreement. Suspicion was not one of Montgomery's better assets. "I guess so," He said with a twitch of his head.

Jud met Eli's cutting cat eyes head-on and didn't budge. The smile remained plastered on his face. Jud could tell it didn't sit right with Dunn. The coachman was hot and tired. His partner had already agreed. Jud knew Eli would go along with the idea soon enough.

"Oh, alright," Eli said. "But you'll have to get the cards. I left them back in the cab under the deck seat."

Perfect, Jud fought to hold back the knowing smile he felt inside. He already knew where the playing cards were. He'd seen Montgomery put them under the deck seat. One of them would have to go out there to get them. And when he did Jud took his cue. "Not me, I'm no errand boy. One of you two go out back and get it. I got my exercise just tossing and turning trying to sleep."

"Oh, hell," Montgomery cut in, rising off his hay pile throne, "what's the fuss. I'll get the cards. A game of cards might be an improvement over listening to you, Dunn."

Eli gave no indication as to whether he'd heard the cut or not. He slumped back in his seat and chewed on a piece of straw. His eyes were cloudy with thought. Courtough watched him carefully out of the corner of his eye. The driver was the smarter of the two and a hell of a lot more suspicious. Jud had to make certain he got caught up in the trap once Jud sprang it. If he didn't...if he hesitated too long, that could throw everything off.

The sheriff dropped into the guard's nest and waited.

The plan would begin soon. In a rush, like a herd of shagtail Texas long horns tearing up a night trail camp. When it did, Jud would be at the head of it. He wouldn't be running, he'd be deciding its route of rampage. He'd see to it that Sheriff Jud Courtough was the heads up, tails down winner - and he alone.

The plot broke wide open in the person of John Montgomery sprinting across the back street, white-faced and sucking back lost breath. The guard raced up the length of the storage shed, missed Jud's stall completely and burst through the back door.

"Jesus Christ, Montgomery, what's come over you?" Eli exclaimed.

"Apaches!" John Montgomery gasped, "They knifed one of the miners. Right back of the feed shed. They just left him propped up against the back of the building."

"How many?" Jud piped in, faking surprise.

"Can't tell, they covered their tracks. Could be only one ... or a hell of a lot more."

"Wait a minute," Eli cut in, "why would they cover their tracks?" The driver's suspicious hairs were up. Jud sensed it immediately. He moved into action.

Jud arose, quickly checking the cylinder of his colt. "I'll tell you why," he said, "to spook us. That's why. They want us to know they're nearby...and waiting. It's one of their favorite tricks south of the border. They'll sneak into an army camp and cut up a couple of the sentries and let everyone else alone. Something like that plays hell with morale." Jud retrieved his rifle and checked its load. "Listen, there can't be more than two or three of them. If it were a larger party they'd have been all over us long ago. It's got to be a couple of bucks wanting to count coup. They've got to be close by, waiting for us to make a wrong move. That or they're gonna try to pin us down until more of their band gets here for the slaughter." The sheriff eyed his companions with a cold stare. His fingers slipped the last of the shells into the rifle tube. "There's only one thing we can do. Get them before they pick us off, one by one."

"I don't know," Dunn muttered, "It don't smell right."

Courtough advanced to his second plotted step. "If you want to see that miner for yourself, Dunn, you're welcome to it. I'm going next door and alert the others. You're either with us or you're out. Suit yourself."

The driver felt anger and confusion at the same time. He still didn't trust the sheriff but Montgomery had been the one to find the miner. The sheriff rose to leave. "You got any idea what it'll be like trying to find some scalp-hungry injun in these ruins?"

Courtough stopped and turned to the driver. He levered his rifle slowly, mechanically. "What do you think our chances are of leaving here alive tonight if they're still around? You think about that. You tell me what choice we got." He gripped his rifle tightly and left quickly out the front doors.

Eli was still grumbling as the sheriff turned out of sight. "John, I don't like the smell of this. The whole thing don't fit together. Apaches wouldn't cover their tracks. Not unless they were the ones being hunted. Not the hunters themselves. I don't trust Courtough. It could be some sort of a trick."

John Montgomery was shaking his head in confusion. They could both hear the sheriff next door. Voices were being raised. The guard lifted his shotgun from his gear. He checked both barrels. "I don't know, Eli," he said, "I think they'll probably believe him. That miner's dead just as sure as I'm standing here. And it wasn't one of us that did it."

"The sheriff could have!" Dunn offered.

"So could I, but I didn't. Why the hell would the sheriff want to kill a nobody miner? I think your suspicious nature is getting the best of you. I'm with Courtough. I figure it's got to be Apaches. And we've got to stop them."

Dunn persisted, trying to convince himself more than his partner. "Old Jacob won't buy that story of Courtough's." The driver had lost his audience. Montgomery was slipping his revolver into his belt.

Eli was still muttering when John Montgomery spoke. "Damn it, Dunn," He said, "either you're with us or shut your trap about the sheriff. Now he's the one willing to fight. It's a Spanish supper for us until we get outta here. The sooner the better. We gotta hunt down those injuns and now."

Dunn watched his partner, his eyes still not registering all that was happening about him so quickly. Montgomery was darn near out the door. "Alright, wait for me," Eli blurted out. He grabbed his rifle and followed his partner out the door.

When the teamsters came in, Courtough had the other passengers bunched in a back corner. He motioned for the driver and guard to come closer. "You're here! Good. I'll go over the plan again. Jacob, you and the cowboy move down this side past the storage shed. Try to flush them out but be careful. Dunn, you and Montgomery head on up this side of the street." The sheriff gestured at the surviving miner. "You can cover your buddy inside the feed shed, then circle around and join up with Jacob." Jud turned to the girl. "Miss, I'm sure you'll be all right if you stay here until we get back. There can't be more than one or two of them. We'll smoke them out. Take this just in case…" He handed Claire his revolver, grasping her hands as he did. A quick smile was offered with the touch. Claire just dropped the piece back into Jud's palm.

The girl reached under her skirt and drew out a derringer, small and harmless-looking in her hand. "'Thank you, sheriff," she said with a smile, "but I believe this will do just as good a job."

"So you've got a knuckleduster," Courtough said grinning. Then the grin turned deadly serious. "It won't do the job. Maybe at a few feet but not where it'll do any good for you out here." He thrust his revolver back into her lap. "Take it," He ordered her, "and don't play heroics."

Claire bit her lip, taking the heavy gun in hand.

Jud resumed his oration. "I'll take the other side of the street. As we move up, Dunn, you and Montgomery cover me and I'll do the same for you." Dunn's response was a hollow look and slight nod. *Christ,* Jud thought, *if there really were Apaches out there, I'd be in one hell of a mess.* Dunn had clearly not taken the bait. "Alright, any questions?"

With the exception of Dunn, the others believed Jud's story. He could read it on their tense, drawn faces. Their white knuckles tightly gripping weapons.

"Let's go then," Jud commanded, moving at a crouch under the groaning batwings. He paused under the swinging gates. Jud wiped a sweaty brow and let Jacob and the cowhand move past him. They padded past the storage shed moving in a crouched stance. For a moment they disappeared between the shed and its neighboring building, then reappeared and entered a partially collapsed adobe and wood structure next door.

"You ready?" Jud threw out at driver and guard crouched behind him.

"Shit!" was all he got for a response. Eli and John Montgomery were past him and running before he could rise up himself. They disappeared into the building next door. Jud took a deep breath, allowed himself one knowing smile then slipped off the porch and sprinted across the street. He ran like the entire Apache nation were sighting in on his backside. He plowed through the broken batwings and landed on the dust-covered floor of the cantina.

Jud knelt on the barroom floor for a full minute, catching his breath, and checking his load mechanically. He perused the room. It had been a much smaller saloon than the Laurel Belle, but its decor marked it as a much better one. The bar ran the length of the room itself. Behind it, large mirrors, most of them shattered, had hung against the wall. Glass shelves had held the rows upon rows of shiny glassware. Intricate designs had been carved on the front of the bar and its footstep was still a shiny metal. It was not copper but another, duller silver color. Jud wasn't sure what kind of metal it was. There was a back room also. Jud could see through its split door. It was cluttered with junk. Probably from the interior of the saloon after it closed. *This is some place! I wish I'd been here when it was open.* He smirked into the pieces of glass, satisfied with himself. *But I'm glad I'm here now instead. Back to the plan.*

As Jud methodically moved shells around his belt loops, bringing them all closer to his front, he took stock of his plan thus far. The others had taken the bait. All except Dunn and he had gone along with the rest. They all believe the Apaches were lurking about and had to be destroyed. They were spread out, moving farther from the girl back in the Laurel Belle and the stock in the storage shed. He'd make his move very soon. Back to get the girl and his map.

Sheriff's Courtough's plan as formulated back in the feed shed was basically simple; get the others away from the girl then grab the map and get the hell away. Despite what he had told the miner back in the feed shed, Jud had convinced himself that Claire really had the map on herself. Either that or he'd take her captive and hold her for a ransom. He could outride any buzzard around. If he left right then, he could ride a while then hole up until dusk when it was safer to travel. He could have the girl safely tucked away in some cave or draw by the next morning and be leaving word with the girl's father by the next afternoon, that Don would not wait long to pay a handsome ransom. Jud might conceivably be on his way to old Mexico in less than two days from now.

Jud had been motionless on the barroom floor for several minutes, concentrating on the girl and the map. He then became aware of the intense stillness of the ruins. Even the persistent, ever present wind did not seem to penetrate the quiet. Jud wasn't a professional tracker but it wouldn't take that much trail experience to find his way to Santa Fe by a shorter route than the stage line trail. He doubted if he'd meet any cavalry patrols along the way. As for the Apaches…Jud tensed. There had been a minute sound … barely heard and registered only to his subconscious. Courtough could pin neither direction nor source to it. His gray eyes searched the room, moving out front into the bright sunlight. Tumbleweed rolled slowly past, pushed by a gentle breeze. *Field mouse probably, or some other four-legged scavenger who's made a home of these decaying ruins. It sure as hell can't be...*

Jud cursed himself. *Apaches? Hell, I started that rumor! Of course there aren't any Apaches around. The sound must have been my imagination. Coffee nerves, that's what it is. I'll have to lay off the stuff until town and get some good rye whiskey to settle my stomach.*

The sheriff rose to his knees and edged up to the front entrance. He peered outside. There! By the livery barn or what was left of it. The driver and guard were just leaving. That must have been the noise he heard. Yes, something old clubfoot Montgomery had stumbled over. Jud's shoulders sagged, relieved a little. Eli looked back at the lawman. The sheriff waved his rifle over the single batwing and exited himself. He walked the length of the store front, hugging the side as he did. Even though Jud knew it was all a farce, he couldn't help feel as distressed as being subjected to a hundred Apache flint-tipped arrows. Playacting or not, Jud would be happy when he was done with it and on his way; the girl or map his companion.

The second store was much smaller than the cantina. It was cramped with junk and debris of all sorts. There were chairs, a pile of timber, wooden crates of leftover goods and other sundry material of a once prosperous hardware store all lying in piles around the room. It must have been a makeshift warehouse while the town was dying. And no one had come back to claim the refuse. Now it was left for time to claim back to dust itself.

Courtough picked his way around the junk littering the floor. Looking back outside, he spotted Eli and the guard exiting their building. They looked for him, pausing a moment, then Dunn waved his partner on to the next building. Back down the other side of the street, Jud could see no sign of Jacob or his partner. Everything was going just according to the sheriff's plan.

Now Courtough would wait a few minutes, double back behind the row of stores and be in the Laurel Belle in less than a minute. He allowed himself a smile again.

The minutes went by. Jud wanted a smoke but didn't have any. The air was tight and very hot inside the building. It smelled rank and dry. Of the death itself that had come to Defiance. His eyes kept watch outside. He saw driver and guard move out of their building, skirt a stone corral and then move onto the porch of an adobe miner's hall. Now it was time for Jud to make his move.

Jud tiptoed back through the mess about him to the back door. He carried his Winchester gripped tightly in his right hand - his gun hand. One finger lay lightly on the trigger. His left hand caught hold of the back door latch. It was unlocked. Loose on its wooden plug hinges. He paused before opening it, smirking again to only himself. *Jud Courtough, you good old son-of-a-bitch, you called this one right. That map is as good as in your hot little hand right now.*

Courtough swung open the door and froze in terror.

Standing no more than three feet away, face level to his chest, was an Apache painted for war. He was carrying a stone axe.

For a split second, they both stood in place, caught completely off guard. It seemed an eternity. A dozen images flashed through Courtough's stunned brain; that pigment-streaked face, black eyes under a red headband - a killer's face. The war axe gleamed sunlight, not bloodied yet.

That quickly, the moment was past. The Apache was moving. His arm shot back to slash at Courtough with his hatchet.

The movement jerked Jud back to reality. Instinctively, born out of years of practice, he reacted. His rifle, already level at his hip, exploded in the Indian's face. Without checking results, Jud spun around on his heels and ran through the junk and rubbish, clawing his way out the front of the store.

Then he was on the porch and pounding down the wooden sidewalk. A long feathered arrow hissed by his head and buried itself into a pillar inches away. Bent-double, Jud ducked inside a door. Another arrow missed his head by inches. Gunfire burst from several stores behind him. Wild yipping arose from out of nowhere. Jud's revolver fanned the air, seeking out a target. He could find none. Down the street, he could see driver and guard running down the front porch walk. Gunfire followed them closely.

Sucking in a gut full of air, Courtough leapt out back onto the porch. He dare not look back. The voices of driver and guard came from across the street. They were yelling at Jud. He didn't bother to turn around. He was running as fast as he could. An unanticipated chair leaned against the store front. Jud jumped it, caught a heel on something and came crashing down in a heap.

An Apache had leapt from out of nowhere to down Courtough with his axe. As the sheriff fell into a heap, the Apache stumbled over him, caught in the momentum, and fell to the porch. Jud lashed out with his feet. A boot smashed against the red man's face.

It stunned him. Jud fired once, his rifle barrel inches away. The blast, powder-burn close, slammed the Indian back against the store front. Jud, instinctively, fired a second time. The brave heeled over dead.

More gunfire snapped overhead. A slug splintered off pieces of the post and showered the lawman with fragments of wood. He rolled over and dropped off the porch. A blurred figure dashed out one building, down the porch, and ducked inside another door. Behind him, Jud could see more Indians moving through the debris piled in the streets. Jud waited his moment, sucking in gasps of air as he did. The attacker appeared again. Jud fired. He missed. The slug sent the archer scampering back inside. From out of nowhere again, another arrow cut the air by his face. Squirming back on both knees, Jud swung his smoking colt back and forth, searching out a target. The Apaches would give him none. Across the street, Jud spotted the stage crewmen darting out a doorway and sprinting down a last stretch of open space to reach the Laurel Belle. It was time for Jud to move out again.

Both driver and guard had made it back to the saloon. Gunfire now blossomed from both sides of the street. Shells ripped into the false store front, tearing out great chunks of wood. Down the last short stretch, Eli and John Montgomery came running faster than they had ever moved before; over broken chairs, boxes, off the last porch, and onto the saloon steps. Apache arrows followed them all the way as they disappeared into the fort. Jud was the only one left outside. From his vantage point directly across the street, the sheriff could see Jacob waving him over.

Digging his legs into the ground like well-oiled pistons, Jud ran across the street. He was in the street. Open space. His backside exposed to every cut throat Apache raider. The realization hit Jud in a split second. He'd been right all along. Defiance was infiltrated with Indians. Pretend had become reality; this farce had become a race against certain death.

A rifle exploded right behind Courtough's ear. Its bullet whistled past his head frying the air. Jud dove down, ate dirt and pitched over facing his attacker. He fired once, twice. The rifleman doubled over and fell off the cantina's porch.

A long black barrel appeared just above the saloon's batwings. It coughed fire and smoke. Jacob's covering fire. Jud hit the porch in two long strides and dove down as more slugs knocked off his hat and laced his vest. The porch came up to slam him in the face. He rolled over. Clambering to his feet, Jud pitched himself forward through the swing doors and crashed onto the saloon floor.

He was safe inside. His lungs were screaming in pain, sucking in the stale, hot air. Everyone had made it back. Jacob and cowboy held the front doorway. Driver and guard were on the sides. The miner was back with the girl, guarding the rear. The siege was on … the real one this time.

Chapter Fifteen

Despite the intense fusillade that sent everyone diving for cover, the Apache attack never materialized. Ten minutes after the attack first began, all was quiet. The hesh-ke were nowhere to be seen. Inside the Laurel Belle, windows were sealed and crammed with wood. Driver and guard ducked next door to watch the stock. On his own, the miner ran back to watch the Concord. Courtough and the others peered out windows, trying to gauge size and location of the enemy. No luck. There was not a sign of the Apache anywhere.

Jacob hunkered down in his corner. He slipped a bit of cut plug inside his check. The waiting had begun. Jacob knew that Apaches usually had little stomach for being drawn into a siege against entrenched whites. They favored instead flanking sweeps and then a tightening of the ring until the defenders were either picked off or overrun, but these hesh-ke were of a different mind. Even a dead place such as Defiance held no fear for them. Perhaps their forces were not as strong as the onslaught first seemed to indicate. Perhaps it was a trick, common to any Indian's form of combat. In either case, the rush never came as everyone imagined. If a ring was being tightened around the neck, the whites hadn't felt it yet.

The silence was a perplexing switch from the initial attack. As the sheriff had fallen through the batwings, shadowy archers had sent long feathered shafts into the false front. Some plunged through the doorway to sink into the back wall. Well concealed riflemen had blasted out the Laurel Belle's front windows. Jacob and the others swung from one side of the windows to the next seeking targets. Wind cleared the air of gunpowder smoke and acid. Heat returned to everyone's consciousness.

A lull settled over the saloon and its defenders. Jud was slumped up against the solid oak bar. Above his head, the wood was cracked and splintered from Apache slugs. The sheriff's breath was slowly coming back. His throat and lungs still burned from the flat-out dash back to safety. He looked up to see the driver coming through a side window. His arm was bleeding.

"Here, let me help," the girl called out. Eli move toward her. Jacob dug out a roll of cloth from his carpet bag and threw it to the driver.

"Your partner alright?" Jud asked.

"He's alright, but you stand warned, Courtough; Montgomery's madder than a gut-shot wolf right about now."

"At what?"

"At you, for not covering us like we planned. Man that tries to save his own skin and not his partners' is no good to anyone. Don't blame you for wanting to save your own bacon, sheriff, but remember you're not the only one here."

Jud leaned forward. "Old man, you got your knickers twisted something fierce for one who didn't believe the Apaches were around in the first place."

"Hey!" Jacob interrupted, "why don't you two cut the jawboning and figure out how the hell we're gonna get outta here."

Courtough grabbed the moment. "I've already given that some thought. I say we wait them out. Once it gets dark, we can make a break for it. We wouldn't stand a chance in bright daylight in the open."

"What the hell are you saying? One Apache is enough to pin us down all day," Eli shot back. Anger fumed in his eyes. Claire tried to settle him down so she could apply the tourniquet but he pushed her hands away. "We can't stay here any longer. Those 'paches aren't waiting us out. They're up to something. We've got to get outta here right now."

"Eli's right, Courtough." Jacob cut in. "Them savages aren't holding back because they're afraid of a fight. They're scheming for your scalp right now. We got no fodder for the horses. No water for ourselves. We can't stay here."

"You're right about that!" a voice said from the back of the room.

A dozen eyeballs darted to a back window, landing on a figure framed in the opening there. It was Ree Bannon. Covered with dust, his hat set at a rakish tilt, the man looked as one who had spent the better part of a night riding hard. Unlapping the Winchester, the breed dropped out of the window ledge and moved to the front of the room.

"We're glad to see you," Claire offered. Her eyes hinted at more than just a friendly greeting. The dark eyes shone anew, at once charged by a current of familiarity. A deep, intense interest in the man she knew so very little about and yet wanted to know so much more about.

Jud Courtough was her opposite. His brooding eyes cut mean stares at the stranger. The eyes sized up the breed, taking in the colt, hunting knife and a new 17-shot Winchester. He possessed all the instruments of a desert fighter; an equal to any Apache bronco wolf around. Jud would need all his brain power and gun skills to deal with that one, he realized.

Unlike the others, Eli Dunn didn't hide behind a facade of numb weariness. He wrinkled his forehead in honest surprise. He wasn't sure how to react to this Navajo cub; once surely gone forever now kneeling beside him. He managed a guttural greeting under breath and let it go at that.

Old Jacob was the only one of the men to greet the half breed with a 'welcome back and just in time'.

Ree had caught the sheriff's harsh stare when he first laid eyes on him. The sheriff was the only one who hadn't seen Ree before. He had to suspect the man. Ree had killed his partners and made tracks as soon as the lawman showed. Courtough obviously couldn't trust someone like that. The sheriff would be a loaded gun aimed at Ree's back all the way to Santa Fe. And Ree was well aware of it.

Quickly sizing up the rapidly changing circumstances; the sheriff tried for a diversion - anything to stall until he could maneuver the group to back him. "You're the one from the relay station, how in hell did you get through those Indian lines?"

"Yeah," chorused Dunn suspiciously.

Bannon rested on his haunches, rifle lapped and ready. He cupped his hands to light a half-smoked cigarrito. "Came over the east ridge. They only left one guard back there. It's clear now. If we leave straight away, head into the mountains, there's a trail I know of. It's about the best chance we got."

Jud cut snake eyes. Eli opened his mouth but could only sputter half-words out; anger choked the rest. Jacob checked his load and listened. Ree was in charge.

"But the Apaches, won't they be waiting for us?" Claire asked.

"They'll be waiting," Ree deadpanned, "They won't be expecting us to ride straight out of here. There's not more than a dozen. They're spread pretty thin. So far, they're all on the other side of the street or farther down the block. We've got to get out of here before they get any closer. Dunn, you and your partner rig the teams. Jacob, you cover..."

"Wait a damnable minute!" Eli fairly shouted, waving his bandaged arm. "Since when are you giving orders around here? I got me no boss on the road ceptin' myself. You aren't tellin' me..."

"Oh, shut up, Eli," Jacob roared, his voice drowning out the hissing stage driver. The old skinner's eyes were aflame with passion. His jaw set firm and controlled. "We're fixin' to die here and you know that as well as me. Unless we get out of here, we don't stand a chance in hell of stopping those hostiles. I, for one, think the lady deserves more of a chance than that."

"Oh, Jacob," Eli returned in a lowered, tempered voice, "I don't want anything to happen to the lady either, but I ain't about to take orders from no..."

"We're wasting time," Ree cut in. "There's no more time for talk. Ma'am, will you be coming with me?"

"We all are coming," Jacob said, flopping on his slouch hat. "What do you want us to do?"

Ree let out a little smile and surveyed the others. They stared back, evenly, waiting for his command. Even Eli and the sheriff seemed resigned to the fact that Ree might be their only chance at escaping the closing ring of death.

"Ma'am, you and the cowboy go back to the shed. You may have to cover the crew as they rig the stage." Her eyes held onto Rees for a moment. They were trying to say something even though she wasn't sure herself what it was. Her hand gripped the heavy revolver tightly.

"Jacob, you take the south side of this street. The sheriff and I will take the north. Burn the building as soon as the stock is clear, then this place. The smoke may give us some cover. Now let's go."

The operation went smoothly. Despite Courtough's suspicious hesitation, Ree managed a sizeable fire between the Laurel Belle and its neighboring building in no time. An occasional shot smacked into wood above their heads but the Apaches made no attempt to rush the spread out defenders. As breed and sheriff came trotting back, black smoke began to replace the first wisps of white. Angry flames licked at the tinder-dry structure. Down the line, they could see the old skinner's handiwork blackening the sky.

More rifle fire was breaking out from across the street.

The stock had been run across the street. Driver and guard were frantically rigging them to the wippletree. Claire and the cowboy contributed to the miner's steady stream of shells flying back at figures milling by the buildings farther down the line. The combination of threatening fire and singing lead kept the Apaches well back of effective rifle range - for the moment.

The Concord was ready to roll in record time. Jud threw his saddle on the roan as the passengers climbed onboard. Dunn wheeled the leaders into a tight circle, heading out for the rough cut ridgeline directly behind the shed. Ree galloped past the sheriff, scooped up a handful of burning hay and flung it into the Laurel Belle's debris-crowded back porch.

Jud threw bedroll over one shoulder and leapt to saddle. As he galloped to catch up with the others, the Laurel Belle was becoming engulfed in flames and thick black smoke. Up ahead, he could see Bannon leading the coach up and over the rocky shelf.

Gunfire grew farther down the line. Figures dashed out of several buildings, each seeking a last shot at the fleeing whites.

Claire held to her window along with the others. She sat, aiming her weapon out the window, not daring to show how very scared she really was. There was too much pride for that. As the coach had topped the ridge, Claire got a quick look at the mounted Apaches whipping their ponies around the buildings. Ree had been right. She counted ten at a glance. They were pressing the attack, driving their mustangs at full gallop. The gap between attacker and game was closing rapidly.

Above the passengers, Eli and John Montgomery were driving as if judgment day was knocking right behind their ears. The teams were running on the thin edge of panic, held back from a flat-out, gut-tearing stampede only by Eli's deft hands and taut reins. Montgomery lay belly slung over the cab's top surrounded by jumping luggage and sought out a target close enough to hit. The Apache wolf pack was holding back, waiting for the coach to spill over on the rough, uneven ground. Bannon and the sheriff rode up ahead, flanking the crude trail.

The breed kicked his lean-bellied mustang out to point. He lead the Concord down a side gully, around a broken-edged bluff and then to the edge of a sharp slope. Both riders paused only a fragmented second then plunged over its edge, disappearing from sight.

"Hold on, inside!" Eli bawled over the thunder of pounding hooves, "We're taking a dip."

The teams poured over its edge and the heavy mail coach was on the gravel slope. It skidded from one side to the other as Dunn rode the brake handle for all he was worth. The teeth-jarring vibration inside the cab flung Claire and the miner over one another. The girl grabbed frantically for a hanging strap but succeeded only in a handful of air. Again she lunged for the strap and managed to loop two fingers through it. She hauled herself up to the window; only to be thrown back down again as the coach lurched drunkenly over to one side. The other passengers faired only slightly better. Each gripped the window frame and held on for dear life. Moments later, they reached the bottom and leveled out onto a back trail leading down to the flats below.

Above the Concord, the Apaches were spilling over the edge of the slope, firing down on the cab. Ree and the sheriff fired back but with no visible effect. A cloud of dust from the stage rolled back up to shield the Indians. The two riders held back, riding drag on the stage. Through the gray cloud, the war party broke in several places. Ree estimated ten for certain, probably more. They were yipping and yelling, urging their mounts down the slope.

Up ahead, Ree saw a canyon. Its entrance was covered with a thick growth of walnut and ash. The roadway passed between several large boulders which stood out and hung over the road. Ree spurred his mount alongside the stage. He motioned Eli to go ahead and not stop. The breed reined back, letting the coach pass through the narrow canyon entrance.

"We'll hold them off here," Ree shouted into the wind. Courtough followed him out of the saddle. They were beside a heap of rocks and twisted piñon trees which flanked the trail.

"Why are we stopping here?" Jud shouted, "We can't hold them off." He traced the breed's steps into the rocks.

"We can try!" Ree said, without looking back.

Courtough was frustrated and angry. Bannon had taken control of the group so quickly that the sheriff hadn't a chance to fight back. If he wanted to get the map, he'd have to be in control. Tension tightened his muscles and churned his stomach. His anger erupted. "Don't think I'm taking orders from you, breed!"

Jud snarled, "You're only riding point because you know these mountains. Once we're out of here, I'll be giving the orders, and I don't want to see your face around…"

A rifle volley smashed into the rocks, singing off in different directions. Jud kissed a rock. Ree allowed himself a slight smile, unmoved by the screaming ricochets. The sheriff cocked a mean eye over in Bannon's direction. His lips curled in a glare. He hugged the rocks closer and shouldered his rifle. Ree let his piece rest on the rock, waiting for the horsemen to get closer.

Dust from the Concord slowly settled over the pair. Through it, war cries filled the air! They were closing in quickly.

No trace of tension surfaced on Bannon's face. His eyes followed the riders unflinchingly. The gleaming Winchester came to rest on his shoulder - a finger curled around its trigger. The sights rose to center in on a large warrior at the head of the wolf pack. The trigger finger began to tighten. Eyes closed to a narrow squint; all attention focused on the lead rider. Courtough was jabbering; nervous chatter. Ree ignored it. A bullet hit the rocks. It sent a shower of splinters against his leg. Ree remained unmoved. He fired off one round. The first Apache wavered then toppled over and rolled in the dust. Courtough joined in with a volley. Another warrior dropped out of the saddle. The surging horde pressed forward. They would not be stopped.

From a short distance behind them, Eli's high-pitched mule scream split the air. Jud spun around. Ree didn't bother. It didn't matter how many Indians had outflanked them. The ones behind weren't going to turn back. Ree knew then it would be a bad fight. His gamble had failed. They were trapped.

"It's the Army!" Courtough shouted, ignoring the Apaches at their heals.

Ree peered back just in time to see a column of blue sweep past the stopped Concord, and charge the pass. Above the din of pounding hoofs and gunfire, Ree could hear the faint sound of a bugle.

The Apaches had reached the canyon entrance, pouring through the narrow canyon walls. As they whirled by, the red men fired point-blank into the pair's fort-up. Clouds of gray dust churned upward, filling the air, drawing visibility in tight. Both men lay, flat-bellied on the ground, their rifles useless.

The column of blue hit surging red tide just inside the narrow pass. Army Springfields bounced echoes through the rock tunnel, reverberating back and forth. They mingled with shouts, war cries and odd cracking of Apache Spencers and Maynards. Instead of breaking off the attack, the Apaches drove directly into the charging troopers and split its ranks up the middle. It was a jolting collision of club and carbine, man and horse. Warriors leapt off their ponies, dragging troopers down into the enveloping dust. Others thrust forward. Their feathered lances cut into trooper and horseflesh alike.

Dunville's squads were caught off guard, expecting the Apaches to turn tail and run. They realized only too quickly these were not tiswin-loaded bucks off the reservation. They were hesh-ke; fanatical hotheads, the white-killers. These Apaches lived only to count coup against the white invader.

Sergeant Flaherty snapfired three rounds at a warrior galloping past. The brave dropped over his pony's side and fired back, creasing the non-com's hat brim. His next shot went wild and before the sergeant could return fire, the man was past. Another warrior bursted out of the choking dust. His pony smashed into the sergeant's gray. They both went down, locked in a fierce struggle. The Apache kneed the non-com, raising his war club for a killing blow. Flaherty blasted him a powder-burning foot away. Before the brave hit the ground, another had taken his place, leaping out of nowhere. The sergeant emptied his revolver into the brave and took an eye-blackening blow to the temple in the process. As he fell to his knees, Flaherty could hear shots and screams rising to a deafening crescendo. He felt his body grow numb. The ground rushed up to hit his face. Everything went black.

The terrible fight with the hesh-ke lasted only minutes. When it was over and visibility grew, it was apparent the price had been great. Scattered like wind-swept prairie grass, the limp forms of red man and white lay frozen in deathly array. The pungent odor of blood, gunpowder, sweat and dying horseflesh was thick in the air. Indian ponies sped away, their single-strand hair bridles whipping in the wind. Army grays kicked in dying spasms or stood obediently, riderless. Groans arose from scattered bodies and wounded troopers slowly regaining their senses. All the hesh-ke were dead, most lying by a trooper taken down with him. According to the code of their secret lodge, none of the hesh-ke had lived to become an Army prisoner. They had fought and died according to their own rules.

Lieutenant Dunville looked in numb disgust at the carnage around him. He quickly counted the bodies of seven troopers who were not moving. Several more lay sprawled on their backs or bellies, trying to move. Stunned troopers sat and stood among their fallen comrades.

"Sergeant Flaherty," Dunville shouted out.

"Wounded, Sir," A corporal answered as he passed by with a fistful of bandages. The officer followed him to the non-com who was just starting to arise. A large blue-black welt was already blossoming on the sergeant's forehead. Dried blood caked his dirty tunic.

"Sergeant, are you alright?" The lieutenant asked as he surveyed his bloodied command.

The sergeant stumbled to his unsteady feet. "I'll live, Sir, don't worry about me. What about the others?"

Dunville shook his head. His eyes were gazing out past the bloodied ground toward the hills wrapped in summer's heat. "It was bad, sergeant, very bad." The officer turned on his heels to the corporal behind him. "Corporal, I want a burial detail, five men. Picket the stock and set up a perimeter guard. We'll move out as soon as the wounded are attended to. See that they are placed in the stage as soon as possible."

Flaherty was cradling his head; showing real signs of pain. "With the lieutenant's permission, I'd like to sit a spell. My head is kind of funny. I feel pretty dizzy." The officer waved him off and Flaherty slipped to the ground and sat hunched over and remained very still.

The Concord had returned as the battle subsided. Lieutenant Dunville approached the crewmen who were checking cinches and straps.

"Driver, I'm lieutenant Dunville. We're in very great need of medical supplies. Do you have any onboard?"

"I have some," A girl's voice came from inside the cab. Claire hopped out on the foot step and quickly dropped to the ground. "It's not much," she said holding up a handful of gauze and cotton bandages, "but it will have to do."

The officer finger-tipped the edge of his battered hat. He spoke with restrained surprise. "Driver, you didn't say anything about a woman being onboard." "Hell, you didn't ask me!" Eli retorted.

Dunville ignored the outburst. He turned his full attention back to the girl. 'Ma'am, I can assure you the United States Army will do its best to protect you until Santa Fe. We haven't a surgeon with us so might I ask you to see what you can do for the men. Some of them need patching up pretty bad."

"Of course, lieutenant," Claire said. "Mister Dunn," she turned to the driver, "if you'll come with me please." The driver narrowed his eyes suspiciously but followed behind the girl immediately.

The other passengers were already at work with the wounded. Claire took command of the situation. She gathered the wounded in a shaded spot under several walnut trees and set a small fire going. Lieutenant Dunville watched the girl out of the corner of his eye. *Such an attractive girl,* he thought. The months at Camp Puerco had eventually robbed his senses of what a pretty young woman can do to a man's heart and mind. Claire certainly was doing just that to the lieutenant. The officer was diverted back to the pair of men who were dog-trotting toward him. It was the two men who had stood at the rocks. Behind them, the officer could see several bodies huddled by the pass where they had rushed through. Bannon and Courtough stopped in front of the officer, both leaning against their rifles. Both men were gray with dust and lined with streaks of sweat.

"We saw your smoke," The officer began, "We've been following you since the Barlow place. I'm Lieutenant Dunville, Third Cavalry, Camp Puerco. We suspected you might have trouble with the Apaches. I guess we were right about that!"

"We're still not in the clear, Lieutenant," Ree said.

"Who are you?" the officer asked with raised eyebrows.

"Doesn't matter. What matters is that these Apaches weren't alone. They were part of a larger war party. The main pack is due west of us. Right now, judging from the size of that fire, I'd say they're all riding hell for leather right toward us."

Dunville's eyes followed the breed's straight arm. A column of black smoke curled upward into the brassy sky. The entire town must have been aflame from the size of that smoke column.

"We haven't got much time if we want to lay some distance between us and them." Ree pointed out

"Alright, Bannon, your heroics are over, "Jud interrupted, "We'll take over now."

"We?" Dunville questioned the lawman.

The sheriff dug a tin star out of his vest pocket. It was dirty and tarnished. "Sheriff Courtough, Lieutenant; out of San Lacita. I was tracking three outlaws when I met this stage at the relay station. The bandits had been killed but I decided it best I escort these folks to Santa Fe."

Claire had just returned from the wounded when she heard the last of Courtough's inflated oration. "Sheriff Courtough," She said in a sharp tongue, "I think you should mention that Ree Bannon did get us out of that town. And that he was the man who stopped those three bandits. If it weren't for him, we might be dead back there." Claire never once turned to Ree, her attention focused on the sheriff and the officer.

Lieutenant Dunville had been watching the two men. Tension was growing between them. The sheriff was keyed up, ready to spring. The other man was loose and calm. He leaned on his rifle to feign complaisency. He wasn't amiable and Dunville knew it.

He hadn't missed the distinct Indian features; the deceiving slouch, the slack shoulders. They were meant to deceive. This one would be the one to watch. The lieutenant straightened his shoulders. "This is a military situation with civilian lives in danger. I'll take command here," he said.

"Good!" Jud piped in, "Now I think we…"

"Sheriff! I said the Army will take command."

Jud Courtough bristled but kept his silence. Claire searched Ree for a reaction. His attention was focused on the officer; straight, direct, and penetrating.

"Lieutenant, if you want to continue calling the shots you best move 'em out right now. You just lost whatever time you had." The breed's arm lifted toward the smoke of Defiance then veered to the right.

Dunville's eyes darted to puffs of white smoke rising up along the horizon. Smoke signals! They had been pinpointed.

Bannon read the officer's mind. "We've got a chance if we move out right now. The ones behind us won't attack…"

Dunville turned quickly; more smoke was rising up from another direction.

"…they'll dog our trail, but they're not strong enough for a frontal assault. We might be able to shake them long enough to reach the mesa. It's not far. It's your choice, lieutenant, but you've got to make it right now!"

Dunville looked at his troopers slowly reassembling into two columns under the barking command of recuperated sergeant Flaherty. He pursed his dried, cracked lips, and his eyes lifted to the breeds. He looked older, the weight of his lost men heavy on his shoulders. "You sound like you know these parts," he said, "which way do you propose we go?"

Ree pointed his rifle toward the gray mountainous folds far off to their left, northeast of the black column of smoke. "I know of an old Navajo trail, narrow but level enough for the stage. It leads through those mountains up to the Glorieta Mesa: from there on, we stand a chance of making it."

The other passengers had gathered around by then. "Better listen to him, Lieutenant," old Jacob broke in, "he's been right about everything else so far."

The officer turned to the driver. "Mister, is that true? Do you know of such a trail through the mountains?"

Eli furrowed his eyebrows, feeling cornered into a hard admission he didn't want to taste. "I've never heard of such a trail." Begrudgingly, he added, "But if Bannon says it's there, I guess I'll have to believe him. Either way, lieutenant, he's right about them Apaches being on top of us soon. We got to get outta here."

Lieutenant Dunville looked at the party assembled before him; the sullen sheriff Courtough, the grizzled looks of Eli and John Montgomery, the composed half-breed and tense young girl. They were now all of his charges … with exception of the breed. He was only his own concern. He was also, potentially, their only key to crossing the mountains.

They were all waiting for him to speak.

"All right," Dunville finally said, "Stranger, you…"

"Bannon."

"Bannon, then, we'll try your trail." Dunville turned to the non-com who had rejoined him. "Sergeant, place half the troops in front of the stage, half in back.

156

You'll ride point with Bannon here. Sheriff, I want you back with the stage. Let's move out. Now!"

Chapter Sixteen

On a stretch of flat playa sandwiched between two mountainous humps, rode the Santa Fe-bound party. They rode at a steady canter, trusting instinct over caution. The troops were worn by the terrible fight against the hesh-ke and now the punishing sun.

The army column with its Concord charge was deep into the mountainous terrain everyone had deemed impossible to cross … all except Ree Bannon. He rode point a quarter mile out. Riding alongside him, sergeant Flaherty puffed on his gnawed down cigar stub and cut eagle eyes back and forth. They exchanged few words. Ree studied the hills for Apache smoke, Flaherty the rough cut ancient roadway for tracks. There was no need for idle chatter between them. They understood their jobs. Each relied on himself and trusted the other. Nothing had to be said.

After traversing the stretch of bottoms, Ree took them up and over the sun baked spine of a narrow ridgeback. The stage team laid hard into their collars, straining to get up the rocky slope. The additional weight of wounded troopers made the going rough. The cab swayed back and forth, its leather thoroughbraces groaning. Tug and slack chains grinded with the force. The wippletree was stretched taut and rock-solid. Eli ran his lines slack. He urged, cursed and threatened the toughened brutes upward. Upon cresting the mountainous spine, Dunn foot-juggled the brake handle and began his descent. He lay back on the reins, trying to keep the stage even and balanced. The party dropped into the valley in a rush of choking dust.

Lieutenant Dunville exchanged outriders on the column's flanks. The new detail moved briskly to the valley's rock walls. There had been no sign of the enemy. The officer gazed back at his command. They were tired and worn. Flanks and shoulders of the Army grays were darkly patched with sweat. The heat was worse there. It boiled up off the valley floor, seemingly thirty degrees hotter than on the plateau. Sweat beaded along Dunville's forehead and ran in familiar creases down his cheeks. He cursed formality under breath, stuck a finger under his collar and ran it around his neck. The kiss of air was short but sweet. His skin was rough and itching. His back was soaked and sticky, his pants the same. The officer twisted back in the saddle to face his corporal riding back from the coach.

"Corporal."

"Sir."

"How are the wounded?"

The trooper nudged his mount alongside the officers. He rubbed a dripping face as he spoke. "Private Owen had gone badly, Sir. He's lost a sight of blood. The girl's doing all she can but it doesn't seem to help. I don't think he's going to make it back."

"And the others?" Dunville asked, in a guarded tone.

"The rest will all make it. You can't tell it by their complaining but they'll pull through. They're third cavalry, by jingle, that's something going for them."

"Resume your post," Dunville said, nodding at the man.

"Sir?"

The lieutenant had started to turn away. Now he looked up at the trooper, caught by his serious tone of voice.

"What made them Apaches act like that?" the corporal asked. "It was like they wanted to die. They could have turned tail when they first spotted us. So why didn't they run?"

Lieutenant Dunville was lost for an answer. He knew he must answer the question. An excuse of ignorance wouldn't do. So the officer summed up the knowledge he'd gathered on the hesh-ke. "Corporal, I don't know why they charged us like that. That's the straight up truth. I don't think any white man would know. They all wanted to die, no doubt about that. I guess it's part of their religion. It's said the hesh-ke have only one goal in mind when they take to the warpath; and that's killin' - anyway, anytime. White or Mex … even friendly Indians. They weren't about to turn their backs on a fight even if it meant their annihilation. It doesn't make sense to us but it did to them." The officer paused, not sure what else to say.

"So it was the only thing for them to do. Yeah, I guess you're right … but Sir, it still doesn't seem right anyway you cut it - our way or theirs!"

Dunville could only shrug his shoulders in agreement.

Trailing the column by a half mile, old Jacob was eating dust and looking for trouble. Riding drag wasn't his notion of fighting Apaches but the young lieutenant had asked and Jacob needed the feel of doing a job. Now was his chance. Up ahead, the party exited its canyon cocoon and wormed up the twisting curl of a ridgeback toward another mesa. The old outrider spurred his borrowed army gray up a rocky shelf just outside the canyon walls. He left his horse rein-thrown and stood in a patched screen of high burnt grass. Nothing stirred except the grass pushed by a northerly breeze.

Ahead of the skinner, moving slowly up the roadless mountain spine, the column blended into the molten brown-gray coloration. Ree and Flaherty had already crested the ridge and were standing to horse. Jacob could see them clearly, silhouetted against a clear blue cloudless skyline. Perched on that spine;

they, like Jacob, had a view of the expanse of plains stretching off to their left and a tangle of mountainous terrain behind them. What lay ahead, only they could tell. Jacob had his rear to cover and something…anything… to look out for.

Jacob hadn't lost his touch. There was simply nothing to see. No tell-tale dust to signal approaching riders. No puffs of blanket-smoke to telegraph their winding escape through the labyrinth of mountain trails leading up to the Glorieta Mesa. Ahead lay the unknown. Behind, only the twin ruts of iron-rimmed wagon wheels lay in the sandy canyon bottoms.

The Apache wolf pack hadn't found them yet… Old Jacob was no fool. It was only a matter of time. If the breed was right about his trail through the mountains, they might stand a chance at reaching the mesa. If not, then the hesh-ke would soon catch up to them. Once the hesh-ke were close, they would make their presence known. Following pattern, they'd root themselves on the high peaks adjacent to the canyon. There they could let the cold chill of their visibility do its stomach-tightening work. When it suited them, when the time was right to die, then they'd come charging down out of the hills and it would be the end. The skinner stepped to saddle and wheeled his gray back to resume his drag-tail assignment. They were bound to come sometime soon. Jacob only hoped he would spot them in time to warn the others.

Onboard the pitching Concord, the wounded soldiers sat stuffed together. Each was wrapped in a layer of dried blood and dust. Only after Claire had reprimanded their complaining, did they turn to disciplined silence. Jammed in tightly, Claire twisted and turned at awkward angles to administer what little help she could give. Private Owen was the worse; a gut-shot wound that hadn't stopped bleeding since the fight. He had lapsed in and out of consciousness. Claire did what she could to comfort him. Up above, Eli and John Montgomery rode in silence. They could feel the tension running the length of the column. It showed plainly on every trooper there. Around them, the hills seemed quiet and somber. They both knew that was very deceiving.

Sheriff Courtough spoke to no one as he rode along. His guts were knotted up with sullen anger. Hatred masked his face with its taut stretched cheek bones and menacing eyes. First Bannon's sudden appearance then the Army's had combined to frustrate all his plans. He'd wanted to get at Claire in Defiance. The hesh-ke had changed all that. He was no closer to the map than he had been back in San Lacita. If his hunch about the girl having it proved wrong, Jud would be one murder-prone shootist: Bannon first, then the driver and guard.

As the pace slowed going up the mesa's side, Jud spurred his mount alongside the cab and tried to make conversation with Claire. She hung out a forced smile then turned back to her charges. Jud dropped back to the others and mulled over another avenue of approach. He remembered Ree had said they might fort-up on the Glorieta Mesa before sundown. If he was lucky, Jud might have a chance to approach the girl then. He might be able to con her out of the map. If not, then it'd have to wait until Santa Fe.

Time crawled by slowly. The wind-swept mesa provided an expansive view of the surrounding land, but it told them nothing of the enemy. Dust would say something, but there was no dust. Sunlight reflecting off metal even, but there was no reflection. Everything seemed to indicate they were alone. Everyone knew they weren't or wouldn't be for long.

The troop angled down off the mesa and swung left to pick up a vague wild horse trail which traversed a broad band of sage-studded flatlands. The trail bordered a series of hump-backed foothills hanging like a necklace around the large, imposing Sangre de Cristo Mountains.

Lieutenant Dunville strong-armed the column to a short noon rest a half hour later. The party was situated by a clump of gnarled Joshua trees, the only shade within miles. He ordered the wounded taken out of the cab and placed under the spare shade. They were given water and their wounds were checked.

This done, the officer set up a perimeter line and picketed the jaded horses in groups of four, each with a trooper. Two privates were sent to clean out the stench-filled cab under the tutorage of Claire. Eli was directed to park the Concord apart from the troops in case of attack. The team horses would spook much quicker than the trained army mounts. Dunville didn't want a runaway stage tearing through his lines if an attack came. Driver and guard watered the teams and then drifted off to find a suitable watering spot for themselves.

"Cold beans and sowbelly," Lieutenant Dunville told the corporal. "Smokeless wood or no fires - we can't risk any smoke."

Bannon and Flaherty were moving back through the hock-deep grass. The lieutenant shaded his eyes to watch them approach. He turned around. Old Jacob was now in sight, moving as a tiny speck against the heat swept land. A loud moan turned Dunville's head around. It was young Owen rolling his bandaged head back and forth. The Corporal was by him trying to administer water. It seemed only a matter of time before the youth succumbed to his wounds. Along the line of walking wounded, stiffened faces held granite-firm without a sound.

"Sergeant, we'll stand to horse in ten minutes," Dunville said as the pair got close. "See what you can do with the wounded then check our supply of ammunition."

Sergeant Flaherty angled around and moved off at a trot. Bannon watched him leave and then turned eyes on Dunville. Beneath the wide hat brim, his pure blue eyes scanned the camp. Men and horses were restless, very edgy. Like a herd of trail-tired longhorns, they were spooky and tired-mean. Dunville noticed the stare. He read the somber eyes, the knit brow. This was Ree's charge now. He was the key to survival - and they both knew it.

The Concord was parked in a depressed outcropping of rock and shale. A heavy aroma of freshly perked coffee turned Ree's attention toward the small, smoke-less fire a short distance from the coach. Eli and John Montgomery sat beneath a Joshua tree. The guard waved Ree over. The breed wanted to say something to Claire but she was busy cleaning out the cab. Crossing over, Ree noticed Jud with the lieutenant; both arguing over some matter. Their backs were to him. The breed drew his mustang in behind the fire.

John Montgomery thrust a steaming cup of coffee in his hand as Ree squatted beside the fire. Both crewmen were cleaning their pieces as the point man settled in.

"This is some trail you've got us following," Eli commented. "You sure that rig of mine is gonna make it all the way?"

"We should reach the mesa before dark," Ree said, his eyes skipping about the camp. His attention was focused elsewhere. Both Dunn and Montgomery noticed it; their eyes locked and tied their separate observations together. The breed was a concerned hombre. It seemed obvious to the pair that more than hesh-ke troubles were high on the desert fighter's mind.

The driver gnawed on a linty piece of cut plug, eyeing the third man. "None of my business, Bannon, but we figure you and the sheriff have got to hit heads soon. One way or another, it'll happen before we reach Santa Fe."

Ree cocked an eye at Eli. "And if it does?" he questioned.

John Montgomery, never one to hedge on a response, answered for both of them. "Listen, Ree, Eli and I hate that son-of-a-bitch as much as he seems to hate you. Now if you want any help, you can depend on us. It's as simple as that. We'll stand up to him with you."

The breed's somber eyes flickered a moment then retreated back to their suspicious selves again. "Thanks, but I don't need it," Bannon stated flatly, his eyes on the coffee. He looked up from the tin. "Thanks anyway." He arose and palmed the rest of his coffee down. He dropped the tin and moved toward the stage. Moments before he had caught the tag end of two troopers moving away from the cab. The girl should be alone now. This might be his only chance to speak to her before the column moved out again. A mere glimpse assured him Jud was still arguing with the lieutenant. Ree would have to be quick.

He found Claire on the floor, mopping up a pool of blood. The rank odor of sweat and blood was still present. It didn't seem to bother the girl. She worked in deep concentration, her back to the breed.

"Miss LeFonte."

Claire paused a moment, her shoulders tense then sagging. She resumed her wiping. She spoke without turning around. "I knew you'd be coming," she said, "I know what you want…"

"You have the map," Bannon stated flatly. "I want it."

Claire then turned and lifted herself up onto the bench seat. She fingered back loose strands of hair out of her face. "How did you know?" she asked.

Ree made sure no one was nearby. The sheriff was still with Dunville. Eli and John Montgomery had launched into their own argument. Ree turned back to face the girl. "It doesn't matter how I found out," He answered. "You've got it and it belongs to me."

Claire was composed, her face displaying strength and confidence. "Whether you believe me or not, I did intend to give you that map the first chance I got. I didn't know I had it until I changed into a new blouse and found it stuck inside. I remember what you said back at the station house about trusting me and all. I want you to believe me that I never intended to keep that map. I always planned to…"

"Ma'am … Claire!"

"We haven't much time," Ree interrupted, "The map, please."

Claire looked at Ree with a perplexed expression. "Well," she said, "If you want it, you'll have to turn around…or do I have to dig it out in front of you?" Ree turned his back to her. He heard the rustle of buttons and underpinnings. Claire tapped his shoulder. She held out the map.

Ree took the map and examined it closely. It was made of smooth dried doe skin, soft and flexible. On its back were the finely drawn lines and Indian symbols of the location of Bannon's quest.

The importance of the map intrigued the girl. "Why is that map so important to you that you're willing to die just to get your hands on it?" She asked. Ree gave her a stern look. Claire persisted. "Well, you can tell me now that I've given it to you. I didn't tell anyone I had it. No one is going to find out."

"There is some gold and silver hidden in a cave, but I don't intend to take it. I'm going to close up the cave so no one will ever find it."

Claire's mouth dropped open. "Close it up? You mean you're not going to keep any of the gold or silver. That's what you were willing to die for…to walk away from a treasure like that? I can't believe it."

"Doesn't matter whether you believe it or not! It's the truth. That's blood money fashioned out of the death and misery of my ancestors. I won't have any varmints take it to war on my people."

Claire leaned in closer, intrigued by the complexity of Ree's mysterious motivation. "I know it is none of my business. I just don't understand why you wouldn't take that gold and silver - if for no other reason than to give it to your people. They can do a lot with money even if it is white man's money. They can buy food or seed for crops."

Bannon moved farther inside the cab, away from the window. He peered once more to be assured the sheriff was still near the troops. Time was scarce. It would only be minutes before the column moved out again. Ree wasn't sure why he was telling the girl all this. He trusted her even when she had the map. He believed her even if he wasn't sure why.

"There's a lot of gold and silver in that cave. It also contains old swords and armament of the conquistadors who tried to make slaves of my people. A long time ago there was an Indian uprising and all the Spanish were driven from this region. Before they left, they hid their treasures in that cave. They intended to return and begin another slave colony. The exact location of the cave was kept a secret. The Indian slaves who were made to carry the wealth into it were then put to death. There was no one alive to reveal the cave's location except the Spanish."

"The Spanish never came back. Not long ago my uncle found that cave by accident when he was hunting mountain sheep. He made this map of its location. He was going back to the reservation to get help to close it up tight so that no one could use the gold and silver to again wage war on his people. He never made it back. He was ambushed by a bunch of buffalo hunters. A miner found him where he had holed up in some rocks, badly wounded. The miner stole the map and left my uncle to die. My people found him before he died. He told them of the map.

When I found the miner, he had been shot by the Easterner and left to die by the Lanker gang. I trailed those three outlaws to San Lacita. They were after the map along with the sheriff. I overheard them talking about robbing the stage and getting the map. I knew I had to get to the stage before them but…"

"What happened?"

"I came across an Army patrol that had been attacked by a war party. I tried to help them. I was too late. I could only rescue an old Navajo couple, my people. I couldn't let the Apache take my people."

Claire sat, open-mouthed. She was transfixed by Bannon's stern determination. Ree could see her mind was troubled.

"No one will know you had the map," he said.

"But what if the sheriff finds out that you have the map now?" Claire asked, "Jacob thinks Courtough might be wise to you. If he is, he'll surely try to kill you for the map."

"I don't think so … not in front of everyone here. The sheriff has still got too good a cover to waste on a foolish move like that. He won't try to get the map unless he figures there's a fighting chance he can escape with it." Then Ree's blue eyes narrowed. They lay on Claire with a firm hold. Claire felt awkward. "Watch yourself, Miss. The sheriff is not a fair-minded man. He'll kill you as quick and clean as he would an unarmed altar boy. Doesn't matter that you're a pretty thing. He's going to try something before Santa Fe. Don't get yourself in his way. Stay out in the open. Don't let him get you alone."

"If he finds out that you have the map he'll be forced to act. He could use that fight with the Fowler brothers as an excuse to take you in." Claire had hardly finished the sentence when she realized what she had said. The revelation stopped her short. She didn't know what else to say.

"How did you find out about that?"

"Jacob was there when it happened. He saw the whole thing. He knew it wasn't your fault."

"Is he the only one that knows?"

Claire bowed her tussled head sadly. "Yes, but he would back you if it came to that."

"It never will!" Ree declared. "Every man in that saloon later claimed it was murder. It was me against four men…and they called it murder. That's white man's justice."

Claire was angry at herself for mentioning the incident. She tried to salvage what she could of the situation. "Nobody else knows about it," she insisted. "You can depend on Jacob and me not to say a word. Believe me, you can trust us. We're on your side."

Ree's mind was working overtime; judging and calculating the odds for and against him. "If Courtough finds out, he'll ask for Army backing to take me to Santa Fe. He'll try to take me back to Spanish Wells … or at least pretend to. If he does that, I'd never live an hour outside of town."

"But how could he find out? We're the only ones that know."

Ree allowed himself a little smile. "There were a lot of people in that saloon. Word got around. There aren't too many breeds around the territory that match my description. There's always a chance one of these troopers might have heard about me - or the miner or cowboy. Any one of them could tell the sheriff for a piece of the reward money."

"What are you going to do if he finds out about you?"

"He won't take the map!"

"You're going to fight him. Do you mean that? It would be suicide. The Army would surely jail you."

"If I have to kill Courtough, I will. He's not going to bring me in."

"No, there has to be another way."

"None that I know of."

"Ree, you can't…"

"Bannon!" A voice called out. It was Lieutenant Dunville.

He wanted to say more. He could sense that she did too, but the time and the place was wrong. She was years too late for his life and he was surely wrong for hers.

Stepping down out of the Concord, Ree noticed Lieutenant Dunville leading the walking wounded back to their cramped quarters. By the depressed rock, a squad was finishing a shallow grave. They carefully covered all signs of its presence and laid rocks on top to prevent scavengers from digging it up. Private Owen would not be going back to the camp. The wounded filed slowly into the cab. The men were a ragged bunch, tired and dirty. Ree moved quickly to his horse. Driver and guard passed him to load up.

The men were loaded onboard. Claire had followed Ree out of the cab. She had watched Ree mount up and ride out toward Sergeant Flaherty who was already on point. Claire didn't notice the man watching her intently from a clump of mesquite, off to the right. She hadn't seen the eyes staring intently at Bannon as he rode off at a rocking canter. They were Jud Courtough's eyes; all the time watching Ree and the girl well enough to guess the gist of their conversation.

The outriders were on the flanks. Lieutenant called to mount. Troopers swung to saddle. Jacob tossed a half cup of coffee and kicked his gray into a gallop. Back to resume his drag detail.

"Ready to move them out, Corporal?"

"Ready, Sir!"

"Move 'em out!"

The cavalry horses pounded on a lope into the dust. The pace was quicker this time, the Lieutenant could sense the urgency felt by his command.

Chapter Seventeen

The hesh-ke came in late afternoon. There were no head-on suicidal charges. No flanking movements to surround the column. Instead a single Apache appeared on the crest of a hill a mile away. He sat motionless on his paint-smeared pony, a tiny dot against the sky. Several more well-armed warriors gradually rode up beside him. They sat watching as the column trudged wearily by.

A murmur moved up and down the trooper's rank. Carbines were checked for a third and fourth time. Dunville turned to the corporal. "Alert the men to stand ready for a forced gallop if more hostiles appear."

The command went down the line.

Dunville kicked his mount back to the sheriff. Courtough was staring ahead, out at the point riders. His companion riders were studying the half-dozen hesh-ke lining the hillside.

Courtough looked over as the officer pulled in alongside.

"Sheriff, I expect we're going to have plenty of trouble very soon. I want you to take charge of the stage. See to it that the wounded are taken care of. The corporal will assist by giving you cover."

"That bull-headed driver isn't going to like that, Lieutenant. He's more ornery than a she-lynx cornered with cubs."

Dunville straightened his back. "I don't give a damn whether he likes it or not. I'm putting you in charge of those wounded and that stage. As long as this unit is under my command, he'll abide by those orders." With that, Dunville kicked his mount to resume his place at the head of the column.

Jud kneed his mount up alongside the Concord. "Miss LeFonte, if there's trouble, the lieutenant says you're to take orders from me. I'll see to it you're taken care of." Then the lawman locked eyes on Eli's hostile stare. Jud cut a mean stare back. "You two hear that? The Lieutenant says when the action starts, you're to follow my…"

A stream of tobacco juice splattered on the ground in front of the lawman. His mount threw back its head and side-stepped the shot. Jud's face turned red, his cheeks taut and mean. "Dunn, you're going to be one sorry son-of-a-bitch before we reach Santa Fe. Believe me; I'll have your bacon."

As the lawman heeled back to his old position, he could hear driver and guard chuckling. Through the corner of his eye, he saw Claire watching him pass by. She carried a stony look on her face.

Dunville studied the grassy terrain where flatlands had gradually turned to meadows. It was wind-swept prairie grass; sunburnt, dry and covering most of the wide valley. The lieutenant guessed it hock-high, four or five inches. Not enough to hide a large force of mounted hostiles, but enough for snipers. He noticed there were now an even dozen warriors lining the higher ground to his left. He saw his outriders dip down, hidden to the waist as they rode down through a gully and then up again out of it.

Arroyos.

Unseen from where the column rode, there had to be draws and gullies off to its right. If those depressions were large enough, a large body of hostiles might be hiding out there waiting for the opportune moment to attack. For all practical purposes, the officer realized they might be trapped. The mounted braves could be a mere distraction for a large force moving in from his right.

The corporal's voice broke the fragile silence. "Lieutenant, look behind us!"

Dunville wheeled around and saw a rider heading for them. It was old Jacob, bent low over his gray, waving his battered old flop hat in the air. Nothing moved behind him. He was not being pursued.

Jacob went straight to the column's head at a dead run. There he drew up sharply, his horse rearing high while he slid off as expertly and smoothly as a Plains Indian. The wrinkled face was alive.

"Lieutenant, we got us a pack of problems. You've got a bunch of hesh-ke dogging your trail and coming up fast. I figure there are a couple dozen by their dust - moving straight and steady."

Dunville's time had come. He was ready for it. Dunville studied the land's rising shoulders. Glorieta Mesa was not too far away. His eyes swept from right flank to left, then came back to the old teamster. "How soon?" was all he asked.

"If they keep their pace, I'd give them less than an hour at the most … unless those critters start something." Jacob pointed his civil war Spencer at the motionless Apaches lining the ridge.

"Get Bannon!" Dunville ordered. He turned back to Jacob. "Did you see any other sign of trouble?"

"Nope! But you can figure if they're showing themselves on the left. Some are sure as hell settled in on your right flank too. I'd guess they're scouting up ahead to find a place to hold up the column. They can box us in until that main party comes up from the rear."

The officer signaled in agreement.

Jacob scratched his dusty whiskers. "Them bronco bastards sure got a lot of confidence showing themselves like that. They're trying hard to spook us - and doing a damn fine job of it too!"

Ree Bannon rode back at a gallop. He had spotted the first warrior on their flank when all that showed was his headband. Now with Jacob back at the column, Ree needed no more explanation. His trained eyes could see the cloud of dust rising up behind them. Riders - a lot of them. The hesh-ke had found the column.

"Bannon, Jacob reports a party of hostiles trailing us by less than an hour. Now how far is it to the mesas top?"

Ree pointed toward the mountainous mass they had been approaching for seemingly hours. Glorieta Mesa! Distance was deceiving. There were no foothills at that spot to gauge their distance and estimate a time of arrival. Only a trained, familiar eye could tell how far away they really were. "We're less than a half hour away from the top right now. There's a trail leading up to the summit straight ahead. If our company has anything planned, it'll have to be soon. This trail buckles up pretty soon. Its sides start to drop off. They won't be able to pin us down up there."

"What are you suggesting then?"

Bannon looked Dunville straight in the face, locking eyeballs. "Lieutenant, if I were you, I'd tie down those wounded, hold on to your kepi and ride hell for leather to the summit. That might hold those varmints on both your flanks long enough for us to make it. We'll have to fort-up once we get on top. No way we can make it to Santa Fe before dusk. Trail's too rough and treacherous." Releasing his stare, Ree finished, "You're asking me. So that's what I'd do."

"That's good enough for me," Dunville shot back. "Corporal!"

"Sir."

"Tell the driver and young lady to mind their passengers. It'll be a forced gallop from here to the summit. See to it that the wounded are made as comfortable as possible, then alert the troop." The officer turned back to Bannon. "Take Jacob with you on point. If there's trouble up ahead, you three will have to deal with it. I will not stop unless I'm absolutely forced to. Is that understood?"

Ree and Jacob smiled and wheeled their mounts to rejoin the sergeant. Up ahead, a faint opalescent haze hung low over the mesa's top. It was dust swept off by wind blowing over the tabletop. It was deceivingly beautiful. A powerful fight was brewing up and Ree was in the thick of it. Feeling for the map tightly lodged in his back pants pocket, Ree wondered if he'd ever have a chance to fulfill his father's wish. Or even see the next day, for that matter.

The battle plan was outlined for Flaherty. The non-com's old crusty face came alive with each detail. He checked his belt loops and hoisted up the carbine suspended from his belt swivel.

Lieutenant Dunville tightened his command. Outriders were gradually, cautiously drawn in, until they were only a dozen yards from the column. The hesh-ke, seeing the change in the troop formation, spurred their mustangs back and forth along the ridge. They shouted taunts and waved their weapons menacingly. Several let out a volley of shots even though the range was too distant. They began riding parallel to the column. Dunville studied his right flank. There was still no sign of hostiles among the draws and gullies.

On top of the Concord, Eli braced his feet for the forthcoming race and checked his revolver. It was a matter of simple self-assurance but Eli needed to do it. John Montgomery checked his load and settled back for the spine-jarring roust that was sure to come. The teams were rested. They showed little sweat from the full load inside. Eli was gambling his rig would hold up on a mountain trail he hadn't seen before.

As predicted, the ground began to buckle up, its sides falling farther back. A natural trail began to rise up out of the grassy plain and wind itself toward the mountainous mass looming ahead of the column. The men were eager for the fight, all eyes glued on the lieutenant and his aide. The hesh-ke came off the ridgeline, drew in close and fired their weapons, then sprinted back out of range. Tempting, Teasing; trying to rattle the troop. Dunville held firm.

The point-riding trio had moved farther ahead, stretching the distance between themselves and the column. Sergeant Flaherty looked back at the lieutenant. Dunville slipped revolver out of holster. It went up in the air.

"Corporal."

"Sir."

"Move 'em out!"

As one cohesive body, the blue column moved out at a canter. Dunn bellowed out a hoarse-voiced command and the teams laid into their collars, picking up the pace. The sound of pounding hooves crescendoed, drowning out all else. The officer glanced back over a shoulder. The dust cloud was growing larger and ever closer. The hesh-ke were coming up much faster than anticipated.

"Alright, corporal," Dunville shouted over the pounding lope of the big army grays, "Let's ride!" With that, he spurred his mount into a gallop. The column surged ahead, the Concord falling into place accordingly.

Up ahead, Ree urged his mustang into a hard-pressed gallop. Flaherty and Jacob rode close to his side. Hostile rifle fire whistled and whined overhead. The Apache horsemen were cutting in closer, between them and the column. There could be no turning back. They were effectively cut off from the column.

Flanking the trio farther ahead, a small party of braves had broken off from the others and were now riding hard for an outcropping of rock and stinted pine bordering the narrowing trail. Their intent was clear; an embattlement to block the party's escape to the mesa top. Bannon knew if those Indian riflemen could delay the column for even a short while, they'd be caught on the narrow, dangerous trail.

The breed quickly estimated the distance the Indians had to go against that remaining between the trio and the rocks. It would be a very close race. The stronger cavalry horses were conditioned for such a hard pull, the shorter Indian ponies weren't. The hostiles had a good head start and rifle fire to cover their dash. The trio had no rifle cover; only the column surging up behind, depending on them to clear the way.

"Sergeant!" Ree called over pounding hooves and ever-closer yipping Apaches, "We've got to beat them to those rocks and secure that position. Cover me."

"The hell!" Flaherty shot back, "we'll all three take 'em together."

Ree wasn't about to argue the point. He dug heels into the mustang's flanks and hung low. Flaherty and Jacob followed suit. The three were in an all or nothing race to the finish. The trailing hesh-ke, seeing this, let out a chorus of war cries and followed it with a fusillade of rifle fire. The racing leaders flailed the sides of their ponies and pushed even harder.

It became a race between the trio and seven bucks up ahead. The remaining hesh-ke broke off their rear attack and turned back to harass the column.

Ree eased up on the reins, letting his mount go at its own gait. He raised his Winchester and let go a shot. It missed. He fired again. Another miss. The pounding ride made accuracy a near impossibility. The red horsemen were drawing farther ahead, lengthening the distance between them and the three whites.

Jacob saw the hostiles draw ahead. He had seen the breed trying to bring down one of them and his shots going wild. Hung low, belly buried in a saddle horn, no man could get off a decent shot. The skinner knew this and also what he had to do about it. Jacob slowed his mount. Shouldering the Spencer solid against his arm, Jacob centered the piece on a tail-end rider. Ignoring slugs thrown back at him, he squeezed the trigger.

A hit. The last rider buckled over and tumbled off into the dust. The others were too intent now on reaching the outcropping to notice their loss. They rode a straight line for the rocks. They concentrated their fire on Jacob.

Ree and the non-com did not see the slug hit home. Twisting around, they saw Jacob flinch once then sit back, straight and erect. He levered his piece then put its steel-shod butt to shoulder again. Ree tried to wave him down. The Indians were returning his lead assault. Jacob ignored Ree's warning. He fired and missed. Cursing the wind, he levered quick, braced, and fired again.

Two shots hit home simultaneously. The first splattered against the last Indian in line. It flung him out of his saddle. The other slammed into Jacob. The force knocked off his flop hat and smashed the Spencer out of his arms. The leather-tough teamster swayed back then slumped over his horse's mane, arms hanging limp at his side.

Flaherty's first instinct was to break off the run and attend to his fallen comrade, but Jacob was managing to stay in the saddle despite the blood spreading across his front side. Flaherty looked to Ree for an indication of what to do. The breed just spun around and urged his pony faster.

The sergeant went to Ree's side, a leg all but brushing up against him. "What about Jacob? He looks hurt bad."

"We can't stop now," Ree shouted back, "He'll have to make it on his own."

Behind the pair, Jacob's trained cavalry gray was keeping pace, tailing the other two army brutes by only a few yards. Jacob was semi-conscious, aware he was dying and not too slowly. The first bullet had hit him center, knocking out his wind, dulling his senses. Only instinct and a primeval sense of survival kept him locked in place. The second shot had sealed his fate. Now he clung to his bouncing, jarring horse and hoped to make the rocks in time.

The distance to the rocks was closing rapidly. All of the hesh-ke behind the outriders had dropped back before the race began. Now Ree could hear gunfire coming from the column. The Apaches were just about to the rocks. It was obvious the three points could not reach the embattlement first. The five remaining Apaches were bunching in tight, cutting between boulders, slowing. In unison, they arose from their low profile. One started to swing down out of the saddle, celebrating success prematurely - and finding death instead.

It was the option Ree had prayed for. Together, Ree and Sergeant Flaherty had slowed their own pace; just enough to steady braced rifle-arms.

Carbine and Winchester exploded as one and then repeated as the first shots hit flesh and bone.

An Indian pony collapsed, its rider sent sailing into a pile of rocks. Another painted mount reared up, its rider sliding off behind a smear of blood. The wounded pony buckled under, falling on the crippled warrior. The other Apaches wheeled around and returned fire, but found instead a concentrated barrage of rifle fire lacing their ranks. Another warrior kissed a slug and screamed out his last war cry. The two remaining braves leapt off their skittish mounts and danced over the rocks. One stopped long enough for a steadied shot at the pair bearing down on him. Orange blossomed out the end of his Maynard and Ree felt a bullet split the air past his nose as the lithe Indian was limped into the rocks, disappearing with his surviving partner.

Seconds later, Bannon and the non-com were to the rocks. They jumped off their jaded mounts and scurried one way then the other into the rocks. Jacob's gray sided up to the other two, its rider still slack in the saddle.

Ree was racing through the rocks, aware of Flaherty off to his right, of the column coming up quickly, of two riflemen waiting up ahead. Somewhere in the back of his mind, he registered the strangely soft, padding rhythm of his desert boots slapping leather against rock. Nothing else. Silence overcame the pair but for a moment.

A shot rang out, sending Flaherty diving for cover. Its echo bounced off the rocks, somewhere to the right of the non-com. One for the sergeant. Where was Bannon's man?

He had been limping, one of them. Perhaps he was lying in ambush close by. The breed leapt over a clump of dead brush and straight into the rifle barrel pocking out a shallow depression in the ground.

Orange-yellow flame flashed out at Ree, burning his side. Acid smoke filled his lungs, choking his breath away. He staggered back, rubbery legs giving way. Instinctively, his trigger finger jerked down hard. Two shells hit the prone figure at his feet. Sage came crashing down on his back and Ree was staring up at cloudless blue growing dim around him.

Ree had no idea how long he laid there. He was vaguely aware of a burning sensation against his left side - a wet feeling lay on his skin there. His left arm felt as if it had been burnt raw by the desert sun. He touched it only to jerk his head away at the pain. Flaherty was calling out to him. Close by. Ree looked back at the horses. The column was still a minute or so away. He must have been unconscious for only a few seconds. Sucking in a mouthful of dust and rank air, Ree bent double and raced for a huge boulder between the sergeant and himself.

Flaherty had tumbled into a shallow bowl of rock; his hand waving at Ree as he closed ground toward it. "Keep down," the non-com warned, "He's in those rocks up there." A screaming slug cut off his words. The spent bullet ricocheted off two boulders before hitting the sergeant. "I'm hit!" came an anguished voice - then silence.

Bannon lay in the dirt, sucking in the ground's hot breath. His head was pounding. The stinging sensation was still throbbing but the pain was a dull irritation now.

The remaining Apache, burrowed into a sheltering camouflage of rock and sage, could hold up the entire column. Jacob was hurt, probably dying back there. Now Sergeant Flaherty was, for all practical purposes, pinned down and helpless. It was up to Bannon alone.

The breed lay against a flat-sided slab of rock. Behind him lay an open stretch to his last kill. Up ahead, a jumble of rocks and he didn't know what beyond.

The shot that had hit the sergeant came from that direction. Exactly where, Ree didn't know. It was a tangle of up-thrust basalt formations laced generously with mesquite and sage. The sniper could be nestled into one of a hundred tiny holes and crevices. A troop of infantry couldn't smoke him out in a month.

Ree's eyes, blinking out stinging dust and reflecting sunlight, gauged the distance from his cover to those rocks. It was too far to run without cover. Any frontal approach was pure suicide. Wiggling back like a mouse in a hole, Bannon backed up several feet and wormed around the back side of his sheltering rock. He saw steep granite incline to a thicket of mesquite trees. There! From that vantage point, the breed might be able to turn the tables and effectively pin down the red man while the column passed.

Without waiting to judge logic or sense of it, Ree was on his feet, legs pumping him in one last desperate dash for the trees - exposed. He scrambled up the first slab of rock, leaping from the top of one boulder to another. Like a ballerina, he was hopping from left to right. His arms were outstretched, balancing his rush. He slipped, his legs sliding down the side of a smooth rock, slamming him down into the rock pile ... and saving his life. A shot, followed by the high-pitched whine of a Springfield, ripped off a chunk of stone and spit it in his face.

Staked on the rock, Ree flexed his legs for broken bones. As none were found, he fought to regain his balance again. Ree knew there would be a few seconds before the sniper could shove another shell into the breech of his weapon and fire again. Seconds that could save his life. Clutching his piece tightly, the breed scrambled up the loose granite slope and reached the trees. Just in time to duck another shot which chipped a mesquite trunk in his face.

Belly-heaving, mind-spinning, Ree wormed back over the crest of the point and buried his cheek in the dirt. The sound of army carbines and Apache yipping was bearing down on top of them. It would be only seconds before the column was there - and the sniper remained.

Ree sucked in more air to steady his pounding chest. Poking an eye over the crest, the breed looked down on the rocks where the sniper lay hidden. There was no sign of the man. Flaherty hadn't made a sound since being hit. Ree didn't know if he was alive or dead. Ree could see Dunville leading his command. The Apaches had fallen back as the trail began to rise. Now they were directly behind the troop, nipping away at the drag line. Dunville had said he wouldn't stop. If Ree managed to delay the sniper, there would still be a pack of hesh-ke wolves baying for his blood once the column passed.

As his mind tossed and turned, Ree's squinting eyes were scanning the rocks watching for any kind of movement - a mistake to indicate any sign of the sniper. It came more easily and out of place than Bannon expected. A flash of brown wiped past a cut in two rocks far from the sniper's lair. Close to where the sergeant lay. Trigger-finger ready; Ree's eyes jumped ahead to gauge where the Indian, stealthy as a panther, might be seen again. He guessed right. A second later, the figure slipped past a low-slung slab of granite. Ree fired. The shadow ducked out of sight. That moment, another shot rang out, and yet another.

"I got him," A voice shouted. "Bannon, I got him."

Instantaneously, Ree was off the bank, careening down over the rocks. He forced his sore, stiffening muscles into movement. He danced over the long, stony escarpment and ran around the rocks that hid the Indian.

Sergeant Flaherty was still lying in his stone bowl several yards away. The barrel of his stubby carbine curled gray smoke. At Bannon's feet, the last of the Apache hesh-ke to make the rocks, lay dying. He was coughing up his own blood and moaning a death chant.

"Are you hurt bad?" Ree asked the sergeant, his eyes glued on the wounded brave.

"Not bad enough I can't ride," Flaherty answered in a gravel-voiced growl. The yellow non-com's strip on his left leg was red with blood. Climbing to his unsteady feet, the sergeant used his rifle as a crutch and turned back to the horses. The column was on them then, the lieutenant waving as they galloped by. Behind their dust, the hesh-ke followed at a close distance. Ree spun around and ended the warrior's death chant. He grabbed one of the sergeant's arms and moved him hurriedly along. Dunville had changed his mind. A squad of troopers headed by the corporal remained behind to cover the trio. The troopers quickly dismounted and formed a tight skirmish line.

The Apache riders, instead of a direct, front-line attack, turned their ponies in a flanking movement and swept around the far side of the rocks, effectively out of range.

"What the hell," shouted the corporal, "now them yellow bastards won't fight!"

"Give them time, sonny," Sergeant Flaherty remarked. "They'll be back, with a hell of a lot more of their own kind." He turned to Ree who was bandaging old Jacob. The old man was pale and breathing slowly.

"Is he going to make it?" Flaherty asked, between clenched teeth.

Ree shook his head slowly back and forth. Jacob had remained intact in the saddle. When the breed slung his slack form off, the spread of blood over saddle and blanket spelled out death. If the old skinner didn't get medical attention now, he would surely die within the hour.

The rear-guard squad, under command once again of the growling sergeant, moved out at a fast clip. More hesh-ke were visible by their ominous dust cloud. The trooper's hard ride brought them up to the column's tail in minutes. They were halfway up the mountainous trial.

The eroded summit trail was more than a wild burro track but less than most had hoped for. Ancient runoffs had chiseled deep grooves across it. Rocky debris was spread everywhere. Eli hugged the jagged wall of rock rising up on one side. The pockmarked roadway narrowed down until the Concord was scraping paint off its polished ornamental side. On the other side, the trail fell off into empty space, a drop of more than a hundred feet. Harness-jingling teams fought for solid footing on the rocky trail and Eli wished to hell he'd strapped on mules before leaving San Lacita. Small rocks were crushed under the wide iron tires. Larger ones jolted and jarred the coach. Ahead and behind the coach, troopers scanned overhanging rocks for snipers and cradled carbines for comfort.

Lieutenant Dunville led the column with sheriff Courtough at his side. Behind the pair, the groaning Concord could be heard along with Eli's continuous coaxing flow of verbiage.

"You ask me, Lieutenant, that breed's got us on a wild goose chase," Jud Courtough complained, "ain't so sure this rut's going to lead us anywhere but into more trouble."

The officer studied his companion with intent eyes. He had sensed at once the animosity felt between Bannon and Courtough. A fire of hatred he dare not let grow. He wasn't as concerned with the breed as he was with the short-tempered lawman. "Right now, Bannon's the only one who has a solid suggestion to go on," Dunville said, "and it just might save some lives. Yours included. That's worth taking a chance on."

The sheriff wasn't buying the officer's line. He muttered something under breath and then cursed the wind.

Lieutenant Dunville drew rein, slowing the column a bit. The sheriff looked over, surprised at the slowdown. "Sheriff Courtough," The officer began, "I don't know what is going on between you two. Right now, I don't care. As long as you're a part of this unit, you'll take orders from me and keep your personal concerns to yourself. If you have a beef with that man, settle it in Santa Fe but not until then. Do I make myself clear?"

"Look, Lieutenant, I got jurisdiction in..."

"Courtough, right now you've got no jurisdiction anywhere."

Silence fell between the two men. Behind them, the troop moved restless in the saddle, anxious to make the top and more steady ground. Eli yelled at the officer to move out.

With a mask of contempt, Jud Courtough spurred his mount into a gallop and moved ahead of the column. Dunville waved the line forward and the procession was moving quickly once more.

Behind the column with the rear-guard squad, Ree and Flaherty were slowly moving their way up the trail, eating dust and watching for the hesh-ke to follow. None came. The small party of warriors whirled and raced back and forth on the valley flats below them. They never ventured up the trail to within gunshot range. Across the flat tableau of sand and rock, the dust cloud was very close. Tiny dots were distinguishable there.

"You figure they'll come up this trail to cut us off before we get very far?" the sergeant asked Ree.

Bannon only shook his head and pointed with his rifle at the neighboring cliff sides around them. "There's a dozen or so trails leading to the summit just like this one. The hesh-ke probably know every one of them. They'd have us cut off minutes after that main party gets here. Only chance we got is to fort-up and hope we can hold them off. There's no other choice as I see it."

Sergeant Flaherty spat into the dust and cursed under breath. "Damn it, man, a fort-up isn't the way to fight them red devils. It's a rigged parlay. We were trained to fight by tactics and superior firepower. Out in the open, where we have the advantage … on our terms."

Bannon didn't indulge the outburst. His voice was settled and calm as he spoke. "Sergeant, we are fighting the Apache on our own terms. They'd like nothing better than to catch this troop spread out across the mesa without cover or ground to move. It'd be a massacre for sure. You know as well as I do that the Apache don't like a fixed fight. They aren't likely to wait us out for any length of time. They must know the cavalry from Camp Puerco and Fort Union are starting their sweep back up from the border. That means they'll be in the vicinity, heading for Santa Fe in a couple of days. Gunfire would draw them sure. Sergeant, believe me, if they want us bad enough, and they do, they'll hit us soon. But it'll be against a stone fort - on our terms."

Sergeant Flaherty tilted his campaign hat farther down over his eyes. "Guess you got a point, Bannon, but it still boils my blood to think of running all this way, fort-up or not."

Lieutenant Dunville reached the mesa's top moments after the sheriff. A steady breeze stirred the junipers and scrub brush lining the edge. Soft grama grass was everywhere. Courtough was sitting on a rock smoking as the first squad fanned out to set up a perimeter defense. There was no sign yet of the hesh-ke on top of the mountain.

Eli let the team pull the coach on the last stretch at their own gait. They were heaving and blowing when he reined back for a desperately needed rest.

Dunville rode over. "Driver, we can't stop here."

Eli Dunn, badly fatigued and strained by the treacherous haul up the mountainside, would hear none of it. "Damnit, Lieutenant, unless you want to carry them boys of yours all by your lonesome, these horses of mine are going to get a rest. They'll never make it to Santa Fe otherwise."

Sheriff Courtough jumped into the argument. "Dunn, you old goat, you heard what the lieutenant said. He's in charge. You take your orders from him!" Jud rested his palm on the butt of his revolver for effect. The driver remained unshaken.

"Listen Sheriff, why don't you kiss the baying backside of a mountain burro, you son-of-a-..."

"That's enough," snapped Dunville, riding between Jud and the coachman, "Driver, you will move out as ordered or be replaced and put under military custody. Now that's an order!" The officer noticed Flaherty and Bannon cresting the trail. He swung around to meet the pair.

"Well done, sergeant ... Bannon," the lieutenant said as he looked with concerned eyes at the slack form of the station master strapped to his saddle. "Is he hurt badly?" he asked.

"Lost a sight of blood," Sergeant Flaherty offered. "He'll need looking after real soon if he's going to make it to Santa Fe."

"I can help him," A voice cried out behind them.

The men twisted in their saddles to see Claire climbing out of the cab and running toward them, her skirt billowing out from her legs. Ree met her before she reached Jacob. He stopped her with out-stretched arms.

"You can't help him now. We'll take care of him until we stop. There's nothing you can do right now. Go back to the others. They need you. Once we stop, we'll fix him up as good as a five dollar gold piece." Claire looked the breed straight in the face, her eyes holding his sparkling blue eyes. His eyes fell away and the girl turned back for the coach and her wounded charges.

"Where do we fort-up, Bannon?" Dunville asked, waving in his perimeter guards.

"There's a place not far from here. Let's go!" Ree swung up into the saddle. All eyes were on him; some trusting, some cautious, some hateful, but all were following him as he spurred his jaded mount once more into a gallop across the stone plateau.

They reached the spot Bannon had designated for a fort-up in less than ten minutes. The flat tabletop had quickly changed to that of more jagged ground making coach travel painfully slow. Flaherty grudgingly admitted to Ree that he was right about making a fort-up. The column could never have made good time across that rough cut terrain. The column picked its way through the cracks and crevices of the broken surface, making its defense practically impossible.

Ree had selected a broken arroyo which split a rising section of ground near the edge of the mesa. The cracked and split topography was probably the remains of a once active volcano cone millions of years before. The sage-studded gully was rimmed on three sides by massive basalt slabs that would provide more than adequate cover for the defenders. The basalt walls were too high and smooth to be easily scaled, the gaps between them thickly choked with brush and mesquite. There was only one easy access to the arroyo and that could be sufficiently defended.

One end of the arroyo wandered off the edge of the mesa, scarring its smooth curvature. The hesh-ke attack, when it came, would most likely come from the front and perhaps the sides. The main arroyo and its feeder gullies were large enough to shelter the troops and their mounts, but not the coach. As the soldiers began filing into the fortification and the wounded were gingerly taken out of the cab, Ree dismounted and approached the sullen coachmen. He told Dunn to remove the teams and leave the Concord out of the line of fire. The coach would have to stay outside the defenses. There was no room inside.

Eli Dunn threw a fit. "What the hell do you mean, leave it outside," He exploded, "I ain't so old I can't see a place for it upside that boulder over there."

"It won't fit."

"Says you. Listen, Bannon, you got us here. I reckon we owe you some thanks for that … but no one … I mean no one … is going to tell Eli Dunn that he's got to leave this here stagecoach out for those blood-hungry savages to put to the torch. I mean to park this coach inside those rocks whether you like it or not. Now move outta my way."

With that, the driver sprang up on stiffened legs, bellowed out a roar and whipped the startled teams into a flying leap forward. The Concord hit the upthrust rock, bounced a foot into the air and rattled over it as the team sent up sparks, pounding iron against rock. Eli brought the Concord up over the rock and down into the arroyo bottom with a crashing, jarring thump. Amid the swirl of dust and blowing horses, Eli stood up and saluted both breed and officer. Ree allowed himself a smile and moved out to scout the defense line. Eli Dunn, that pigheaded, stubborn old gaffer would be one hell of an asset when trouble arrived … and that would be very soon.

Chapter Eighteen

It had been more than an hour since they reached the arroyo. Lieutenant Dunville, accompanied by Bannon, walked the perimeter line and assigned pickets to guard the stock. A curl of smoke from the enlisted men's coffee fire lifted straight up. There was not a breath of wind anywhere. No need to hide the fire's smoke. Everyone knew the Apache were close by. Troopers sipped coffee, cursed the heat and waited for the attack they knew would come.

Lieutenant Dunville had noticed Ree's waist wound when they first unhorsed. He suggested the breed attend to it promptly. Bannon waved the inquiry aside. Now Dunville realized the bleeding had stopped at least temporarily. The two men stopped by the rear defense line. "That may be a flesh wound, Bannon," the Lieutenant began, "but you best take care of it. It could get infected quite easily. Gangrene can kill just as sure as an Apache ironwood arrow or a slug."

"Bleedings stopped...it'll take care of itself," Ree answered with a shrug of shoulders.

"Nevertheless I suggest you watch it. Everyone here is depending on you. Especially that girl, I would imagine."

Outside the busy perimeter line, the heat-wrinkled terrain looked quiet and peaceful, vacant of any sign of life. Neither Ree nor the lieutenant believed it. Both knew looks said one thing but experience cautioned something else. An attack could come at anytime from any direction. Since the fortification's steep sides needed fewer guards, most of the troopers were in front where it was lower and more vulnerable to attack. Still Dunville worried about an Apache favorite tactic, the flanking sweep. He and the breed discussed adjusting the troopers' positions, but decided to leave them as is. The officer separated to complete his tour.

Ree surveyed the front defense line from his position near the rear of the arroyo.

What worried him most was its flatness. The arroyo was shallow there and the approach to it, relatively level. The Concord had been parked back in a front curve of the arroyo wings, yet it was the highest level up front. Flaherty had already positioned one scout trooper on top the coach, behind a barricade of luggage. His trail-worn eyes would have to see more than the others. He would be the early warning signal that just might save a lot of soldiers' lives.

Even more worrisome to Bannon were the loosely scattered boulders and heavy matting of ocotillo and chaparral that laced the bottom of the flanking malpaís.

It would prevent a mounted attack there but would also provide more than adequate cover for Apaches sneaking up on foot. They might be able to accent the flanks undetected. Covering fire from their ranks could conceivably prevent troopers from returning fire from a frontal assault.

Sliding off his stone rest, Ree went past the makeshift corral. The corporal was with the stock, supervising their care. Little water remained for the animals, and no forage. Men and animals stood with bowed heads and sweated profusely.

Ree moved up to the edge of the high table land and nestled in a sunburnt curvature of rock and soapweed. He trained his watchful eyes out across the front perimeter. A slight breeze picked up but only lifted more heat off the rocks. Both Sharps and Winchester lay at Bannon's feet. With hat brim tilted deep down, Ree's mind wandered back to Santa Fe … then to the Sangre de Cristo Mountains and the hunting he'd done there.

"The Lieutenant said you were wounded! Why didn't you tell me?"

Ree looked up, taken off guard. The swaying skirt of Claire approached. The girl knelt down beside him, reaching out to examine his bloody waist.

Ree's calloused hand grabbed the girl's.

"Oh, stop it!" Claire snapped. She unlocked Bannon's grip and tore away the dirty rag of a shirt above his handcrafted gun belt. Ree sat still, his eyes locked on Claire's face as she worked. She had brought over a canteen which she sprinkled over a clean cloth and then gingerly dabbed away the crusted blood.

"It's only a flesh wound," Ree protested.

"I can see that," Claire said, "but it still needs to be cleaned so you don't get an infection."

"Well, I don't think…"

The girl looked up, her eyes defensive and alert. "Well, what? Are you some sort of shaman that you're immune to blood poisoning? Don't be that way. I'm only trying to help."

"The others need looking after…not me. I can take care of myself."

"Oh, be still," Claire snapped in a motherly tone of voice.

Ree began to grumble but stopped when he caught a flash of the girl's terse stare.

Claire finished cleaning the wound in silence. She removed a strip of cloth from her vest pocket and wrapped it around the breed's waist, under his tattered shirt. When Ree didn't bring his arms up quickly enough, Claire pushed them up. Bannon sat back and let her work. She was the first woman he had let handle him like that. If Claire had looked up she might have noticed the faint trace of a smile cross his face.

Claire finished her work. She wiped her brow and sat back, letting out a sigh of exhaustion. "That'll keep you until we reach Santa Fe."

"You've got confidence, I'll allow you that. I've never met someone like you."

"You sound like I'm the first woman you've ever encountered. You must have had a woman in your life before."

Ree said nothing.

"I don't want to pry…"

"But you will anyway."

"I'm just saying…"

"No."

"No?"

"I've hunted and trapped and done odd jobs. I've never had time to settle down and have a…"

"That's too bad, Ree. A man like you needs someone in his life. Someone to take care of you…"

"I don't…"

"Everyone needs someone in their life."

Ree shrugged his shoulders. "You've been talking to old Jacob too much. He'd tell you it's springtime weather now and waters aplenty if that's what he thinks you'd want to hear. He's the eternal optimist."

Claire's face turned cold.

"What's wrong?" Ree asked.

"I'm sorry Ree, Jacob's dead."

Ree stared at the girl. Claire let out a crestfallen sigh and her shoulders fell. All the pressure of the harrowing ride and attack surfaced, intense and overpowering. Claire looked exhausted and scared - *like a frightened little girl in need of a father*, Ree thought.

Ree was lost for words. He wanted to praise the old man he had grown to respect and admire. He couldn't. He wanted to tell Claire what Jacob represented to him, more than a trail companion and a fighting comrade. He still couldn't. It wasn't in him. Neither his nature nor culture could find the well from which to draw out the right words. He remained silent and troubled.

"I think I loved him," Claire said, "like a daughter loves her father. Even in this short a time."

Ree's eyes said he understood. Claire managed a weak smile, her first for a long time. The air buzzed with insects but neither Ree nor the girl unlocked eyes off one another. Beads of sweat formed and ran down familiar creases on both faces. The spell faded away. Claire looked back at the soldiers lining the stone defenses. "Have you ever been to Santa Fe?" she asked the breed.

"Couple of times. For a little while. It's a nice place. Man could get into a rut there and maybe even like it, I reckon."

"Even a man like you?" Claire asked, without hesitation.

Ree smiled for a moment. "Don't know. Maybe … in time."

"I love it especially in the winter," Claire said, "When the Sandias are covered with snow and all look so pretty."

Ree shook his head. "Too cold then!"

"Not during the day. Especially if the sun is out. It can get warm in the afternoons. I've gone shopping for our supper many a time during the winter months and only worn a shawl."

"For you and your father."

"That's right. My mother died when I was young. I have no brothers and sisters. How did you know?"

"Didn't! I guessed it. There's a lot of your father in you."

"You're a strange man, Ree Bannon, I wish I could understand you,"

"Don't try."

"Why not'? Why must you be so different? My father was just like you are until he met my mother."

"And now I've met you. Is that what you mean?"

The girl wasn't sure how to reply to Ree's frankness. "I'm not sure if I should be insulted or not. I wasn't comparing us, really, I…"

"No offense meant," The breed assured her, "You're a remarkable lady. I respect you."

"You and I are a lot alike."

"I don't think…"

"No, we are," Claire insisted. "I'm sure you can't see it now but we are."

"You're a strange woman, Claire LeFonte Martinez…a strange woman, indeed."

Claire smiled at Ree. He smiled back at her. Their eyes spoke in hushed tones that even the wind could not hear.

Claire blushed at her own boldness and looked away, "Will they come soon?" Her eyes scanned the stone stockade they were in.

"Yep, before dark if I guess them right. They're out there right now…watching us and waiting."

"For what?"

"The right time…their right time... It doesn't pay to second-guess the Apache. They don't think like whites do."

"Giving advice again, Bannon?" A voice cut in, hard and cold.

Claire spun around in surprise, caught off guard. Jud Courtough was standing a few feet away. He'd come down from around several large obtrusive boulders. He had surprised the girl but not the breed. Bannon had heard someone approaching moments before. He guessed it to be the sheriff. Ree had caught the looks and cutting stares Courtough had bombarded him with since their first encounter back in Defiance. His outburst back at the narrow canyon entrance hadn't gone unforgotten either. If Jud hadn't suspected by now that Ree was also after the map, he was a lot more stupid than Bannon thought.

"What's your business, Courtough?" Ree asked calmly.

"You."

"Meaning what?"

"I seen you talking to the girl before. Wouldn't have been about a map, now would it?"

No response.

"You know what map I'm talking about. The one that was taken off a dead miner outside of San Lacita a few days back. I think you have that map. I'm guessing you got it from Miss LeFonte here. By my authority as marshal of San Lacita, I'm claiming it. That map is the property of the territory until someone can lay a rightful claim to it. So hand it over!"

Claire was incensed. "Just what do you mean butting in here with that kind of accusation? I feel like…"

"No!" Ree cautioned her, "Let him go jawboning. Those are empty words. They mean nothing."

"Nothing, huh? I seen you two jabbering nonstop back there. I'm not stupid. You had more than enough time to exchange goods. Don't tell me you were just talking weather."

"What we were discussing doesn't concern you, sheriff," Ree said in a firm voice.

"Are you going to hand it over or not?" Jud demanded to know.

"No!" Ree said.

Claire watched the sheriff intently as Jud sized up the breed.

Ree still cradled the Winchester on his lap. His hand lay across its trigger guard, fingers loose but ready. Courtough wasn't foolish enough to miss the signs. Ree could tell he hadn't, and he knew the odds. The lawman backed off, but not without a last stab.

"Bannon, there's something about you that don't set right. I've had a feeling stuck in my craw since I met up with you back in Defiance. I know you from someplace...or heard of you maybe. Now I mean to find out what it is. When we get to Santa Fe, I'm placing you under arrest for holding stolen property. You stand warned!" Jud turned and strutted down the incline.

Claire watched him leave with fire in her eyes. "What right did he have coming here like that? I'm of a mind to tell the lieutenant..."

"Tell him what? That the sheriff has bad manners? That he threatened me? Don't bother. Courtough didn't do a thing that would involve the military. Besides, young Dunville's got enough troubles on his mind for ten officers." Ree dropped his head to chest, eyes staring down at his worn, dirty boots. "Let it be. Forget that the sheriff even came over."

"I don't understand you. You let him go on like that. And you didn't say anything to defend yourself."

"What's to defend? I do have the map. Besides, I don't fight well by arguing. So why try? There's another language he understands much better. So do I. If we ever fight, it won't be with words."

Claire was exasperated. "I thought you weren't like all the rest; the gunfighters, the drifters, all those wanderers who pass through Santa Fe in search of someplace better." Claire's face hardened. "Now I don't know if you are different than any of them." She arose, scooping up her things as she did.

Ree cast his somber eyes up at the girl. Her dark eyes, under a knit brow, stared back down on him. Her eyes spoke of disappointment. His said nothing. Claire read him and turned away.

The breed watched her go. Sundown was close. Ree sat motionless for a few minutes; watching, listening, waiting. He cautiously arose on silent feet and ambled down toward the stock and his hobbled mustang. The pony had worn badly racing to the rock enclosure. Ree wanted to feed and water him. There were a few forage scraps in his saddle bag. The breed was halfway to the stock when the Apaches made their move.

It didn't seem like a concentrated attack at first - just a sudden, withering blast of rifle fire and rush of ponies and footmen charging the fort. The lookout hadn't seen a thing before the first volley sent him diving for cover. Spilling off both sides of the front line attackers, shadowy forms darted through rocks and thick chaparral, running in short zigzag sprints. A few of the flankers fired shots, but most ducked and rushed closer before disappearing out of sight.

The attackers charged at a dead run. Dunville held back fire and let them come. Bullets screamed off rocks and boulders, whining into the air as wounded ricochets. Unchallenged, the Apaches poured over rocks and brush, dashing straight at the defender's line. At near point-blank range, Dunville's men opened fire.

The first volley slammed into many of the front line Apaches and brought scores down. As quickly as they fell amid dying and wounded ponies, other warriors filled in their depleted ranks, carrying the attack forward. Another volley laced the bloodied ranks and still the wave of yipping hesh-ke surged closer; a red tide of death sweeping over everything in its path.

Then the trooper's fire broke cadence, every man firing at anything moving, desperately trying to smash the human tide before it flooded over their defense line. Screams of dying animals mixed with human voices. The air was thick with choking dust of swirling forms and gun powder. A trooper stationed on top the Concord tumbled off the rig, an arrow through his neck. Another soldier climbed out of his rifle pit to help. He caught a slug in one leg. Crawling on hands and knees, he struggled to the rig before collapsing unconscious.

Dunville moved behind his men; snapfiring, yelling encouragement and shouting instructions. His voice rang out loud and strong above the din of battle. Troopers heard and responded. The officer dove into a shallow rifle pit alongside the sergeant, firing as he moved. The red tide was topping the perimeter line when it broke apart. One moment the hostiles were on top of the line; the next they were stumbling back, grabbing dead and wounded as they fled.

A joyous shout went up from the defender's ranks. One young soldier jumped out of his rifle pit, snap-firing his carbine at the retreating Indians. His pit partner joined him, shouting and laughing.

"Get down, you two!" Dunville yelled, "That's an order!"

Before the words were out of the officer's mouth, flanking snipers opened fire. One soldier caught a slug in his face, the back of his head flying off in a flash of blood and bone. His companion; too intoxicated by the killing and drunk at the prospect of victory, kept on firing, ignorant of their danger. Dunville yelled again. No good.

Bullets chipped the ground at his feet. Flaherty was out of his pit, racing toward the trooper. Another bullet slammed home. The trooper doubled over, clutching his stomach. Flaherty leapt over the dead soldier and grabbed the wounded man around his waist. Another bullet ricocheted off a stone at his foot and hit the trooper. He was dead before the non-com got him to shelter.

Flanking sniper fire laced the arroyo and tore great chunks of white ash off the parked Concord. Eli spat out curses like great breaths of fire, watching his beloved rig being methodically chewed to pieces. He realized the Apaches were not conserving their ammunition as they usually did. He could only reason they had enough to pop away at his rig and still launch another attack. Apache riflemen were now settled into strategic positions on both sides of the frontal perimeter. Their fire kept all heads below ground level, effectively cutting off most chances of spotting another buildup.

Lieutenant Dunville lay back against the dirt wall and reloaded his service revolver. Flaherty, beside him, did a flash inventory of his squads and estimated visible dead and wounded.

"Get me a headcount, sergeant."

"What about the Apaches, Sir?"

"They'll know soon enough, sergeant; I want to know right now."

The voices rolled in; tired and pained. Often there was silence where there should have been a response. Silence that read six dead and two dying; then four more wounded increased the total. Heavy losses in one attack and Dunville knew more were to come.

Ree Bannon had been by the stock when the attack began. He had made it to a front corner position before getting pinned down by the riptide of lead. He joined Jud Courtough and the two coachmen there. Claire had been back by the pit where old Jacob and the wounded were kept. As the attack collapsed and sniping picked up, Ree sprinted back toward the girl's shelter. He slid into the depression, his feet sending up a swirl of dust. Propping himself up ever so slightly, he quickly surveyed the scene and saw no one was hurt during the attack. Several of the wounded gripped revolvers and lay against the slope, guarding their companions. Claire's eyes met his and showed welcome relief. The sniping persisted overhead, making everyone edgy.

"Did we hurt them?" Claire asked.

"Can't tell for sure. They took most of their dead and wounded away."

"Will they be back?"

Ree's face showed resignation, "Yeah, We must have hurt them but they'll be back with artillery flanking their run. They'll try to pin us down while others charge. It's gonna be very hard to stop them."

Claire was relieved at the honesty of Ree's answer. She already knew what the answer had to be. She had watched the charge collapse and the foolish troopers fall prey to the Pino Alto snipers.

"I'm sorry I got angry at you back there. Please forgive me?" she said in a soft voice.

"Can't remember a thing," Ree returned. Ree realized the smiles were coming easier now. He felt warmth whenever he was near the girl. She was different from the rest. The first real lady he had ever known. It gave him a good feeling … and that worried him.

On both sides of the fort, troopers lay in trenches barely a foot deep, surrounded by dingy green sagebrush. There was enough shelter from sniper fire but not enough cover if they had to stand the crest against an attack. Gradually the sniper fire died down. There were a few random shots and then uneasy silence returned. It seemed an alien sound to their gunshot-battered ears.

Ree wormed over the back side of the depression.

"Where are you going?" Claire asked.

"I'll be back," he said, then disappeared over the top. All Claire could hear was the shuffle of his boots, carrying him away.

The girl had barely begun to change dressings on several of the wounded when she saw Eli and John Montgomery wriggling past. They waved a greeting and kept crawling along, heading for the arroyo's backside.

Claire watched them go; two old men clutching heavy weapons, crawling faster than most men half their age. She considered her own father, the Don, and how he must be worried. Her stage was so long overdue and he had certainly heard the rumors of rampaging hesh-ke. There wouldn't be any word or help from the Army at Camp Puerco. He must be pacing their sitting room floor right now, worried sick. Her heart then turned to Ree Bannon. The gazes he gave her. The feelings she got when he looked at her that way. It was a funny feeling, it was different with Ree. Her body felt strong with desire when he was around. Claire's gaze moved across the top of her pit and came to rest on none other than the smile of Ree Bannon himself, just cresting the slope.

"You're back," she said in surprise.

"You worried?" Ree asked.

"Well, yes, I mean no. I just thought … well, where did you go?"

A canteen landed on the girl's lap. Claire's eyes lit up. "Oh, water, where did you get it?"

"Off a couple of mounts. Their owners are dead. Use it sparingly with the wounded. It does funny things to a hurt man in this heat - they get crazy for more." Ree rolled over to watch the stagehands complete their crawl to the back of the fort and then slid down the side of the depression.

"Do you still have your revolver?" he asked the girl.

"Yes, I've got it handy."

"Good. Keep it close just in case. Now I've got to go."

"Ree?"

"Yeah?"

"If we get out of this alive … I mean when we're back in Santa Fe, I want you to meet my father. I think he would like you."

"Sure, if we get back."

The girl's voice hardened. "I mean it, Ree, when we get back…"

Ree looked at Claire, his eyes holding hers. She was serious, her eyes wanting. Anything he said would have been wrong right then - for him and for her. He touched fingertip to hat brim, then turned and was gone over the edge.

Eli Dunn and John Montgomery were fed up with the waiting and even more with the frustration of having to see their rig being slowly reduced to kindling. By the time the sniping had ceased, the Apaches had blasted apart the brake lever, a door, a wippletree attachment and parts of the exposed wagon tongue. The coachmen would have one hell of a time rigging their team for the long pull home. Disgruntled, they jumped at the lieutenant's suggestion they relieve the troopers guarding the arroyo's backside. Though the air was no better there, they were alone and off the front line.

Dunn was first to see the breed slipping back toward them. He carried his Sharps buffalo gun in his hand. The Winchester was strapped to his back. Eli sized up the man as a determined and well-armed fighter.

It happened so quickly, Eli wasn't sure what occurred in what sequence. Bannon was inching towards them, being careful not to expose his backside to sniper fire. His belly was flat on the ground when, without warning, he was up on one knee, throwing the Sharps to his shoulder. The rifle flashed and sent a slug screaming past Eli's head. The driver spun around to see a painted Apache, only feet away. His upraised axe was coming down fast. John Montgomery had started yelling, blazing away at the mesa's edge. The dying warrior collapsed over Dunn, his axe skipping down the driver's face before sinking into his chest.

Pain shot through Eli's body, numbing him. Instinctively he made a border shift, switching gun hands and flinging the broken body off. His eyes watered and he couldn't see properly. He tried to rise but couldn't. More Apaches were slithering over the edge of the rocks, firing at the pair. Bullets sang by Eli's head. He tried to rise again but fell back on rubbery legs. Montgomery had moved away, edging toward the perimeter rocks. Dunn could see at least two or three bodies, sprawled in deathly poses, behind his partner.

Ree appeared by the driver, urging him to seek cover. Eli cursed him off, firing at darting brown forms that swarmed over the perimeter rocks. Pain mounted inside, doubling him over. Gathering a burst of energy, Dunn staggered to his feet and stumbled after the breed, firing at figures now turning back, slipping over the edge, and disappearing.

Eli never saw his partner die. Stumbling forward, he kicked up against something by the perimeter line. Looking down through sweat-blinded eyes, he found John Montgomery lying in a space between two boulders. The guard was cradled there as if he were asleep. When Eli turned him over, he saw the tiny bloodless hole in his partner's shirt just below the left breast. There was a calm, satisfied look on his face. He looked like he knew he had stopped the attack and perhaps saved the troop and themselves. The driver slumped down against a boulder, numbing shock running the length of his body. He sat there for a long time, stunned, and sick with grief.

Ree Bannon returned, his Winchester still smoking. The breed bent over Montgomery's still form. He looked at the driver. A mute expression of pain and suffering lay bare on the man's face. Weariness ran the length of his wrinkled forehead and sagging chin. Around them, troopers were coming back from the rear line, mumbling among themselves. The attack had been beaten back. The guard was the only casualty, but the soldiers were all the more uneasy. Lieutenant Dunville was talking… words would not gather together for Eli digest.

"What happened?" Dunville asked the breed.

"They flanked us, Lieutenant. Came up a sheer wall of rock right by the mesa's edge. Don't ask me how. I didn't see any of them until they were right on top of us."

"How many were there?"

"Well, I counted five dead. Figure a couple more were dragged away. There must have been at least a dozen or so that hit us. They won't try it again if we mount a guard here."

The officer shook his head doubtfully. 'We're badly spread out right now. Any more men assigned back here will only weaken our frontal defenses even more."

"Lieutenant, I'm afraid you really don't have a lot of choices. The Apaches will try a probe back here again. If we don't have some troopers to stop them, the next time they might overrun that position. If they do, this troop would be finished in a matter of minutes."

"Alright, Bannon, I'll assign a couple of men back here. You'll have to float, keeping a watch on the girl and back here. I can't afford to send the sergeant on that task."

"Anything you say, Lieutenant," Ree answered with a smile.

Dunville turned to his sergeant. Flaherty saluted. The non-com was confident of the breed. Together they turned and slipped back among the rocks toward the front lines.

"You saved my life, Bannon," Eli said. "I owe you."

Ree looked to the driver who was staggering to his feet. The breed extended a hand but it was waved away.

Eli growled, "You know it's funny. John always claimed he'd outlive me by a dozen years; said he'd be long retired to a ranch someplace while I'd still be skinning mules someplace."

"I'll take him back with the others." Ree offered.

"No." Eli snapped, stumbling toward his dead companion. I'll take care of him. He's my partner."

Ree turned to leave.

"Bannon!"

The breed turned back to Eli's mean eyes. "You remember what I said about the sheriff. I seen him talking to you and the girl. He's getting worse. I've been watching him. This siege is working on his mind. He means to try something right soon. I'm warning you to look out."

"Thanks for the warning, old timer," Ree said and turned away.

Just then a shot rang out. Ree spun around in time to see Eli gripping his chest and falling backwards. The breed fell to one knee. He swung his Winchester up at the mesa and powered off three rapid shots. A lone Hesh-ke toppled off the rock face and bounced to the ground.

He rushed to the driver. Eli looked up at him with dying eyes. "You're alright, breed, you're all…" Eli's eyes rolled up. Ree gently laid him down and bowed his head. Ree allowed many moments to pass.

Ree moved to the stock to check his mustang. His eyes swept the skyline. The distant hills were dark gray and lavender at dusk, the sun nearly to the horizon. Its elongated shadows stretched great distances across the mesa top. A gentle breeze brought with it the first hint of relief.

A trooper approached Bannon. "The lieutenant wants to see you… Right away!" he urged.

The officer was situated in a rifle pit near the left flank of the perimeter defense line. Flaherty and the corporal were with him. Bannon slid into the hole and dug a cigarette out of his shirt pocket. "You wanted to see me?' he said.

The officer did not look in his direction at first. He had his hat off, feeling the wind stir his thinning hair. His gaze was far away but his question straight to the point. "Bannon, I need to know when they're coming back…and where."

Ree did not hesitate. "Right soon, and probably right up front like before. Dusk is fast approaching. Hesh-ke don't know anything but to fight. You may have hurt them the first time around - and that second time back of the mesa, but they're committed now. Unless we can empty their ranks so they figure it isn't worth that high of a price. That isn't likely. I give them less than an hour and they'll be back."

"I was told Indians don't like fighting in the dark," the corporal said.

"Comanches and hesh-ke do. They're crazy … not regular Indian crazy … worse than that. They'll fight in the dark alright. Don't you mind about that."

Dunville slipped his hat back on and realized it felt very intolerable in the heat. "We've got half the patrol killed or wounded. Several horses down and the stage shot up. If the hesh-ke make another concentrated attack like their first one, we might not be able to hold them off."

"Does the lieutenant want some advice?"

Lieutenant Dunville lifted his bloodshot eyes toward the half-breed. "Such as?"

"Set up two lines of defense. When they come, you pull back with the first line. It might fool them into believing you're pulling back to reassemble your forces. If they buy that, they'll charge straight up, without hesitation. It might make them careless. You'll have a second line of artillery waiting. That might chop them up badly enough to think twice before attacking a fourth time."

Sergeant Flaherty was all ears. "It just might work, Sir," he offered.

Dunville agreed. "It's worth a try. Bannon, I want you to continue floating. Corporal Sweeny can cover the rear defenses. You stick close to the girl and the wounded. They might need a steady rifle if this plan doesn't work. The driver and guard can help…"

"They're both dead."

The lieutenant paused for a moment. "Let's move out," he said softly.

Ree touched fingertips to hat brim and was gone. *The lieutenant is finding his own,* Ree thought. *He's finding out what he can do as a man, and an Army officer under fire. He'll be alright. The lieutenant's gonna do right fine.*

Claire had finished redressing the wounded men when Bannon slipped into her pit. Two more wounded were crouched in separate corners, standing guard. The others were too hurt to hold weapons. They lay in the sand and suffered with clamped mouths - army-tough quiet.

Claire motioned the breed to move a few yards away. She seemed eager to talk. "I meant what I said before about meeting my father, Ree In fact, you could have a job on the ranch if you want it - just for the asking."

"I earn my own jobs. Thanks."

"You're still coming with us to Santa Fe, aren't you?"

Ree's face grew serious, his voice lowered, knowing what he had to say would only be misunderstood by the girl. "No, now let's be honest with one another…"

"What is it?"

"We come from different tribes, Claire. Mine is of mixed blood. You're a fine young woman. You'll be wanting a good man, a supporter; someone to give you children and a fine home. I'm not that man. I'm a drifter. I've dusted too many a trail to change now. I've never had a home or even a place to call my own - just a lot of stops here and there ... some white ... some Indian. Do you understand what I'm trying to say?"

Claire leaned forward, her eyes intent and alive. "I understand what you're saying. I don't agree. I'm of mixed blood too. My mother was a New England Yankee married to a Spanish landowner. You see we really are quite alike. Your past doesn't have to make any difference. It's how people feel inside. That's what counts."

Ree was crouched in a shaman position, in such a way he appeared to be meditating on the girl's arguments. His blue eyes were staring at the girl, but seeing beyond the two of them.

Claire noticed the sheriff watching them from his position near the front lines. "Are you sure it isn't Courtough and that map that is making you say these things?"

The breed unlocked his gaze. "That too," he admitted. "He's not going to get the map unless he kills me for it."

"No!"

Blue eyes met frightened ones. "That's the way it has to be," Ree said.

Claire lowered her eyes. She felt crushed. Ree read her mind. He felt helpless and uneasy. He wanted to tell her he still cared.

A rifle blast took him off the hook.

It smashed into luggage on top the Concord and sent a shower of splinters into the air. "They're coming!" was all the lookout could say before he was struck down, his dying voice all but drowned out by a chorus of rifle fire and Apache yelping. The hesh-ke surge rushed forward.

Dunville had done his homework. Along with ten troopers and the non-com, the officer held the front line. Behind him about ten yards, the remainder of his command lay in concealment, their rifle barrels hidden in cracks and crevasses, ready for a signal to fire.

The attack had come at dusk as Bannon predicted. In the ruts and crevices, riddled with mesquite and yucca plants, Apaches swarmed forward, firing as they ran. The flanking snipers were charging also, pitching through tall pitahaya. It was to be a full force attack.

Lieutenant Dunville could see auburn bodies gathering in the hummocks not twenty yards away. He directed his fire in that direction but with no visible effect. The swarthy forms melted into rocks only to reappear several yards closer and still laying down a tight pattern of shells.

A trooper along the line screamed in pain and fell. Flaherty only briefly eyed the man. "Now it's eleven," he muttered. Another soldier slipped quietly to the bottom of the trench. Flaherty didn't bother to count anymore.

The rush of bodies was drawing closer. Carbine fire was doing nothing to stop it. Dunville elbowed the non-com. "Let's go," he ordered. They pulled back, firing over their shoulders as they ran. The attacking Indians saw the line falling back and let out a shriek of war cries. They arose, dancing over rocks, rifles and stone axes ready for the coup. Another trooper stopped a slug and pitched into the officer's path. The others stumbled over him in their frantic dash back.

The Apaches were approaching the line. Like an army of red ants, they swept over the rifle pits, firing down into them. Two warriors leapt onto the stage and climbed on top. With certain victory in their grasp, the Apaches rushed toward the retreating soldiers.

"Fire!" Dunville screamed as he pitched into the second line trench.

A withering blast of carbine fire smashed into the Apache's front ranks. Hardened eyes peered down rifle barrels and fired at point-blank range. Bodies fell and were trampled over as more and more Indians leapt over falling comrades to press home the assault. Gaping holes appeared in the leading ranks. Still they came. They broke the line in several places, crashing into troopers with flailing hatchets and knives. It was hand-to-hand fighting at close quarters: the suicidal, fanatical hesh-ke against the organized soldiers.

Lieutenant Dunville sidestepped a mounted lancer and blew out his backside. He turned back in time to see an archer loose an arrow at him. The shaft burned past his arm, ripping open his sleeve. He fired his carbine at the brave once before it jammed. Flinging it aside, he unholstered his revolver. Another warrior, flat on the back of his pony, skimmed in front of the lieutenant. Dunville downed his mount and then the man as he fell off. He glimpsed more Apaches running toward the wounded. Shots rang out and they scattered. Ree was holding his position.

Lieutenant Dunville leapt over a pile of rocks and stumbled against the small shape of Corporal Sweeny. The man lay with his revolver still gripped tightly in his hand, his eyes wide. Off to the left, Dunville could hear Sergeant Flaherty shouting a warning. Instinctively he ducked as a lance cut past his head. The lieutenant fanned his revolver, lacing the warriors back three times and was moving again before the Indian was falling off his horse.

On and on the officer ran; dodging mounted braves, shouting encouragement, keeping the straining line intact. His eyes watered from the dust and burning acid of gun smoke. A pony clipped his shoulder and he fell, slamming into rock. Pain shot up his arm. There was blood where an arrow had torn his shirt. A rider raced by and he fired. The rider wheeled around and Flaherty blasted him. Dunville rushed back toward the line.

The firing dropped off. Swirling brown forms melted back into the night, leaving many dead behind. Peripheral sniper fire tried to cover the Apache's stumbling retreat. Dunville, bloodied and bearcat angry, wasn't about to let the hesh-ke off the hook that easily.

The officer raised his piece, shouting, "Follow me, men, after them." He rushed down from a cluster of rocks after the escaping Indians. Others quickly joined him, firing as they ran. The line of troopers rushed past the Concord laying broken and smoldering from the gunfire. Flames crackled and licked at its polished oval body. More troopers stumbled to their feet, joining the others. They pursued the bloodied warriors, showing no mercy to stragglers. After a run of twenty or so yards into the darkness, Dunville signaled a halt. "Reform the men, sergeant. I think we've taught them a lesson they won't soon forget."

"Lieutenant, listen!"

The officer cocked an ear to the muffled sound of ponies riding off. The Apaches were riding away.

"It might be a ruse, sergeant, we'll take no chances. Set up a new perimeter and tend to the wounded. We'll stay put until daylight…and only move once we've made a reconnaissance of the area."

Ree Bannon lay in his makeshift rifle pit, exhausted and sore. In front of the crude pile of last-minute-assembled rocks, lay three Apaches. The close proximity attested to the nearness of their success. On either side of his pit, another warrior lay, stopped cold in his tracks. Now the breed lay, spent and sore, sucking in sweet air and thanking the stars he was still alive. He crawled to his knees, then his feet. The ground wavered a little then became steady. He turned to see if Claire was all right. Ree hadn't gone a dozen yards before a voice stopped him cold in his tracks.

"One more step, injun, and the girl gets shot!"

Ree froze. His gun hand sank to his waist.

"Try it and you're a dead man!"

The hand stopped moving. Ree forced his strained eyes but could not spot the location of Jud's voice. Heavy cloud cover made the dust darker than usual. Ree took a step toward a large boulder, darting his eyes back and forth, hoping for a hint of the sheriff's location.

"One more step, Bannon," Courtough snarled, "just one more."

There was a pause followed by the sound of shuffling bodies. The girl spoke up. "Ree, please don't do anything foolish. He'll kill you for sure."

"Claire, are you alright?" Ree asked.

"She's alright, Bannon. For now! But she won't be unless I get that map. Now drop your gun belt."

Ree had to stall for time. He still couldn't spot the sheriff but obviously the fugitive lawman had drawn a bead on him. Lieutenant Dunville would be back in minutes. Ree couldn't risk the girl's life. He had to stall until then. "How do I know you won't kill us both after you get the map?" Ree asked.

"The gun, damnit, now drop it," Jud shouted. Courtough was not an easy man to fool. He had run the thin edge of death and danger for too long and too often not to sense a stall. The sound of a pistol being cocked seemed very loud in Ree's ear. He could hear the girl catching her breath. He could taste the fear Claire must have felt then.

"Alright, I'll give it to you," Ree said. The gun belt came off slowly and fell to the ground.

"Take it slow and easy, Breed." Jud warned. "The girl's life depends on you."

Bannon held out the map. He was now certain Jud was near a cluster of rocks and sage not more than fifteen yards away. The excellent camouflage there, along with darkness, provided more than adequate cover.

"Toss it in front of you," Jud ordered, "Then turn around and step away."

Ree did as he was told and turned, stepping forward a few feet. He could hear footfalls coming up behind him … heavy boots … alone. Courtough must have left the girl behind in the rocks. A plan quickly formed in Ree's head. When the footsteps were close, far enough from Claire to matter, Ree would make his move.

In one leap, Bannon dove for an upthrust of rocks a few feet away. Jud fired wildly. Slugs whined off rocks, screaming off into the air. Ree raced around the stone formation, intent on circling around and reaching the girl. He heard heavy boots coming up quickly, following him around the formation. Ree scampered up a sheet of rock, throwing himself behind a clump of sage there. He gripped his hunting knife, crouched for a killing leap if need be.

The sheriff came around the corner at a run. He carried his .44 colt upraised, ready. Ree's side wound had split open in his leap. He could feel blood breaking through the dried crust, soaking into his shirt and pants. Courtough was directly below him now, straining eyes to see in the black rocks. The breed tensed for the leap.

The sheriff was passing him now. Ree felt his bunched muscles exploding as he sprang out and down on the gunman. A split second before that something caught Courtough's attention. The lawman spun around, spotted the breed already in flight, and fired. Orange flame leapt out of Jud's gun barrel straight into Ree's face.

Lightning struck Ree in the head. He was aware of a collision with Courtough, the ground slamming into the both of them, a struggling body then sweeping darkness. Claire's voice was off someplace. It seemed miles away. She was shouting for help. Everything grew dim, it was a deep, black well. Ree was falling, falling, deeper and deeper until everything became nothing and he fell unconscious.

Consciousness came and went several times before Ree was able to grasp enough reality to stay awake. Soft fingers were rubbing his neck and pressing a bandana tightly across his forehead. There were others in front of him; dimly lit individuals he didn't recognize. Their voices were garbled.

"He'll be alright, Miss," a voice was saying. It was Lieutenant Dunville. Helping hands grasped his arms, leaning Ree up against a rock. The girl was applying a new bandage to his waist wound. A canteen was thrust into his open hands.

"Take a big swallow. You deserve it. You pulled us through. The Apaches aren't likely to be coming back." The officer turned to his second. "Sergeant, see to the line."

Ree upended the canteen and let the sweet liquid pour down his parched throat. His vision had settled a little. Things were taking shape in the darkness. The non-com was leaving, the officer standing close by, smoking a cigar. Claire hovered nearby, washing out the bloodstained cloth she had removed from his waist. The lieutenant was addressing him again.

"Sheriff Courtough is gone. I guess your hunch about him was right all along. Miss LeFonte tells me he tried to kill you. I'll have Flaherty and a party set out after him at dawn. Most likely he'll head straight for Santa Fe."

"Don't bother," Ree said.

Dunville and Claire both eyed the breed strangely. The man was slowly twisting his head to loosen the tightened cord of muscles in his neck. His eyes rose to meet those of the pair. "The hesh-ke haven't all left," he explained. "Some are still around. They're waiting for something foolish like that to happen."

He turned to the officer. "You hurt them bad; lieutenant, but you didn't break them. Most likely they'll be gone by morning - but not before. Even hesh-ke don't rank that kind of firepower a bargain. If they saw the sheriff ride outta here, and I'm betting they did, then he doesn't stand a ghost of a chance to live ten minutes in the saddle."

The Apaches were gone by daybreak. As the troopers lay in their rifle pits, itchy fingers resting on triggers, Bannon slipped out and made a reconnaissance. The area was clear. All the dead and wounded had disappeared. Even the arrows which had landed short of the fort had been taken away. Except for the blood that still colored the ground, there remained no trace of the battle that had taken place there just hours before. The bodies of the hostiles were buried in shallow graves and dead troopers tied to their mounts. The column was formed up and moved out. The Concord was patched up; its wheels luckily untouched.

Not long into their final journey, they came across the remains of Jud Courtough. Bannon had been right. Although the sheriff had gotten farther than expected, the hesh-ke had caught up with him in the end. They had shot his horse out from under him, then dragged his kicking body to a mesquite tree where they tied him, hanging upside down. They set the tree afire. Claire looked away in disgust. Ree squinted against the morning sunlight. The clothes had been all burnt away. The dead carcass of the army gray was stripped of its saddle and bags. There was no sign of the map. Claire noticed it right away as they filed past.

"What do you think happened to the map?" Claire leaned over and whispered to Ree.

Bannon settled back in the saddle and his tired face relaxed. "It's gone. The hesh-ke have taken care of it for me."

Claire was confused. "What do you mean? Now that they have the map, they'll find the cave and all that gold."

"But you forget one thing," Ree explained, "That's white man's gold and silver. Indians have no use for it; especially if they're Apaches and it is the gold of the conquistadors. They'll find the cave alright, but they'll bury it better than I could ever do."

"Then your job is done," Claire said, her face alive with possibility, "It's over. You're free to do whatever you want."

"Whatever I want," Ree repeated out loud.

Claire's eyes settled on Ree's peaceful face. She began to whistle a little ditty, just loud enough for Ree to hear.

Ree Bannon; too long a man alone, a man with no tribe, liked what he heard and began to whistle along.

THE END

ABOUT THE AUTHOR

Denis J. LaComb is a storyteller.

Dissatisfied with a single title such as novelist, screenwriter or playwright, Denis decided that the most apt description of his work would simply be 'storytelling'.

No matter the genre; novel, play, movie or children's books, the essence of Denis' work is storytelling in its purest form. While the characters may change and the theme may vary, at the core of all of Denis' work is a story to be told. A story that might involve mystery, passion, conflict or the intricacies of relationships.

The catalyst for Denis to begin writing full time was a decision to wind down his video production business. With the threat of retirement looming in his future, Denis went back to work on a Western novel he'd written forty years earlier and a new career was born.

Denis has three published novels and several more close to publication. He also has a number of plays and screenplays in treatment form. Denis is also writing scripts for television movies which he is shopping around for the proper venue.

Writing has become Denis' new passion; defying the notion that the ups and downs of being a struggling author is a younger man's game..

Denis and his wife, Sharon, divide their time between Minnesota and Southern California with long layovers in Colorado where three of their grandchildren live.

Connect with Denis online

Official Website
www.DenisJLaComb.com

Facebook
www.facebook.com/denisjlacombofficial

Blog
denisjlacomb.blogspot.com

Twitter
@AuthorDLaComb

Other Titles by Denis J. LaComb

Apache Death Wind (Jeb Burns Series, Volume I)

Love in the A Shau

Other Projects in Development by Denis J. LaComb

Debris

Follow the Cobbler

Volume II of the Jeb Burns Series
(Sequel to Apache Death Wind)

Trans Con

Wake: The Musical

Sweet Pea & The Gang

Siloso

Printed in Great Britain
by Amazon

25595010R00116